THE BLUE FIRE PEARL:
THE COMPLETE ADVENTURES OF
SINGAPORE SAMMY, VOLUME 1

George F. Worts

OTHER BOOKS IN THE ARGOSY LIBRARY:

Alias the Night Wind
BY VARICK VANARDY

Clovelly
BY MAX BRAND

Drink We Deep
BY ARTHUR LEO ZAGAT

The Gun-Brand
BY JAMES B. HENDRYX

Jan of the Jungle
BY OTIS ADELBERT KLINE

Minions of the Moon
BY WILLIAM GREY BEYER

The Moon Pool & The Conquest of the Moon Pool
BY ABRAHAM MERRITT

Tarzan and the Jewels of Opar
BY EDGAR RICE BURROUGHS

War Lord of Many Swordsmen:
The Adventures of Norcross, Volume 1
BY W. WIRT

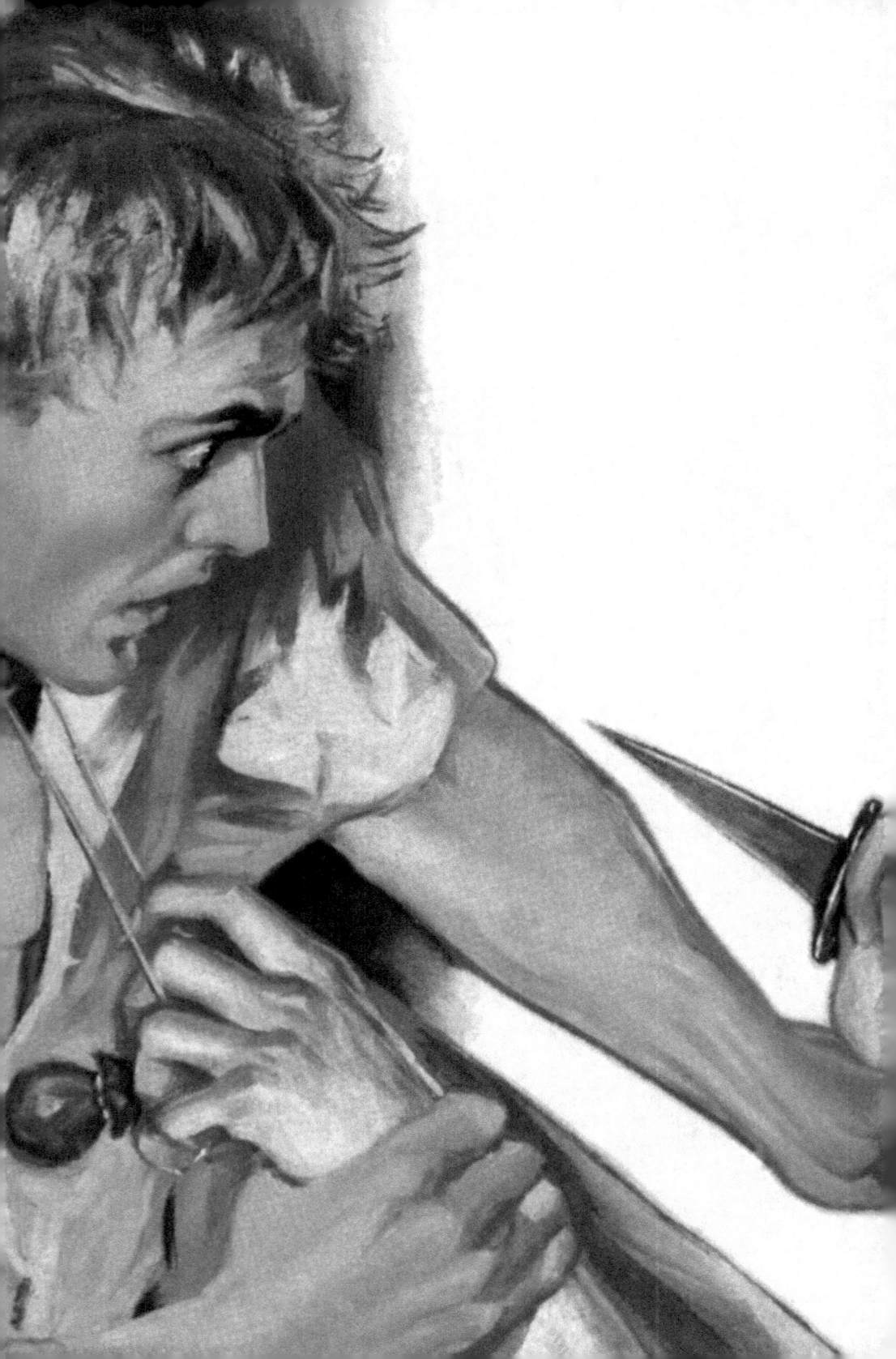

THE BLUE FIRE PEARL

THE COMPLETE ADVENTURES OF SINGAPORE SAMMY, VOLUME 1

GEORGE F. WORTS

ALTUS PRESS
2017

© 2017 Steeger Properties, LLC, under license to Altus Press • First Edition—2017

EDITED AND DESIGNED BY
Matthew Moring

PUBLISHING HISTORY
"The Blue Fire Pearl" originally appeared in the March 10, 1928 issue of *Short Stories* magazine (Vol. 122, No. 5).
"Cobra" originally appeared in the May 25, 1928 issue of *Short Stories* magazine (Vol. 123, No. 4).
"South of Sulu" originally appeared in the June 25, 1928 issue of *Short Stories* magazine (Vol. 123, No. 6).
"The Pink Elephant" originally appeared in the October 25, 1928 issue of *Short Stories* magazine (Vol. 125, No. 2).
"Octopus" originally appeared in the May 10, 1929 issue of *Short Stories* magazine (Vol. 127, No. 3).
Cover illustration originally appeared in the December 12, 1931 issue of *Argosy* magazine (Vol. 226, No.15). Copyright © 1931 by The Frank A. Munsey Company. Copyright renewed © 1959 and assigned to Steeger Properties, LLC. All rights reserved.
"About the Author" originally appeared in the August 2, 1941 issue of *Argosy* magazine (Vol. 309, No. 5). Copyright © 1941 by The Frank A. Munsey Company. Copyright renewed © 1968 and assigned to Steeger Properties, LLC. All rights reserved.

THANKS TO
Gerd Pircher

ISBN
978-1-61827-309-3

Visit *altuspress.com* for more books like this.
Printed in the United States of America.

TABLE OF CONTENTS

The Blue Fire Pearl 1

Cobra 39

South of Sulu 87

The Pink Elephant 147

Octopus 193

About the Author 266

|

THE BLUE FIRE PEARL

*A Stiff Right Punch Unlocks a Jungle
Jail for Singapore Sammy*

IT WAS CHRISTMAS Eve in Malobar and "Singapore" Sammy was going to be murdered. He did not know that it was the night before Christmas, nor was he aware that he was going to be murdered. But he had his suspicions. It all depended on whether or not he escaped capture; and his capture was almost certain. He had heard rumors all over the Far East that the Maharaja of Malobar was a cruel monarch who enjoyed scenes of torture.

The moon was just coming up. A faint, hot breeze stirred the palms. And a shrill chorus of small and large insect life came from the surrounding jungle. From far away came the shrill trumpeting of a wild elephant, the answering squeal of a female.

Singapore Sammy—otherwise Samuel Larkin Shay, American born but at present citizen of the world—listened to these sounds, glanced anxiously at the marble palace on the hilltop and advanced on stealthy feet toward the teakwood temple which loomed in the clearing. He heard the heavy breathing of the great beasts and the occasional clanking of the chains which held them captive. There must be a dozen sacred elephants in that temple.

The young adventurer felt his heart thumping with the excitement of this moment—a moment that might crown with success the efforts of five years of desperate search. He knew that he was in a dangerous situation. The mule on which he had ridden into this forbidden territory was tethered to a tree

at the edge of the river. Singapore Sammy was certain that that mule would not live much longer. It was a very sick mule. Certainly, it was not strong enough to carry him back through that horrible stretch of jungle to Chigatti. He would rather die than undertake that journey again. His face and hands were scratched and swollen and he had had a dozen hairbreadth escapes.

All about him, in the light of the rising moon, buildings made their appearance, as if they had crept furtively out of the jungle to watch him. It was Sammy Shay's first visit to this remote kingdom in the heart of the Malayan jungle, and he did not at all like the feel of things. But that may have been due to an overactive imagination: he had heard so many bloodcurdling tales bearing upon the cruelty of the Maharaja of Malobar. If Sammy was captured, the maharaja would certainly put him to death.

Cautiously, Singapore Sammy approached the elephant temple. He hesitated under a sago palm and searched the black, arched doorway with anxious eyes. Then he approached the doorway.

Out of the black shadow just within, a long white form materialized. This guard, a dark faced man in a white robe, uttered a cry of alarm. Sammy spoke to him softly and rapidly in Malay.

"Hearken to me, Heaven Born! Hush! I am a friend. I am nothing but a seeker who wishes to find an old man who—"

He got no farther than that. The "heaven born" uttered another shrill cry and whipped a long curved dagger from a fold of his robe. With a savage gesture he raised the knife and lunged at Sammy.

Sammy did not hesitate, but struck the white robed man full in the jaw. The man in white went down. Men came running into the clearing, half naked brown men with fuzzy black hair. They seemed to come from everywhere. It was as though they had been awaiting this moment; had been hiding in every shadow, behind every bush and tree. And they came swarming down ladders from nipa huts on stilts.

Sammy met the first of his attackers with a terrific right swing to the jaw. The next little brown man to approach he doubled up with a straight left punch in the solar plexus. Then they had Sammy surrounded. Skinny brown hands clawed at his face and shoulders. Mad little eyes glittered in the moonlight. He was pulled to the ground. Men fell upon him.

Kicking and cursing, Sammy was borne to the maharaja's bamboo and iron jail. He was locked into a cell and once again was left to meditate upon the folly of doing his acting first and his thinking afterward. Supposing he had found the old man? What then?

A HAMMERED brass lamp, suspended by a fine brass chain in one corner, cast faint, uncertain light about the cell. Sammy at once began a tour of inspection. The cell was a cage made of stout iron bars. There were bars even along the bamboo wall.

Sammy perspired in the jungle heat, which even at night was furnacelike, killed scorpions, somehow endured the rancid smell of copra and wondered what form of murder the Maharaja of Malobar would select. He listened to the stamping of the albino elephants in the teakwood temple and regretted that he had gone near the great beasts. But he had had to visit that temple. When a man has dedicated his life to a quest, he must accept gracefully such fillips of misfortune as the stars arrange.

The roof of the Malobar jail was nipa thatch, which harbored a multitude of small crawling things. Most of them were fleas, many of them were scorpions—there were only a few tarantulas, perhaps a hundred thousand altogether!

With horrible accuracy a scorpion would now and then drop down from the thatch upon Singapore Sammy, or so close to him that it counted for a direct hit. When the glittering black thing fell on Sammy's head or shoulders, he would convulsively brush it off and stamp on it. If it fell near him, he would quickly crush it under his heel.

The brass lamp afforded enough light during the night for Sammy to see the scorpions just in time to kill them. From the hour of his arrest until late the next afternoon, he killed scores of them. In the same length of time he annihilated perhaps a pint of furry black spiders with red bodies redder and bigger than a full sized maraschino cherry. He was half starved. His body ached with sleepiness, and his eyes felt as though they had been dipped in sand. The time might come when he would welcome any fate the Maharaja of Malobar had in store for him. Anything would be a relief from scorpions—and the copra.

The smell of copra had always made Sammy slightly ill. And just outside the jail were mounds of copra. There was no breeze, and the reek of the decomposing coconut shells crept through the air like the stain of a squid creeping through still water. It penetrated the jail until it seemed to Sammy that his hair, his clothes and his flesh gave off the sickly odor.

ON SILENT feet, a Chinese boy of sixteen or seventeen crept down the corridor. It was not his first visit. All day long he had been coming into the jail, walking slowly past Singapore Sammy's cell, and staring at him with oblique aloe eyes. Each time he passed, Sammy grinned amiably at him.

This time the Chinese boy carried a black lacquer tray. Sammy looked at it with great interest, for he had had nothing to eat since the night before. And this time the yellow boy stopped before his cell and in a low voice said:

"This is your supper, master. Rice, boiled river fish, and number one oolong tea."

Singapore Sammy reached through the bars for the three bowls. There was no furniture in the cell; there was not a stick of wood. So Sammy arranged the three glazed bowls on the floor, cast a final watchful glance over his shoulder for scorpions, and fell to with the chopsticks. After five years spent in Far Eastern ports and hinterland, he could manipulate chopsticks with the skill of a native.

"I cooked it for you," said the boy.

Sammy looked up and grinned.

"You're a great little cook, brother. Where did you learn all that English?"

"In the mission school in Bangkok, master."

"In Bangkok, eh," said Sammy, tasting the river fish and finding it good. "What are you doing in Malobar?"

"I am a prisoner of the maharaja, master."

"Can that master stuff, buddy," said Sammy Shay, "and call me Singapore. What's your name?"

"Lee Yang May."

"Hi-yah!" said Sammy. "You're from the mandarin country. So you went to mission school in Bangkok, and you're a prisoner of his royal nibs. How did that happen?"

The yellow boy shrugged.

"What the maharaja wants, he takes. The Chinese are very honest. His last personal servant, who was a Chinese, died of beri-beri. He wanted another Chinese. One day when he was in Bangkok he saw me in front of my father's store on Cherern Krung Road. He asked me to work for him. I said no. I have learned not to say no to maharajas. I have been here almost a year. That maharaja is a devil, master. He beats me. I want to go back to Bangkok. Will you help me, master?"

Singapore Sammy looked at the Chinese boy with amiable blue eyes. He gulped hot tea, and said:

"Sure, I will, kid! Just climb up here into the cockpit beside me and we'll fly to Bangkok in time for a movie!"

The Chinese lad did not understand. He remained serious and lapsed, in his excitement, into coast pidgin.

"You allatime help me; me allatime help you!"

"Maskee, maskee!" Sammy laughed. "You scratch my back and I'll scratch yours! You get me out of here and I deliver you to your old man in Bangkok. Is that the big idea?"

"Is it not fair, master?"

Sammy uttered a sharp exclamation; dropped his chopsticks, brushed off a clinging black horror that had fallen on his left shoulder, and crackled it under his heel.

He returned to the rice bowl. He did not answer Lee Yang May's question for a while longer. Sammy seemed to be thinking things over. He said finally:

"You're not the kind of lad, are you, Lee, who would lure me out of this dump so the maharaja would have an excuse to shoot me in the back for bein' an escapin' prisoner, are you?"

"I would not dream!"

"All right, buddy; don't get excited. How we goin' to work it?"

Lee Yang May came closer to the bars. He looked up with glittering eyes into Sammy's.

"Yesterday, just after tiffin," he said in a tense voice, "one of your countrymen made his escape from this jail."

"From this dump?"

"Yes, master."

"If you helped him, why aren't you on the way to Bangkok?"

"I did not help him. I did not trust him. But he proves that it is possible to escape."

"Which way did he go?"

"I do not know, master. He entered the jungle and has not been seen again."

"Where does this river run?"

"To Praklat."

"Can you get a boat?" said Sammy.

"Yes, master. And at Praklat there are Chinese fishermen who will take us to Bangkok. The captain of the maharaja's guard has the key to this cell. But a chance will come. You will help me, if the chance comes?"

"I'll take you along," Sammy promised, "if I can make my getaway. And you can depend on that."

The Chinese stepped quickly away from the bars and whispered:

"Someone is coming! I must go."

CERTAINLY, THERE was no doubt that someone was coming. His approach was being heralded by an outburst of eloquence that made Singapore Sammy's eyes glisten. The newcomer was speaking, not English, but waterfront American. He was damning Malobar and all living creatures in Malobar and with seething epithets consigning them to sections of the inferno that even Sammy, with his wide acquaintance with cusswords, had never before heard of.

Two brown skinned men in the dirty blue uniforms of the maharaja's army presently appeared with a tall, red faced white man between them. He wore a khaki sun helmet, a blue flannel shirt open at the neck and chest and exposing much hair, corduroy riding breeches and snake boots.

The soldiers pushed him into the cell across the corridors from Sammy and clanged the iron barred door shut upon him. The soldiers walked away, and two pairs of blue eyes stared across eight feet of space at each other.

"As I live, breathe and die," panted the tall, red faced man across the way, "if it ain't another white man! What have they got you in for, stranger?"

"I crashed the sacred elephant temple last night at midnight," Sammy informed him. "The top mahout thought I meant trouble, and I busted him in the nose."

The man across the way stared at him through the bars.

"My name's Tom Burke. What's yours?"

"Sam Shay."

"American, ain't you?"

"Cairo, Illinois," said Sammy.

"Been in these parts long?"

"Going on six years, Mister Burke."

"You ain't the guy they call Singapore Sammy, are you?"

"I'm the guy."

"Well, can you tie that!" said Mr. Burke. "Everywhere I go, I keep hearin' about you. They say when you get drunk you cry into your beer about your father. And when you get mad your eyebrows crawl around your forehead like red mice."

"I never notice my eyebrows when I get mad," Sammy said.

"Is it true that you've been lookin' all over the South Seas and southern Asia for the past five years, tryin' to find your old man?"

"Yeah, it's true."

"And the only clues you got is that he's nuts about pearls and elephants?"

"That's right," Sammy said tonelessly. "I haven't seen my old man since I was two years old. I don't know what he looks like.

The Blue Fire Pearl

He used to be the top elephant man with Bartrom and Bradley's circus. He was nuts about pearls and he was nuts about elephants. I figured I would find him somewhere where pearls and elephants grew in their natural state. Down in Singapore last week I picked up his trail again, after losin' it for over a year. A Hindu temple architect told me about an old white man who was up here takin' care of the maharaja's white pigs. He said this old guy was carryin' around a fortune in pearls. I knew that was him, so I hotfooted it up here. I got excited last night when that number one mahout got stubborn, and I busted him one. That's why I'm in here."

The young man in the cell across the way stared at Sammy as if fascinated.

"So you're Singapore Sammy!" he said. "Sometimes, Mister Shay, I cry into my liquor myself when I hear about the way you're goin' up and down and back and across this country, tryin' to find your father. I didn't have much use for my old man, but I hand it to any guy who's so fond of his father that he'll wear his ankles out lookin' for him, like you're doin'."

Singapore Sammy said nothing, but he looked suitably sentimental. He always did when people sympathized with him. He preferred not to have people know that the reason he was looking for his father was that the old rogue had in his possession the will of Sammy's grandfather which bequeathed to Sammy a comfortable fortune, and without which Sammy could not possess that fortune. Incidentally, Sammy's father had deserted him and his mother when Sammy was two years old, taking with him every penny of his mother's savings.

He did not know what he would do to his father when he found the old rat. But he would say, "So you are the man that ran out on my mother and me when she was so sick she couldn't get out of bed, and took all her money and that will! Where's that will?" If it wasn't promptly forthcoming, Sammy would simply let nature take its course.

THE YOUNG man across the way was cursing. Every word

was bright purple. He finally calmed down sufficiently to explain why he was swearing.

"Yesterday, Mister Shay, I made my getaway from here. I bribed a dirty little skunk to borrow the keys from the captain of the maharaja's guard. I gave him twenty silver *ticals*, a clasp knife, ten big rubber bands and half an ounce of mandarin opium. He squealed. They followed me into the jungle. My hunch was to break through to the railroad and pound the ties to Penang. Brother, it can't be done. Even if they hadn't caught me, I wouldn't have made it. These jungles are so full of panthers and pythons and elephant leeches that a man with ten eyes might just as well be stone blind! Well, learned my lesson in them hills. When your chance comes to make a break, go down to the Gulf of Siam."

Sammy recalled what the Chinese boy had said, and felt comforted.

"What did you say the maharaja had on you?" he asked Burke.

"I didn't say. I'm a spy."

"Dutch?"

"I don't know, Mister Shay. I don't know and I don't care if I never know. He was an oil guy, that's all I know. It's enough to break your heart, if you want to hear how it happened. You don't happen to have a cigarette on you, I suppose."

Sammy did happen to. He flipped a white cylinder across the corridor. Mr. Burke caught it deftly and lighted it. He inhaled gratefully.

"If they don't have cigarettes in heaven," he said, "I'm going to have my passport visaed for the other place. To begin with, do you know much about this maharaja?"

"I hear," Sammy said, "that he's a tough egg"

"He thinks he's Nero," Mr. Burke said. "That's all. He thinks he's the greatest king in the world. Did you ever hear about the Burmese he caught trying to steal one of his dancing girls—and threw into a pit with two starved black panthers?"

"No," Sammy said. "Is that what he's going to do to us?"

"We'll find out soon enough. He'll think up something good, you can bet your shirt on that. Brush that scorpion off your hair, Mister Shay. I'll bet they take to that red hair of yours. From over here it looks like the port light on an ocean liner. It sure is red."

Burke took another long drag at his cigarette while Sammy was exterminating the scorpion.

"It seems that the British heard about that panther incident, and they sent up a gunboat to Praklat and ordered the maharaja to come down and go aboard and explain. A big admiral was aboard the gunboat, so the maharaja came hotfooting it down. If you think that brown little devil ain't smart, let me tell you what he did. He knew he was goin' to get into plenty hot water. So first he lied himself blue in the face, and said he had no knowledge of any Burmese bein' tossed to the panthers—and he speaks English just like you and I do, if not better.

"Then, when he got all through, he pulled this little bottle off of his hip or somewhere. It was a round glass about four inches high, and it was full of a thick brown liquid that looked like molasses. And he said to the admiral:

" 'Admiral, I brought this liquid along to show you, because it mystifies me. Some of my subjects have found it gurgling out of an area of black rocks in the northern section of my State. Can you tell me what it is?' "

"Oil!" Sammy exclaimed.

"You guesed it, brother. Oil! Crude oil! The admiral took one sniff of the stuff in that bottle—and forgot all about Burmese lady killers and black panthers. You know how England loves her oil! And mebbe you know about the international fight goin' on, with the U.S.A. grabbin' an oil lease here, the British grabbin' a lease there, and the Dutch grabbin' a lease in between. The world has gone nuts about oil. And here was a new oil country!

"Do you get it, Mister Shay, do you get it? That bottle of oil was nothin' but a slick way of gettin' the admiral's mind off that

Burmese panther banquet. There ain't a drop of oil in the whole of Malobar. Or if there is, it certainly ain't bubblin' out of the ground anywheres. I looked. I know!"

"Where did that bottle of oil come from?" Sammy interrupted.

"**THE MAHARAJA** probably got it off some Standard Oil tanker. Well, I was in Batavia, Java, when the story reached certain parties over there. Oil in Malobar! Well, I am a T. T. T., Mister Shay, and if I do say so, I know my way around jungle countries. A fat guy with pink whiskers came to my boarding house and told me he would weigh me down with so many florins I couldn't stagger, if I would go to Malobar and prove up on that oil story. I made him put it in writing, see? And like the sap I am, I kept the letter on me. The maharaja's men grabbed me—and he got the letter. And that made me a spy, didn't it?"

"Not to an American consul, it wouldn't," said Sammy.

"Well," said Mr. Burke, "I got particular reasons for not going near any American consul. Maybe an American consul could get you out of your jam."

Singapore Sammy grinned.

"I ain't on speaking terms with American consuls," he said. "How long has the maharaja had you in here?"

"Almost two months. And all I've been doin' is killin' scorpions and puttin' on boxin' exhibitions for the maharaja. He is hipped on boxing matches. There's nothin' he likes better than to see two guys stand toe to toe and slug. It's a novelty to him. After he got the admiral all hot and bothered about that bottle of oil, the admiral turned his ship inside out showin' him a good time. The admiral showed him the first movies he ever saw, but the maharaja didn't fall for 'em. What he fell for was some boxing matches the admiral had the gobs stage on the fore deck. He was so tickled with those slugging bees that when he went ashore to go home, the admiral presented him with a set of six-ounce gloves.

"And that's where I came in, Mister Shay. When the maharaja got me locked up in this dump, he came in and asked me a million questions. When he found out I know how to box, it was all settled. I had to put on the gloves with every strong boy in Malobar. Some of them looked seven feet tall, but they were easy to take. They didn't have any science, and by the time they knew what it was all about, they were on the canvas hearin' the birdies.

"The maharaja has a big pink marble room up at the palace where he puts the bouts on. He's got a roped off ring and a padded canvas floor. The rest of it is like something out of the Arabian Nights, no foolin', with all them cute lookin' janes from the harem settin' around all lit up with diamonds and rubies, and a couple o' black boys wavin' a big peacock fan over the maharaja to keep him cool. He thinks I'm the heavyweight champion of the world—and what do I get out of it? A chance to stay in this dump, killin' scorpions!"

Sammy shook his head commiseratingly.

"It makes me sick," said Mr. Burke. "Two good guys like you and me, rottin' away in this dump! Do you know what day this is?"

"No," said Sammy.

"It's Christmas! Do you remember the Christmas trees you had when you were a kid?"

"I never had a Christmas tree in my life," Sammy said. "But just the same, I hate spendin' Christmas in a jungle jug. How are we goin' to get out of here?"

"Ask me!" said Burke, and he laughed bitterly. "I'm an expert at gettin' out of here, ain't I now? Take it from me, Mister Shay, we better get busy quick and dope somethin' out. The maharaja's goin' to treat me mean for that getaway, and he's goin' to treat you meaner. If you knew how he dotes on them pink eyed elephants!"

"Just before they brought you back," Sammy said, "a little

Chink boy was in here. Says he's got a boat. Says he'll help me out if I paddle the boat down to Praklat."

"You mean that one named Lee?"

"That's the one."

"Forget him," urged Burke. "I learned not to trust yeller boys. That one's nothin' but a little sneak."

Singapore Sammy recalled that the Chinese boy had said quite as emphatically that he did not trust Burke. He wished he had asked Lee why. Some instinct made him feel that Lee was more to be trusted than Tom Burke. Burke had mean, shifty eyes and a cruel, selfish mouth.

Without relying on one or the other how, Sammy Shay wondered, could he escape from this jail—and continue his quest?

A SOLUTION to this difficult problem was shortly forthcoming. Preceded by the rich Oriental smell of frangipani, three men came along the corridor and stopped between the two cells. Two of them wore the dirty blue uniform of the maharaja's service; the other was a plump brown little man who wore a white silk shirt, O.D. jodpores, and a white pith sala topee. At his thin, dark lips was the most engaging, most innocent smile Sammy had ever seen. He would learn in good time that the smile of the Maharaja of Malobar was undoubtedly the most deceiving smile in the world. His eyes were like currants, and he wore, just above that cherubic smile, a wisp of black, waxed mustache.

The little black eyes seemed to sparkle merrily as they took Sammy in, and the smile became gayer. Then the maharaja addressed his attention to Tom Burke.

"Well, here I am, your majesty—back again!" Burke said weakly.

The Maharaja of Malobar slowly nodded his well chalked pith sala topee.

"So I see," he said amiably. "And you"—he turned again to

Singapore Sammy—"you are the man who attempted to kill my head mahout last night. What have you to say for yourself?"

"I was lookin' for my father," Sammy eagerly explained. "I haven't seen him since I was two years old. All I know about him is that he is nuts about pearls and elephants. I've been on his trail, now, for almost six years, and he always keeps a jump ahead of me. Last week in Singapore I heard he was up here. So I came up to look for him. Has an old white man, crazy about elephants, been up here, your majesty?"

The maharaja was still smiling the smile of an innocent child.

"An old white man, a white man, such as you describe, came and went months ago. In forcing your way into my elephant temple at the hour of midnight, was it necessary for you to half kill my head mahout?"

"Your majesty, it happened to be midnight, because I only got here then. And that mahout made a pass at me with his knife. I just let him have it on the button. If he hadn't flashed that knife—"

"Silence!" barked one of the guards, in Malay. "His majesty has investigated. He has acquainted himself with the details of your savage attack on the mahout. You have violated his majesty's laws. The penalty for your crime is death."

The maharaja had a leather riding crop in his left hand. He was softly tapping with it upon the palm of his right hand. And he was still smiling at Sammy.

"What is your name?" he asked.

"Samuel Larkin Shay, your majesty," Sammy huskily answered.

"What is your nationality?"

"American, your majesty."

"What is your occupation?"

"I'm a gas engine expert, your majesty. But at present I'm just looking for my old man."

"But you have had experience as a boxer?"

"I—I used to do a little boxing, your majesty."

The maharaja's smile became even more indulgent. He was looking dreamily, not at Sammy, but at the end of the corridor.

"Who is that hiding there?" he said quietly. "Bring him here."

The two guards passed out of Sammy's line of vision. They returned, dragging between them the Chinese boy, Lee Yang May. He looked up at the maharaja with terrified eyes. In his terror, he was babbling in his native tongue. Some of it Sammy understood, He was trying to say that he meant no wrong.

His protests were interrupted by decisive action on the part of the maharaja. He lifted the riding crop and brought it whistling down on the boy's cheek. A long red welt instantly stood out. Then, at a word from the maharaja, the guards turned Lee about and ripped his blue silk blouse down to the waist.

Sammy looked from that naked back to the maharaja's face with incredulity. The maharaja's smile had not hardened. It was as soft and amiable as ever. He brought up the crop—and then brought it hissing down.

Sammy turned his head away. He felt suddenly sick. If he could have reached through the bars and seized the maharaja by his fat brown throat he would have done so, but he was helpless.

A dozen times he heard the crop fall on Lee Yang May's back, but not once did he cry out. Then the maharaja spoke, very amiably.

"Go, now," he said.

Lee Yang May, released by the guards, fell to his knees. He hid his face in the crook of his elbow. He struggled to his feet and staggered away.

SAMMY DREW a deep breath. The maharaja's twinkling eyes and childlike smile returned to Sammy.

"So you are a boxer?"

"Yes—you—your majesty," Sammy said with great difficulty.

The maharaja spoke sharply. The guard who had spoken so harshly to Sammy produced a silver cigarette box and lifted the lid. The maharaja selected a cigarette and held it in the match flame which the other guard quickly provided.

"Two boxers!" he said, with a soft little chuckle. "How delightful! You shall box one another tonight. We will make it a sporting proposition. The man who wins will be given his freedom. The man who loses will be put to death."

The maharaja had plunged his right hand into a pocket in his jodpores. A scorpion which had fallen into Sammy's thatch of red hair he brushed off absently. He was watching the maharaja with fascination.

"And the man who wins," the maharaja went on dramatically, "shall win—this!"

And from the pocket he drew forth a round, blue thing. It was a pearl, and it was such a pearl as Sammy had never before seen. Fully a half inch in diameter, it was as blue as a Chantaboon sapphire. In its silky blue depths fire glowed. In the murk of the tropical twilight, it glowed like an evil eye seen at a window.

Sammy knew pearls. He knew that a sapphire blue pearl was rarer even than a sapphire blue diamond. It should be worth enough to ransom a dozen maharajas.

The maharaja was holding up the pearl in the little cup formed of the tips of four fingers, delicately balancing it. He twisted his hand about so that the blue pearl glowed with a divine fire.

Sammy gulped. For the moment, he forgot everything else in the world but that glorious pearl. Tom Burke was similarly moved. He was clutching the bars of his cell door. His eyes were bulging. He was licking his lips.

The maharaja glanced from him to Sammy. His currant eyes narrowed until wrinkles, like little streaks and arrows of silver, shot out from the corners. His smile was one of pure delight.

"Freedom and this pearl to the man who wins; death to the man who loses!"

A moment longer he held up that priceless blue pearl for the two prisoners to admire, then, swiftly, he thrust it back into his pocket, turned about and walked away.

Sammy Shay and Tom Burke stared at one another for a long time.

"Buddy," Burke said in a hoarse voice, "how much do you weigh?"

"A hundred and sixty-five."

"Yeah? Well, I tip the beam at a hundred an' ninety-eight. Buddy," Burke said again, "if I was in any better shape, I'd send a challenge to Gene Tunney. What you just heard that little brown devil say—that was your death sentence, buddy."

Sammy swallowed and found that his mouth was suddenly exceedingly dry. Tom Burke began to laugh, and his laughter was not pleasant to hear.

"That pearl, buddy—that pearl is worth a fortune. Did you ever see a pearl like it in your life?"

"No," said Sammy.

"It would sure make a nice Christmas present to give your old man," said Burke, and he laughed again.

"Listen," Sammy interrupted. "Maybe you can lick me and maybe you can't. Right now, we've got to think about something else. We have got to get out of here, and we have got to get that little Chink out of here, too."

Burke's stare was one of frank amazement.

"I know you feel the same way I do about it." Sammy went on. "I can't stand by and see a poor kid beat up like that. We've got to get Lee out of this place. Did you see those old welts lower down on his back? All they do is beat—"

"Say, listen," Burke broke in, "what the hell do I care about him? Who is he in my life?"

"But they beat him!"

"Well, what of it? What I'm interested in is this fight. How much fightin' have you done?"

"I used to be light-heavyweight champion of the Pacific Coast," said Sammy.

The smile vanished from Burke's face.

"Professional or amateur?" he snapped.

"Amateur."

Burke's mouth relaxed.

"Say, you ain't lyin' to me, are you?" he asked.

Sammy shook his head. He wasn't lying, but he wasn't saying that he had won the amateur light-heavy weight championship through a series of fantastic accidents, and that he had lost it in the first fifteen seconds of his next fight. A champion, so to speak, for fifteen seconds!

BUT IT was evident that Burke was no longer pleased with the situation. His smile had disappeared. His eyes were full of speculation.

"I don't know," he said, "but what we ought to get together on this proposition, Mister Shay. I could lick you with one hand tied behind me, but what of it? Here we are, a couple o' good American guys, gettin' all hopped up to hate each other's guts, just because this near-Nero shows us a lousy pearl."

"Yeah?" said Sammy.

"What we got to do," Burke went on convincingly, "is to get together and stay together. We got to help each other, and we got to help Lee."

This change of front was so startling that Sammy stared. He agreed with Burke, but he didn't like Burke's mouth. Burke went warmly on.

"What we got to have is a gentleman's agreement," Burke announced.

"To do what?" said Sammy.

Burke was beginning to betray the symptoms of eager, innocent enthusiasm. He was softly pounding one iron bar with his great brown fist. His eyes in the dusk seemed to shimmer.

"I'll tell you, buddy! We'll go into that ring tonight and give him a boxin' exhibition. What we need is time. We'll pull all our punches. We'll slap each other loud where it won't hurt and make it sound noisy and dangerous. We'll fall down and get up again. See? It'll look to him like the most terrible sluggin' match that was ever staged—and we'll fight ten rounds to a draw."

"And then what?" said Sammy.

"Then, maybe, he'll let us go. Anyhow, he won't kill the two of us. It'll give us time to work somethin' else out—a getaway for us and Lee. To hell with that lousy pearl!"

Sammy didn't feel at all that way about the pearl. He wanted the pearl, but he was certain that he could not win it from Burke in open combat. Sammy looked searchingly at the red faced young man. He considered his mean eyes and his selfish, cruel mouth.

Now, five years in the Far East had made Sammy Shay very wise. He did not know that a great Oriental sage had once said, "The friendships of the day are those of self-interest alone." Or that another famous Oriental thinker had succinctly stated, "A rat knows the way of a rat." But in his own direct, clever way, Sammy Shay had arrived at both those conclusions.

Singapore Sammy did not trust Tom Burke. He was sure that Burke, with his greater weight and longer reach and professional experience, could knock him out in the first few seconds of the first round. And that would mean that Sammy would be murdered. He didn't dare appeal to an American consul, because of a certain little affair that happened in Shanghai.

"You're thinkin'," said Burke, "about the pearl. Forget it! We got to stick together. We're a couple o' good American guys— and we gotta stick together. And we gotta help Lee. If you play, I'll play."

BUT SAMMY couldn't dismiss the pearl so easily. If he could win the pearl, he would sell it. The proceeds would enable him to travel faster. And the only way he could hope to catch up with his father was to travel faster and still faster.

"What do you say?" Burke urged. "You ain't got a thing to lose, because I've got you licked if I want to lick you. I could take you in the first few seconds of the first round—and you know it. But you're a good guy. I like you. I don't want to be responsible for sendin' a good American kid like you into a pit with any starved panthers."

Sammy was watching him warily, especially his mouth. But what Burke was saying sounded so convincing that Sammy half believed he actually meant it.

"I'm leary about fixed fights," Sammy objected.

"If we fix this fight," Burke argued, "we take each other's word as two straight shooters that it stays fixed, don't we?"

"Yes, but—"

"Listen, kid," Burke assured Sammy. "We will go in there tonight. We will slap each other around. First you will push me and I will fall down. Then I will push you and you will fall down. We will stagger back up, and we will make believe we are knockin' hell out of each other. And when it's all over, there we are, both on our feet. There won't be any dirty work. Well, what do you say?"

Still Sammy hesitated. A fixed fight was a fixed fight. A decent fighter never fixed a fight. And Sammy had known of too many crooked fights that hadn't ended as they had been fixed. A fighter who would fix a fight would stoop to double-crossing.

"I don't know," he said.

Burke sadly shook his head.

"Gee, kid," he said, "don't you trust me? Don't you see it's only that I don't want to see a nice guy like you thrown to starving panthers? I'm givin' up that pearl, ain't I, to give you a break?"

"But I don't see why," said the skeptical Sammy.

"Why? Because I want to help you and that little Chink friend of yours out of this jam. Why? Ask me why! Because you're an American and a good guy—and this is Christmas. A fine guy I would be to let one of my own countrymen down on Christmas! How do you suppose I could look my white haired old mother in the eye next Christmas and say, 'Ma, just a year ago, I knocked out a clean young American kid, knowin' they were goin' to feed him to the panthers.'"

"I don't know," said Sammy. "If it wasn't for that pearl, I'd say all right. But that pearl is worth money. It's worth more money than I ever saw in one place in my life. If that pearl ain't worth forty thousand Mex, I'm crazy. And you want it as much as I do."

"Let me wise you up on this maharaja a little more," Burke said. "He showed you a swell pearl."

"It wasn't an imitation," Sammy interrupted.

"I ain't sayin' it was an imitation. All I'm sayin' is that, even if you were to lick me, you wouldn't get that pearl. He knows what that pearl is worth better than you do. Even if you won it, you wouldn't get it. He'd give you a Japanese imitation of it—or nothin' at all."

"I've done business with these guys for five years," Sammy answered. "They may try to crook you or kill you, but they never go back on their word. Whoever wins this fight, wins that pearl."

Burke looked angry.

"Nobody is gonna win this fight, Mister Shay! We're goin' in there and put on a fancy slappin' exhibition, ain't we—so nobody will be thrown to the panthers? To hell with the pearl!"

"All right," Sammy gave in. "To hell with the pearl! Now, how are we going to stage this?"

BURKE GLIBLY outlined the plan he had in mind. At the stroke of the bell for the first round, they would rush out from their corners and exchange a noisy but harmless volley of slaps. He, Burke, would go down and roll about as if he were stricken.

"Who referees these fights?" Sammy interrupted.

"The maharaja. He's been studyin' up on the rules."

"Do we fight the Marquess of Queensbury rules?"

"We do. You knock me down, see? I roll around. At the count of nine, I get up and slam into you. We swap 'em. I drive you into a corner, I put over what looks like a haymaker. You drop. You take a count of eight or nine. And so on. That'll get the maharaja fuzzy eyed. When we get him going, we push each other all over the ring, and take turns fallin' down and gettin' up. But at the end of the tenth round, we're both on our feet, see? We've both taken the same number of knockdowns. We both have the same number of points—who's this?"

A slim shadow had crept up the corridor. It stopped before Singapore Sammy's cell. Yee Lang May's face was a pale blur in the light of the brass lamp. He told Sammy that he had overheard the conversation with the maharaja about the fight.

"You must win, master. If I stay here longer, I will die. You saw him beat me. He hates the Chinese."

Sammy looked down into the pale, upturned face and patted the hand that clutched a bar.

"Cheer up, buddy. I'll get you out of here somehow. Now, you listen close. You're goin' to steal a boat, understand?"

"Yes, master."

"A good, husky boat. I'll tell you where to be waitin' with that boat. Down the river, on the other side, is a big mahogany tree—biggest mahogany tree I ever saw. It's below a *sala* that's empty. You savvy that tree?"

"Yes, master."

"You be waitin' there tonight with a boat big enough for three."

"Yes, master. Who will be the third?"

"This gent across the way. He is a friend of mine."

"Very well, master."

"How long a paddle is it down to Praklat?"

"Only a few hours. We should reach Praklat by dawn."

"All right, kid. We will be seein' you under that big ma-hogany. Run along before that old devil-devil catches you and beats you again."

"Very well, master." The eyes of Lee Yang May were worship-ful. The boy stared at him—and vanished.

"It's all fixed," Sammy said to Burke. "After the fight, Lee will be waitin' for us under that big mahogany tree below the bridge."

"Which one? The river is lousy with mahogany trees."

"That big one below the *sala*."

"I know the one, buddy. But how are we goin' to get there?"

"Supposing," said Sammy, "we plan to make our getaway during the fourth round. Four is my lucky number. We fight the first three rounds the way you said. We get the maharaja all excited. In the middle of the fourth round, we both fall down. We jump up, jump over the ropes and run like hell."

"Buddy," Burke said admiringly, "you're clever. I hand it to you. We'll do just that."

THEY WERE still discussing the details of this daring plan when a dozen of the maharaja's guards came to escort them to the palace. The cells were unlocked. Each of the Americans was surrounded by guards.

Sammy, as they approached the palace, took in as much as he could of the lay of the land. He marked the clearings and the palm groves through which they passed. There was no moon, but the stars were very bright. His favorite constellation, the Southern Cross, burned with an almost fiery light and somehow gave him hope. Sentimental Sammy was a pagan, but there was something about the blazing Southern Cross that had an almost religious influence upon him.

He saw that the palace, on its hill, was not more than two hundred yards from the river. Burke had told him that the pink marble room in which the fight would take place was in the north wing, the wing on the river side. And it was on the ground floor, of course. Arched doorways, Burke had said, gave upon a terrace from which numerous paths ran down to the river. They would have to swim the river, risking the alligators. But Sammy was eager to take that risk.

At the entrance to the pink marble room, they were met by more guards. Sammy looked beyond them—and softly grunted with astonishment. It was his first glimpse of the interior of an Oriental palace, The great room was a golden glare of candle and lamp light. His first impression was of a lofty room as pink as a child's birthday cake, then he observed details. The walls fairly crawled with the bizarre creations of some long-dead artist's fancy. Here was a five toed dragon from whose mouth golden fire spurted. There, a gigantic land crab done in inlaid ebony and silver. There were snakes and fish and dancing women with eyes of semiprecious stones.

Smoke rose in thin cobalt-blue stems from great braziers, and the air was heavy with the rich flavor of smoldering sandalwood dust. The air was hot, stifling. All about the room sat brown skinned men in black and women in the most brilliant colors that the hand looms on the not far distant Irawadi could achieve—burning reds, sinister purples, dazzling greens and blues and yellows. And these women, Sammy presumed, were the women of the maharaja's harem, his wives and dancing girls. Some were young and pretty. Others were older. Dusky eyes looked at him and Tom Burke and gleamed with excitement. Their voices filled the air with a chirping as of hundreds of hungry sparrows.

They squatted, Oriental fashion, upon the floor. Bracelets and anklets of heavy hand-hammered gold clinked and clanked. Precious stones flashed and twinkled. Sammy had heard that the Maharaja of Malobar was one of the wealthiest of Oriental potentates. How easily he could spare that fire-blue pearl!

In the very center of the amazing pink room was the only familiar thing that Sammy saw—a squared ring! It had a canvas floor. There were ropes fastened to stout ebony posts at the corners. And in the center of the ring stood the maharaja, smiling amiably.

Sammy grinned involuntarily—a nervous, tight grin. The maharaja was wearing a green silk *engyi* and a maroon silk *longyi* with a white silk sash about his plump waist.

The two Americans climbed through the ropes and the blue uniformed guards threw themselves down on the floor just outside the ring. And Sammy did not like this arrangement in the least. The guards would be watchful. They would be prepared to cope with the slightest gesture toward a getaway. Sammy's heart began beating a little more rapidly. The only solution was to dazzle and confuse the guards by such an exhibition of fighting as they had never before seen!

THE MAHARAJA had in one hand two pairs of blackened six-ounce gloves. His other hand was doubled into a fist. Still smiling, as Sammy and Tom Burke approached him, he opened his fist.

On his palm lay the fire-blue pearl. It was a perfectly round ball of blue fire. Sammy caught his breath. In the golden glare of candles and *dongs,* the blue pearl was even more beautiful than it had been by daylight. It was a live thing. It seemed to tremble, to shiver. It might have been a ball formed by fiery blue tropical sky, or of valley mist lacquered satiny blue by an Oriental magician.

In his ear, Burke whispered to Sammy: "To hell with *that!*"

The maharaja was saying:

"This—to the man who wins. And to the man whose loses—death! Do you understand?"

"Yes, your majesty."

"Strip to the waist and remove your shoes."

The two men obeyed. When their superfluous clothes were stowed outside the ring, the maharaja said:

"You will fight according to the Marquess of Queensberry's rules. I warn you that there must be no fouling. A man I see fouling will be taken out and given one hundred strokes of the lash—and then sent in here to fight again."

Sammy observed two things: The maharaja retained the blue pearl in his fist; and Burke looked fat. His belly muscles did not stand out in ribs, as Sammy's did; for Sammy had always kept himself in good condition.

"Rounds," the maharaja was saying, "will be three minutes long. Rests will be one minute long. Avoid clinching—and fight clean. This fight must be won by a knockout. Do you men understand?"

What Sammy did not understand was how the maharaja could continue, no matter what he said or did, to smile like an innocent child. He would never forget how sweetly the maharaja had smiled when he was bringing down that riding crop on Lee Yang May's naked back.

"Yes, your majesty!"

"Go to your corners and wait for the bell."

Burke and Sammy went to opposite corners. Sammy seized and tested the corner ropes. He swung himself up and down, flexing his muscles and limbering his joints. The gloves felt funny on his hands, because his hands weren't taped. They felt loose and strange.

The bell rang. Sammy pivoted away from his corner and came rushing out. Burke also came out with a rush. They met with a brisk thudding of gloves on flesh, but there was no sting in these slaps.

They clinched. They parted. Sammy sent over a wild right swing which Burke caught with a loud slap on the glove at his chin.

Down went Burke. It could not have been more realistic if Sammy had actually landed that punch on Burke's jaw.

The chattering of the maharaja's sparrows had now become the cackling of vultures. The maharaja's wives and dancing girls were screaming and yelping with excitement. Under that sustained high note was the harsher sound of men's voices. It was

the old, familiar roar of the crowd—human hounds baying at
the kill. All the world over it sounded the same and it had
always, Sammy supposed, sounded the same. Two gladiators,
met to slay each other, whether they met in the Roman arena,
or in Madison Square Garden in New York, or in the pink
marble room of Malobar, drew from the crowd that same
hungry roar.

THE MAHARAJA was bending over Burke, with a watch in
his hand. The fist clenched upon the blue pearl rose and fell, as
he had no doubt seen the admiral's fist rise and fall.

At seven, Burke got to his knees. At nine, he was on his feet.
Sammy rushed him. They met again with a wild slapping of
gloves.

"Down you go, buddy!" said Burke, in a hoarse whisper. A
glove slapped him loudly between the shoulder blades.

Down went Sammy. He closed his eyes. He writhed and
twisted. He opened his eyes to see the maharaja's fist rising and
falling with its precious invisible burden.

"Four—five—six—"

Sammy sat up. And at nine he was on his feet, and as he had
rushed Burke before, Burke now rushed him.

Again Burke fell. Again Sammy fell. And the ruse was
working. It was working perfectly. So excited had the maharaja become when the bell rang to end the first round that he
had almost stopped smiling. Beads of nervous sweat stood out
on his brown plump face and ran down in trickles. His currant
eyes glittered. His teeth flashed.

A brown man threw a bucket of cold water on Sammy.

The bell rang for the second round. History repeated itself.
The two Americans rushed out and met in ring center with
convincing slaps. Burke and Sammy each went down three
times in that round.

Sammy wondered, as he retired to his corner at the end of
the round, if Burke could stand much more of this. They weren't
hurting each other, but they were using up a tremendous amount

of energy. Sammy had discovered in the clinches that Burke was as soft as lard. His muscles were flabby. He didn't have much wind. Once or twice he had staggered.

And Sammy realized that Burke had very cleverly saved his own neck when he had been offering with such apparent generosity to save Sammy's. Burke was soft. Despite the difference in their size and weight, Sammy was reasonably certain that he would have had an even chance of beating the big man.

But Sammy was not resentful. Burke had got away with it. Burke had done all that clever talking to save his own life. And Sammy had thought that he was pretty clever when he had given in to Burke's suggestions!

It was too bad. Sammy had wanted that pearl. Now, neither of them would have it—but they would both have their lives.

Clang! Third round. Burke did not rush out. He came out cautiously. Sammy's rush carried him almost over into Burke's corner. Later, Sammy wondered how he could have been so gullible, so easy. He had been letting himself get more and more careless.

When he rushed over to Burke's corner, he left himself wide open. He expected Burke to slap him harmlessly in the chest, as he had done so often before.

Burke surprised him. The expression on Burke's face should have warned Sammy. Clever as Burke was, he could not conceal his intention entirely. His eyes were needle points, glittering. His mouth was skinned back in the hardest of fighting grins.

Sammy saw that punch coming. It was coming straight for his jaw. He did not try to block or dodge. He did not even draw his head in. He was sure, if he thought at all, that Burke would, at the last split second, slow it down, pull it.

But Burke did not pull that punch. It landed with a brittle smack on Sammy's unprepared and unprotected jaw.

Sammy went down with a thud. For a single startling second he saw not only his favorite constellation but all of the others and a few that he had never seen. Then blackness flooded down.

ONLY THE resiliency of his tough young body saved him from utter annihilation. It had been a scientific punch and a hard one. He was not entirely unconscious. It was as though he were tied down by ropes, against which he was violently struggling. From a great distance he heard the faint but clear voice of the referee.

"... Two—three—four—"

Sammy struggled up through a dozen thicknesses of night. The ropes held him back. He could not throw them off. His heart, his brain, his entire nervous organization was instinctively fighting for him, trying to snatch him back to consciousness—and safety! Only the spark of his consciousness was lacking. It flickered feebly.

"... Five—six—"

With a violent effort, Sammy threw off those ropes. He was lying on his back, staring straight up into the grinning, brown, wet face of the maharaja. Past him the pink ceiling wheeled. It suddenly steadied. A million bells were ringing in Sammy's ears. A billion anvils were clanging. Behind all this were voices—roaring, screaming voices.

Sammy sat up. He rolled over to his hands and knees.

Sammy shook his head. The maharaja was bending over him with his most delighted smile. At the count of seven he said, "Get up and fight, you white dog!" And kicked Sammy in the left kidney with his pointed shoe.

That insult, plus the injury, drove the rest of the fog wisps out of Sammy's enraged brain. He came lurching to his feet. Burke rushed at him with swinging gloves.

Sammy felt the strength surge back into his legs. Perhaps he was suffering from an hallucination. No matter. Never before in any ring had he felt so strong. Never had he felt so agile, so nimble. Burke's size no longer counted.

Sammy met him. There was a thud of wet gloves striking wet flesh. The two men stood toe to toe and slugged, and these were no longer love taps. In the eyes of the treacherous Burke were visions of starving blank panthers. In the eyes of Sammy Shay glowed a fire brighter than the fire of the blue pearl.

Sammy drove past the big man's guard. He was unconquerable now. He had been betrayed. He would not be betrayed again. He beat Burke's gloves down. He pounded his biceps and triceps. He launched a terrific straight punch into the big man's middle. Before Burke could double up, Sammy carried that punch ripping upwards to Burke's loose and sagging jaw.

Three of Burke's teeth flew out.

Burke went down with all the majesty of a monarch of the forest that has been severed at the butt by woodsmen. He crashed to the canvas.

Sammy, with the lust of battle shining more brightly in his eyes, now turned his attention to the maharaja. The maharaja was smiling at him with amiable amazement.

Sammy reached out as a cat reaches out for raw meat; clamped his fingers about the pudgy brown fist containing the priceless pearl. With his right hand he struck the Maharaja of Malobar fairly and squarely in the nose.

When the maharaja went down, he lacked one glorious fire-blue pearl.

Sammy stuffed that handsome gem into the right-hand pocket of his pants.

The pink marble room was in an uproar. Women were screaming. Men were shouting. For the moment Sammy was ignored. He reached down and picked up the limp Burke; tossed him over his shoulder and carried him to the ropes. Swiftly he climbed over and hauled Burke after him.

Then he used the unconscious fighter as a battering ram. He charged through guards and harem women. A knife flashed close to Sammy's neck, but he was not even aware of it.

Somehow, through all that confusion, he staggered out into the open through an arched doorway.

Sammy could have escaped easily and left Burke behind to be murdered at the maharaja's pleasure, but his conscience would not let him. Burke was a double-crosser, a scoundrel, a river rat of the lowest variety—but he was a white man, and Sammy could not desert him.

A TIDE of men and women, all shouting and screaming, swarmed out on the terrace as Sammy staggered across it and found a path.

Something that was little short of a miracle saved Sammy— and Burke. Sammy started down the hill. It was a steep slope to the river. He started to run. Now, if you ever wish to discover new meanings in the laws of momentum, try running down a hill with a hundred and ninety-eight pound man on your back.

If Sammy had lost his footing, all would have been lost. But, miraculously, he did not lose his footing. Perhaps the power of mind over matter was accountable for this. At all events, his legs moved faster and faster and still faster, until Sammy, with his burden, was running down that hill with the abandon of a runaway locomotive. A twig would have upset that delicate balance between running and falling. But there were no twigs, or roots, or even pebbles.

The steep path ended in a right hand turn into a narrow dirt road which ran along the river—a road pounded flat by the feet of countless elephants.

But Sammy did not take that turn. On and on he flew. An hibiscus hush blocked his direct flight into the river. But Sammy and Burke flew through that hush as though it were nothing but air.

As the bank was high at that spot, they must have struck the water at least fifteen feet from shore.

They struck the black water with a tremendous splash, a splash which must have frightened every crocodile a mile up and down the tropical stream. But it could not have been heard, as events proved, by the screaming and shouting hunters who came swarming down the hill.

The violent entrance into the river had at least one other

happy result. It startled Burke back to consciousness. The water was warm. It was sickly warm. But the violence of his entrance into it restored to that scoundrel his faculties.

Burke began automatically to swim.

"Where the hell am I?" he sputtered.

"This way, you rat," said Sammy. And led him with swift, over arm strokes to the opposite bank.

There they found another elephant road. They paused and looked about. Lights were flitting about in the trees on the other side like fireflies gone mad. It did not evidently occur to the pursuit that Sammy and Burke had crossed the river.

That was why it was so fortunate that all those frantic Malays were screaming when Sammy and Burke plunged into the river with that tremendous splash.

Again to his confused companion, Sammy said contemptuously, "This way, you rat!" And Burke meekly followed him down that path, past the bridge and the *sala* Lee Lang May had mentioned, and so to the great mahogany tree.

The Chinese boy was waiting for them under the tree with a long narrow outrigger canoe—a hollowed out breadfruit log with outrigging of bamboo.

In the shimmering light of stars he came running to Sammy and said:

"You won, master, you won!"

"You bet your sweet young life!" said Sammy. Then, briskly, "Climb aboard, Lee." And to Burke, "Get aboard, you dirty double-crosser!"

When they were aboard, Sammy jumped into the stern, picked up a paddle and pushed off. Behind them, in the *kampong*, torches blazed and shrieks rang out. Several rifles were fired.

SAMMY PADDLED briskly until the jungle on either side of the river grew deep and thick beyond the possibility of paths.

Then he rested and began slapping mosquitoes. Lee Yang May lay at his feet looking up at his bloody face in the dim light.

"Burke," Sammy said, "I should have left you back there for those panthers to make shredded wheat out of."

A whine came from the bows of the breadfruit log.

"Buddy, will you listen? It was an accident."

"You're a liar. The only reason I carried you out of there and saved your worthless life was because this is Christmas. I am soft-hearted. I can't help it."

"I was afraid you would knock me out," Burke growled. "It was every man for himself. I knew you had it on me. Besides—didn't you get that pearl?"

"Did I?" Sammy snapped. "If I did, I earned it all right."

The Chinese boy at his feet spoke up.

"The blue fire pearl?"

"That's the one, buddy."

The moon came up over the trees with the suddenness and brilliance of an electric light switched on.

In its hard, cold light, Sammy examined the pearl. Even in this icy light, the blue pearl burned. To Sammy's fingers, it was as smooth as satin.

"It is an evil pearl," the Chinese boy said. "It will bring you nothing but harm and danger and trouble."

"Not me," said Sammy. "I'm going to sell it."

"You must sell it quickly, master. Take it to the Société Anonyme Belge, in Bangkok. They will pay you a fair price for it. You will be a rich man. With the pearl in your possession, you will know nothing but unhappiness. I know the history of that pearl, and of its mate."

"Do you mean," Sammy gasped, "there is another pearl like this in existence?"

"I have heard of it. An old white man came to Malobar about two months ago who told me of these two pearls. He knew that the maharaja had this one, and he said that a tribal chieftain of the Moosars in far northern Siam had the mate. They were once owned by the Gaekwar of Baroda. Three of his wives wore them in turn—and each died of the black plague. It is said—"

"Hold on," Sammy excitedly interrupted. "How long did this old white man stay in Malobar?"

"About a week, master."

"Tell me about him, kid. Quick!"

"There is little to tell, master. He was interested only in pearls and elephants. The maharaja did not like him. He made him go away. But before he went he told me of the blue pearls."

"Where did the old man go?"

"To Praklat. He said he was going on to Siam for the spring elephant drive at Ayeuthia. It takes place this year, master. King Rama will—"

"Never mind King Rama, kid. Was this old man about my size? Did he have blue eyes?"

"Yes, master. He wore the yellow robes of a Burmese Buddhist, and he carried a begging bowl. He said he had begged his way all over India and Burma and Indo-China."

"That old man," Sammy said excitedly, "is my father, buddy! This is the closest I have ever been to him. This is the first time I have known how he rigged himself up. A begging priest, eh? The old boy is clever. Lee, I have been trying to catch up with him for five years. Each time I get within jumping distance of him, he vanishes like a puff of smoke. But I will find him in Siam!"

Sammy slapped a few more mosquitoes, and he drank cool water from a gourd which Lee Yang May had provided. Then he said, bluntly:

"Pick up that paddle, you rat, and get busy. We've got to reach Praklat by dawn. And from there on you walk. *Alone!*"

Burke meekly obeyed.

II

COBRA

*Another "Singapore Sammy" Story of
a Night's Adventure in the Far East
That Led to Pearls and Snakes*

AS DARKNESS FLOWED over the Singapore waterfront, the man who stood under a date palm and dreamily whistled an old Malayan love song was hoping that the American he was going to kill and rob would not be late.

The man under the palm had a slender olive face, adorned by a wisp of black mustache, the innocent smile of a child—and the eyes of a king cobra.

Bronzy-silver eyes were these. And their color and expression did not change. The king cobra, no matter what he may be thinking about, never changes the expression in his eyes. It is a steady, wicked stare—perhaps the steadiest, wickedest stare in the whole world.

This man was part Portuguese, part Malay, and part God knows what. In him, the West met the East and became a power for unlimited malice.

The night air for some distance about this human cobra was stained with the perfume he used—jasmine—and by the acrid fumes of the white Burmese cheroot he was smoking. Through the trees to his left twinkled the lights of Singapore Town, and to his right, beyond the sea wall, stretched the black, star-spangled waters of the roadstead, where lady liners and tramp steamers from all the ports of the world, sailing ships and Chinese junks, Malay proas and Japanese sampans rode at their anchors.

The man with cobra eyes puffed at his cheroot and from time

39

to time inspected the large glowing spark at the end of it. He frequently flicked off ashes, so that the spark would be brightly glowing when it was needed.

Perhaps fifty feet along the path from the date palm were two hibiscus bushes in blossom, one on either side of the path. Behind each of these bushes a dark-skinned man in a black sarong crouched. These two were footpads, and the manner in which they generally went about their work was very interesting. They would wait in concealment for their victim to appear. When he passed their hiding place, they would follow him, their *klungs*—wooden sandals—setting up a lively clatter. And when they were sure that they were not observed, they would quickly step out of the sandals, run forward silently and swiftly on bare feet—and pounce! Almost invariably, they got their man.

The man with cobra eyes had selected these two for his evening's designs because of their unusual strength and their proven experience. There were no two cleverer footpads in Singapore that night!

The plans of the man with cobra eyes were elaborate and sure. When the American for whom he was waiting came walking in this direction, he would pass a distant street light. He would be recognized by the man with cobra eyes, who would send the white cheroot in a soaring arc into the water. The two footpads, waiting for this signal, would fall in behind the American. When he was abreast of the date palm, they would pounce. When the stabbing was done and the American was dead, the man with cobra eyes would step out and attend to the robbery.

Typically Oriental, this was a plan that could not fail. It had stood the acid test of centuries!

The man under the date palm, softly whistling the old Malayan love song, puffed at intervals at the cheroot to keep the glowing coal alive—and waited with the patience of a king cobra at a waterhole.

SINGAPORE SAMMY SHAY, the proposed victim of this program, was just finishing his dinner on the veranda of the Raffles Hotel. Having signed the check and tipped the waiter, he lighted a cigarette and arose from the table. He secured his sun helmet from the door boy, settled it upon his wild red hair, and went out for his customary after-dinner stroll.

For the past two weeks, since his return to the Straits Settlements, it had been Singapore Sammy's regular habit to take a nightly walk which lasted until one in the morning.

He would proceed through the Chinese and Burmese districts, where pearl and elephant men foregathered, peering into bright shop windows, peering into faces, searching, always searching for a graybearded old man in the yellow robes of a Buddhist begging priest, carrying in one hand the familiar begging bowl, carved from a gourd.

At midnight, when the crowds grew thin, Singapore Sammy would return to North Beach Road and follow it to Tanjong Ru, a point of land overgrown by fantastic beefwood trees. Here, in the warm scented breeze blowing through the magical night from Java, he would stroll along the Tanjong Katong and try to forget his troubles until it was one in the morning, or bedtime.

It chanced that on this particular evening, Singapore Sammy—otherwise, Samuel Larkin Shay, United States citizen but for the past six years a restless rover of the Asiatic tropics—carried in the right-hand side pocket of his white drill coat, a small automatic pistol.

For reasons best known to himself, he seldom went armed; but he had, that afternoon, received a letter, a taunting, maddening letter, and tonight, when he reached the hangouts of the pearl and elephant men, he wanted to be prepared. But he was destined not to keep that rendezvous with whatever excitement fate might have had in store for him.

His hand was in his pocket, absently folded about the lump of cool metal, when he left Beach Road and struck off down the path along the waterfront. And because his mind was deeply

preoccupied with that taunting letter, he paid no attention to
the clattering of wooden-sandals on the hard path behind him.

Proceeding along the path, Sammy was only subconscious-
ly aware that the clattering abruptly came to an end. He was
not thinking of footpads; his thoughts were miles away.

Now came an impression, likewise vague, of a strong perfume.
Jasmine. And he supposed indifferently that some Malay girl
had preceded him along the path by a few minutes. Malay girls
love sickening perfumes.

It was a sharp hissing of indrawn breath behind him that
warned Singapore Sammy that all was not well.

In the next split-second, a terrific blow was delivered on his left side just under his armpit.

The force of the blow sent Sammy staggering along the path a half dozen steps. Violently, his head snapped back. His sun helmet fell to the ground.

Almost senseless, with the wind knocked out of him, the redheaded adventurer sprawled to the path. Fortunately, he had, in the violence of his fall, yanked out of his coat pocket the automatic pistol. It now lay beside him, covered by his right arm.

The footpads pounced. With nimble fingers, they stripped open his shirt collar. A hand plunged down between chest and shirt. There was a sudden profane muttering in Malay. Then a hand reached into his inner coat pocket and plucked out his leather wallet.

Limp from the blow, Sammy could not move. But his senses remained remarkably clear. He was fully aware that the pistol was under his arm—if he only had the strength to grasp and use it! And their whispers, in Malay, came to him distinctly.

"It was not there, Master."

"What have you?"

"This, Master—a wallet."

"Give it to me!"

"Yes, master."

The numbness in Sammy's left side was replaced by a sharp, throbbing pain. And he knew he had been stabbed and was probably bleeding to death.

AS THE pain increased, some of his strength returned. He moved his arm until his fingers found the butt of the pistol. Quickly, he released the safety catch, sat up.

Two brawny black shadows loomed at his feet. He put three bullets precisely into the middle of each of these. He looked for the third man, the one addressed as "master."

An automobile's headlights flicked across the scene and momentarily lighted the face of a slim man who was looking down at him and hastily backing away.

Sammy's black wallet was in his hand, but Sammy hardly saw the wallet. He was staring at the man's face. It was a strange face, but it was one that Singapore Sammy would never forget, with its wisp of black mustache and its bronzy-silver eyes. It was like a face vividly seen in a lightning flash. And the steady wicked stare of the bronzy-silver eyes remained long after the headlights had swept on.

Sammy gurgled an oath. He aimed and fired at the place

where those cobra eyes had been. A crackling in the underbrush answered him. The man with cobra eyes was getting away!

The redheaded American fired the remaining bullets in the clip after these sounds. He staggered to his feet and followed. He tried to cry out, but his voice came husky and muffled, as though a hand were being held over his mouth. And some liquid came from his lungs.

The pain in his back was now almost unbearable. Reaching behind him, his fingers closed loosely on the handle of a knife. He tried to pull it out, but it was lodged so tightly that it would not give.

Away off to his left, he heard the man with cobra eyes crashing through bushes. Sammy could not follow. He knew that he was bleeding internally; knew that he must somehow get to a doctor quickly.

His legs began to give out. All feeling went out of them. He was conscious now of nothing but the brutal pain of that knife in his back.

He staggered and fell. Half conscious, he dragged himself toward the nearest light on hands and knees. Constant hard exercise in the jungles and at sea had toughened his muscles, given him superhuman endurance. And it required superhuman endurance to remain conscious while he dragged himself, sick and senseless with pain, toward the street light. Blood was coming now in little bubbles from his lips. Even in his torturing pain he knew it was blood—a sinister warning that he had little time to lose.

With his head hanging down like that of a beaten animal, he dragged himself onto Beach Road. The pain in his back and side was blotting out everything. Only dimly did he see a double ricksha, with a naked-legged coolie between the shafts, swing into sight; a figure in white seated on the wide seat.

A man's voice gave a sharp command in Malay. And a moment later, Singapore Sammy was absolutely sure that the pain had unseated his reason.

The man was helping him to his feet, and the light was full on his face—the face of a man who had once been closer to him than a brother could have been: a lean, pale, aristocratic face, with dark eyes, a proud mouth, bracketed with deeply carved lines which bespoke dissipation.

But it was a face seen in soft focus. The man's dark eyes stared at him with recognition and amazement.

The outlines of the face in the fog were familiar. But Singapore Sammy could not be sure—and he would not believe!

With a handkerchief the man was wiping the blood that dribbled from Sammy's mouth. His agitated voice said, "Get into this ricksha quick, Sam!" Then he saw the haft of the knife sticking out from under Singapore Sammy's left shoulder, and gasped, "Good God, fellow!"

Singapore Sammy, like a man so drunk he can hardly maintain his balance, stood and stared and swayed. He shook blood from his lower lip with a savage shake of his head and spat out in a spray of blood:

"You—rat!"

He could not yet be sure that it was Ted McAlister; he was sure only that he hated Ted McAlister and never wanted to see him again.

"Get away from me, you rat!" he said thickly, and tried to push the young man away, but all his strength was gone. He would have fallen if Ted McAlister had not been holding him up.

"Let me alone! I'm all right."

The young man's expression had hardened, and his dark eyes had narrowed. Through tight lips he said: "Don't be so damned stubborn, Singapore. I'm going to take you to a hospital."

And in a sharp voice he ordered the coolie to help. Still standing between the shafts, the coolie was staring at the bleeding white man with grinning interest. Life is cheap in the Far East—but a white man's death is a laughing matter.

He came grinning over. Hatred, resentment ebbed low in

the redheaded American. A devil was astride his shoulders, swinging a pick with a point like a vulture's beak. In measured strokes, he swung the point of the pick into a hole, four ribs down, on Sammy's back.

THE VICTIM of circumstances came out of this nightmare a few minutes later to be conscious of a shoulder on which his head was resting, of a voice cursing. His head was on Ted McAlister's shoulder and Ted McAlister was cursing at the coolie, ordering him to go faster. The fat brown calves of the coolie were twinkling.

Singapore Sammy tried to lift his head but could not.

"Be quiet," said Ted's voice. "We're almost there."

"I'd rather die," Sammy grunted, "than have to be thankful to you for anything. Stop this ricksha and I'll prove it!"

"I thought you were up in Siam," Ted said irrelevantly.

"You rat!" said Sammy.

This angered his old friend.

"Look here, Sam; if you want to row in the state you're in, I'll row. Just because I don't happen to look at things the way you do—"

"Hell!" Sammy broke in. "After solemnly promising me to live decently like a white man, you go to Shanghai and get in the worst possible mess; first drink, then opium. Play fall guy for a bunch of suckers, tag around with the rottenest crowd East of Suez…."

"Oh, snap out of it, Singapore. I know I owe you a whole lot for straightening me out, and I'm not forgetting it either. But I can explain all the Shanghai business if you'll only—"

"No," Sammy shouted. "I won't listen to any more of your glib excuses. Let me out of this ricksha. I don't owe you anything but trouble. Get that?"

"Keep still, will you?" begged Ted McAlister. "That knife's in a bad place. Stop that squirming."

But the obstinate redhead, who hated this man as he had hated few men, would not subside.

"Look here, Ted. Are you in wrong?"

Ted hesitated. "Yes," came the reluctant answer.

"I knew it!" Singapore Sammy growled. "I knew you'd get in wrong without me to look after you." Sammy struggled to sit up, but fell back with a groan against Ted McAlister's shoulder. He had sworn he would never acknowledge Ted McAlister's existence as long as he lived.

But he said no more. The demon with the pick was astride his shoulders once more. In a red dream shot with pain he saw the square brick posts of the hospital entrance flit past.

Then he was being lifted down and half carried, half dragged into a large, gloomy reception room, badly lighted. There was a dark flight of steps to the right. Beyond, a courtyard, with a thin moon hanging over a sago palm. On the left, an old oak desk behind which sat a Malay with stupid eyes.

Slumped down in a chair, Singapore Sammy took in impressions as through a dozen layers of heavy gauze. The world was nothing but throbbing pain. Even the light over the desk jumped with each throb.

He heard Ted's angry voice. He was giving the desk boy the devil about something. Where was the doctor? Well, why wasn't he? The desk boy dumbly disavowed all responsibility.

"Doctor giving party, savvy? Doctor busy, savvy?"

"Well, for crying out loud!" snarled Ted McAlister. And he was gone with a banging of heels on bare wood that reminded Sammy of a machine gun burst.

Things grew worse for Singapore Sammy. He tried to tell the human ox at the desk to pull the knife out of his back. The ox sat there and stared at him with dull indifference. Damn Malays! Damn 'em all!

A disagreeable faced white man in the white peajacket of the formal Briton in the Oriental tropics came in. There was another machine gun burst, then Ted again, indignant:

"It's a damned outrage, Doctor! Somebody ought to be here to attend to emergency cases like this. A minute may mean the difference between life and death. This man was stabbed at least twenty minutes ago!"

The doctor looked at Sammy, looked at the handle of that knife sticking out his back. He reached down and gave it a tug. Sammy groaned and Ted growled.

The doctor turned on him with a dark scowl.

"Are you related to this man?"

"No."

"Kindly give your name and address to the registration clerk. This is a police case. You will be wanted in the morning for questioning. You can go now."

"I want this man to have the best of everything."

"He will get it."

"I'll be back in the morning," Ted said.

"No," Sammy managed to groan. "No."

He was not aware that Ted was gone. His next impression was of being carried up, rolled into a bed. There a final terrific throb in his back; then he sank into oblivion. He didn't know that the knife had been pulled out; but it had. That knife, as he learned later, had split a rib. Its keen point had pierced the fourth rib and punctured the lung. Well, the footpad's aim had been bad. Singapore Sammy had missed death by a small part of an inch.

SINGAPORE SAMMY did not waken until mid-forenoon, with the bright equatorial sun shining in the leaves of tamarinds and breadfruit trees outside his windows. A check-up showed that he was resting comfortably. The pain wasn't bad—if he didn't move around.

He was in a private room on a corner. A breeze drifted through the double copper screened windows and faintly stirred a lock of fiery red hair that had fallen across his forehead.

The door opened and a pretty nurse in white came in. He grinned amiably.

"Hullo, sister." She had a nice smile.

"Hullo, redhead. Comfortable?"

"Yeah. How come I rate this private room? I'm a charity case."

The nurse continued to smile. She had heard all about her patient's all-night battle against the forces of death.

"I don't know. Someone wants you to have the best of everything. Don't you deserve it?"

"I deserve what I get, sister. That's me—the kid philosopher!"

"Did you deserve that knife in the back?" She was shaking down a thermometer.

"It gives me," said Sammy cryptically, "a good excuse to get well. Have I had any visitors?"

She smiled again and slid the thermometer under his tongue.

"The chief of police, two detectives, a worried young man and a snooty young official from your consulate. Please relax, Mister Shay. You're not out of danger yet, you know."

Sammy relaxed. When she withdrew the thermometer, he said:

"I'll see the police force, but I'm not in to that worried guy. Get that, sister. It goes for all the time I'm here."

The nurse stopped smiling.

"Very well, Mister Shay. The young man from the American consulate is waiting downstairs. You can see him for ten minutes—then no more visitors today."

"That's jake with me. Are you the floor nurse or a private?"

"Private."

"Who's paying your salary?"

"I don't know."

"But you know I'm flat broke?"

"Yes, I know."

She went out. Puzzled, Sammy relaxed. He discovered he

was hungry. He wanted a thick juicy beefsteak smothered with onions, a platter of buckwheat cakes with real maple syrup, and some of those little sausages. This meant that he was homesick. Six years away from America. Dead broke. Friendless in an alien land.

The door opened and a tall, thin young man with pale-blue eyes came in. He had no chin to mention. He was bold and thin lipped. He looked mean. A brief acquaintance proved that he was every inch as mean as he looked.

There was a certain cold fishiness in the look he bent upon Sammy as he closed the door, pulled up a chair and sat down. He removed from his pocket a slip of yellow paper on which were some notes. He consulted these with a faint, irritated frown for some seconds, then bent a frown that was even more irritated upon Singapore Sammy.

In a thin voice, he said, "Your name is Samuel Shay?"

"Yeah," said Sammy, and wondered.

"I am the American vice-consul," said the young man. "My name is Victor Halloway."

"Yeah?" said Sammy, and stopped wondering. Hooray for the Stars and Stripes! Let the good old eagle scream. It would—and promptly did!

"The consul looks upon you as a troublemaker, Mister Shay," said the vice-consul, clearing his throat thinly. "Last night two natives were found shot to death beside a path running along the waterfront on Raffles Plain. A trail of blood from that spot led to Beach Road—where you were picked up in a ricksha and brought to this hospital. You shot those men, Mister Shay!"

"But holy suffering catfish," said Sammy, indignantly, "look what they did to me! They stabbed me with intent to kill. They stripped me!"

"Did they get that pearl?"

Sammy pretended he didn't understand.

"What pearl?" he asked innocently.

THE VICE-CONSUL, beneath his disapproval of Singapore Sammy for being the kind of American he was, seemed embarrassed. But his curiosity got the better of him.

"I heard a story that you had won a fabulous blue pearl—a blue fire pearl—in a fist fight several months ago up in Malobar. The maharaja offered it as a prize, and you won it. Isn't that story true?"

"Yeah," Sammy said.

"Is it true that you carry it in a chamois sack at the end of a copper wire around your neck?"

"It *was* true," said Sammy.

"You mean—they got it away from you last night?"

"No, they didn't get it. I have it parked."

The pale-blue eyes were gleaming.

"In Singapore?"

"Who wants to know?" asked Sammy.

The vice-consul seemed flustered; then his irritability and his haughty disapproval of the adventurer returned.

"The consul has requested me to tell you that he wants you to keep that pearl away from Singapore."

"That's a laugh," said Sammy. "Why?"

"Because wherever you take it, it causes trouble."

"You tell your boss," said Sammy, "to keep his nose out of my business."

Mr. Halloway stiffened indignantly.

"Mister Shay," he said hotly, "I could have you locked up for that little affair of last night."

"Then why in hell don't you?" shouted Sammy. "You trot along and tell your boss that!"

The pale-blue eyes of the vice-consul were shimmering with fury.

"You forget that the consul and I are the official representatives of the United States in Singapore—and that we are responsible for the actions of Americans here!"

"Says you!"

Mr. Halloway leaped up.

"I wish you to understand, Mister Shay, that nothing but my—my fellow feeling for you, as an American, a countryman, prevents your arrest at this moment for the murder of those two natives last night!"

Sammy, in his amazement, tried to sit up, but he fell back with a groan.

"Can you tie that!" he gasped. "Those footpads jumped me and stabbed me and rolled me for every dollar I had—and you stand there, you pop-eyed parrot, and talk about havin' me pinched! Get the hell out of here!"

The vice-consul considered him with frosty hate.

"That's your story," he said. "But we notice that every time you come to Singapore, you start serious trouble. When you are discharged from this hospital, I want you to clear out and stay out!"

"Listen, big shot," snapped Sammy. "I'm an American citizen, understand? Last night, while I was takin' a peaceful walk, mindin' my own business, three natives attacked me. I got two of 'em. The third got away. Instead of pickin' on me, why aren't you after him? How long you been in Malaya?"

The vice-consul glared at him and licked his thin lips.

"Two years," he said.

"In the course of your travels—ever see a king cobra?"

"What has that—"

"Answer yes or no! Ever see a king cobra?"

"Yes! Certainly!"

"Know what a cobra's eyes look like?"

"Yes!"

"Know a man in this town with eyes like a king cobra's; halfcaste, Portuguese blood, thin olive face, little black eyebrow mustache?"

"I never saw such a man!"

"When you do, let me know. That's the guy who had charge of this surprise party last night. Just get me his name and address. I'll attend to the details when I'm out of this dump."

The vice-consul backed to the door.

"When you're able to leave this hospital, you're going to clear out of Singapore—and stay out!"

"All right," Sammy snapped. "That goes double for you while I'm in this room! Hit the grit before I ruin that tree out there with you!"

Mr. Halloway cleared his throat dangerously, but said nothing more. It was obvious that he considered himself too superior socially to Sammy to stoop to vulgar squabbles. He put on his sun helmet and departed.

THUS, WHEN the door opened again, a few minutes later, Singapore Sammy was in a ripe mood for argument with anybody who entered the room. And it chanced that the newcomer was Ted McAlister. Ted, in rather seedy looking white drill and a rather seedy looking pith sala topee. His smile was uncertain and his dark eyes were miserable. He carried in either hand a heavy suitcase.

Sammy's resentful blue eyes glared at the suitcases, then settled hotly on Ted's thin white face.

In a nervous voice, Ted explained.

"I brought them over from the hotel. They said downstairs you might be here for three weeks. So I checked you out at the hotel and brought your stuff. I packed everything."

Ted was avoiding Sammy's eyes.

"You've got more brass in you," said Sammy, "than the big Buddha at Kamakura. I told you last night not to come back."

"I had to come back, Sam."

"Yeah? I told the nurse not to let you in."

"Sam, you've got to listen to me."

Sammy, looking at him, grunted.

"There's nothin' you can say," he said, "that I want to listen to. Roll along, you rat."

With an air of desperation, Ted seated himself on the bedside chair. He looked at Singapore Sammy hopelessly.

"You give everybody else a square break, Sam. You used to stand back of me."

"Sure! Before I got wise to you."

Ted grinned. He was sitting dejectedly. Even his hands looked dejected. He took out a cigarette and lighted it.

"Light one for me," said Sammy.

"The nurse said I wasn't to let you have any."

"Oh, she did, did she?"

"You've got a hole in your lung."

"And I got a hole in my face, and I'm gonna use it. I suppose you're the mysterious party who's payin' for this room and the nurse."

"Yes," said Ted wearily.

"Well, what the hell's the big idea?"

In discouraged tones, Ted answered.

"Do you suppose I could let my best pal be sick in a public ward, in this rotten town, without doing what little I could? Stop putting chips on your shoulders for a while, will you, and let me explain."

Singapore Sammy looked hard at him.

"I'm listening," he muttered.

"Well, why do you hate me like this?"

"Do we have to go into that again?"

Ted nodded grimly.

"I want to have this out with you."

"All right, old-timer! When that crowd of Shanghai rotters first got hold of you, I was just finishin' up a job that had taken me the best part of two years—makin' a man of you. It took me, as you may remember, two hard years of bullyin' and nursin', but I broke you off the black smoke, and I broke you off the booze. I could finally stand back and say, 'There, by God, is somethin' to be proud of!' And you promised me, didn't you, to never backslide on me. Did you backslide?"

"Singapore, listen," Ted hoarsely began. "I went to Hongkong. After you disappeared. I got a job with Hannibal, the exporter and importer—"

"Hing Sing Tai Pan—on Ice House Lane?" Sammy broke in.

"Yes. Hing Sing gave me a job and moved me up as fast as I learned the business. And then—Hannibal shifted me to Canton; gave me charge of the Shameen office.

"Well, that was the end of everything. You know that Shameen crowd. I couldn't keep away from booze. Then one night I came home so tight the coolies had to carry me in. By the end of the year, I was coming home that way every night. I couldn't stop it. And I was playing poker with that Shameen crowd—table stakes."

TED McALISTER stopped. Singapore Sammy wasn't looking at him, and his mouth was grim. Ted went on.

"I tried to get in touch with you. I knew that if anybody could snap me out of it, you could. So I wrote you to Japan, Java, India, and God knows where. Why didn't you answer?"

"I tore 'em up."

"Without reading them?"

"Without reading 'em."

Ted's mouth was twisted queerly.

"All right, fellow," he said thickly. "You feel the way you feel, and nothing I can say will change you. I've wanted to get straight with you for a long time—to show you that I've done my damnedest not to go back on my promises to you. But why argue about it? You hate my guts. I'm rolling along." He got up. "So long."

"Wait a minute," Singapore Sammy barked. "You've been sick, haven't you?"

"I've been sick as hell ever since I went on the wagon."

"You're on it this time, are you?"

"I'm on it for good."

"How about the black smoke?"

"I haven't touched it since that night you wrecked that joint in Shanghai—and beat me up."

Singapore Sammy held out his hand.

"Kid," he said huskily, "I'm crawling. I want to apologize. Shake my hand, will you? That's a boy! So you're in a jam, are you? Well, whatever it is, just leave it to me, kid. We'll find a way out. Damn your lousy old hide, it sure is good to see you again! Stop worryin'. What's the jam? Let's hear the rest of it. Let's hear the worst."

Ted McAlister's eyes were somewhat moist, but he was grinning.

"Well, Sam; you know that kind of poker I play."

"Do I know the kind of poker you play!" Sammy exclaimed. "Buddy, are you forgettin' the times I've yanked you out of poker games by the scruff of your neck? You never had the self-control. Your idea of a conservative game of poker was stud with the twos, treys, fours and the one-eyed jacks wild."

"It's not my game. I know it, but I couldn't keep away from it."

"Using Hing Sing's money?"

"No. But signing chits."

"I smelled that comin'. How deep are you in, kid?"

"I've got fifteen thousand worth of chits in circulation."

"Holy mackerel!" said Sammy.

Now, in China, an I.O.U. is called a "chit." Any white man in a responsible position can sign chits for almost any sum he wishes. The native bankers accept the chits at their face value. They go into circulation and are, among the natives, as good as money. Occasionally, they are presented to the man who signed them for payment. If he doesn't wish to pay, they go back into circulation. It is the most perniciously easy way in the world to get deep into debt. And a man cannot honorably leave the country for good until all his chits are paid.

"What it boils down to," said Sammy "is that we have got to raise enough money to redeem all those chits."

Singapore Sammy gazed scowlingly at the ceiling. "Kid, do you know what I used to tell you? You don't belong in China. You are one of the guys who never learn to fit into these countries. Where you belong is South Bend, Indiana. Are your folks still down on you?"

"No," said Ted. "I had a letter from my father about a year ago, begging me to come home. He's getting old, and wants me to come home and learn how to manage the factory. But I wouldn't go then."

"Too much pride?"

"Yes."

"I don't blame you. Would you go now?"

"How can I?"

"That's up to us," said Sammy. "As long as the door to South Bend is open, we'll find a way of boosting you through it."

"Well I've had enough of China," Ted sighed. "I hone to see America again. By the way, Sam, did you ever find your father?"

"Look in the pocket of that coat I was wearin' last night," said Sammy, "and see if those footpads took a letter that was in there."

TED WENT to the closet and found the letter. A corner of it was black with dried blood.

"Read it," said Sammy.

Ted opened the letter and read:

> *My dear son:*
> *Stop being a sucker. Stop wasting your time trying to catch up with me. I don't want to see you and I'm not going to let you see me. The hand is faster than the naked eye. You might try putting grease on your heels, lamps on your eyes and scoops on your ears. A wise*

man knows the aim of a bottle. Your loving father.
   Bill Shay.

Ted looked over the top of the letter at Singapore Sammy.

"What does he mean by, 'A wise man knows the aim of a bottle?'"

"It's an old Siamese saying," Sammy answered. "It means, a hunch to a wise guy is plenty."

"Do you know what your old man looks like?"

"Yeah. He dresses in the yellow robes of a Burmese Buddhist priest—begging priest. He sports a long gray beard. I got that in Malobar."

"Singapore, why are you so anxious to find him? It was the one thing you'd never talk about."

"I'll tell you! He's got my grandfather's will, leavin' me about a million dollars—and I can't get the million without that will. But I'll get him! I'll get him if it takes me the rest of my life!"

Singapore Sammy stared moodily at the ceiling, then snapped his fingers.

"Let's get down to business, kiddo. We've got to get you out of China and back to South Bend. We've got to raise better than fifteen thousand dollars, Mex. I'm broke. There was close to five thousand dollars, in Straits money, in that wallet those footpads got last night. How're we gonna raise fifteen or twenty thousand bucks? Say! What you doin' in Singapore?"

Ted fumbled in his coat pocket; brought out a tiny red lac-quered box—about an inch square it was—and opened it.

On a white satin pad lay a pear-shaped black pearl. Singapore Sammy looked at it.

"Listen, Ted," he said. "Did you ever hear about the blue fire pearl of Malobar?"

"Yes."

"The story got way up to Canton?"

"Yes."

"Do you know what that blue egg is worth?"

"I heard it was priceless."

"I've turned down twenty-five thousand, gold, for that pearl, kiddo. I'd almost rather part with my life than lose it. But I'd sell it now—to get you out of hock, Ted. I'd sell it, but how can I? It's locked up in the steel safe of a friend of mine who runs a rice mill in Bangkok. And where's the guy who owns the rice mill? In Paris! And won't be back for three months! So we can't sell the blue pearl. We've got to raise the money some other way. But don't worry, old-timer, we'll raise it!"

"Singapore," Ted said nervously, "I'm going. You've got a temperature. You've talked too long."

"Wait a minute," Singapore Sammy picked up that black pearl and examined it minutely. "Where'd you get this?"

"I bought it four years ago in Shanghai from a sailor who didn't know what it was worth. It's worth three thousand in Hongkong. I was taking it to Ceylon. I could get four thousand for it there."

"Maybe," said Sammy. "Did you figure you were going to make enough profit, out of going to Ceylon, to pay for your return trip from Hongkong?"

Ted nodded. Singapore Sammy shook his head.

"I question that this pearl is worth even three thousand. It would be almost impossible to match, because of the way it curves in at the neck. Leave this pearl with me. Let me sleep on it. Let me see if I can hatch an idea out of it. How much cash have you?"

"Just about enough to pay my hotel bill and your hospital bill for three weeks. Singapore," Ted growled. "What can we do? You can't get up for weeks. How can we possibly raise twenty thousand?"

Singapore Sammy grinned.

"Kid, I get a good idea once in a while. I want you to do something for me. I want you to look for a guy. I'll do the worrying if you'll do the looking. Did you ever see a king cobra?"

"No," Ted told him. "I hate snakes."

"Never mind. This guy I want to find has eyes just like a cobra. Sort of silvery, sort of bronzy, see? I never saw a pair of eyes quite like 'em. Cold and wicked and snaky. He's about your size, and he's olive skinned, and he wears a little black mustache. He's part Portuguese, I'd say, and part native. He dresses well. Last night he was wearin' a suit of Shantung silk."

"Who is he?"

"All I know is that he is the guy who engineered that little raid on me last night. He must know the town well. Puttin' this and that together, I'd say he belongs here. Find him for me!"

"But how shall I go about it?"

"Go down to Jochore Road, where they sell the animals. Get some storekeeper to show you a king cobra. Take a good look at his eyes. Then look all over town till you find a guy whose eyes match the cobra's."

Ted arose.

"I'll try, Singapore. I'll do my best."

"And don't worry. We'll find a way to get you back to South Bend. So long, Kid."

"So long, Singapore."

IT WAS a discouraged and hopeless young man who left the Singapore Hospital that blazing noon to follow the instructions of a man who, he was certain, was suffering then from a touch of fever. But Ted did follow his instructions. He forswore his usual noon siesta, without which life in Singapore is almost unbearable, and proceeded to Jochore Road to look into the eyes of a king cobra.

A Chinese shopkeeper took him to a cage made of fine but strong brass wire mesh, and Ted experienced the doubtful pleasure of looking into the bronzy-silver eyes of the most vicious reptile in the world.

Still uncomfortable from the steady cold hatred with which the cobra had stared at him, Ted went out into the blast furnace—which is Singapore at noon—and began his search for an olive-skinned man of about his own height, with a wisp of black mustache and eyes that matched those bronzy-silver ones he had just seen.

Ted's search proved very discouraging. He reported daily to Singapore Sammy, who daily showed marked signs of recovering from that villainous stab in the back. But that redheaded optimist would not be discouraged.

"I have a hunch he's in this town," Sammy once said. "'A wise man knows the aim of a bottle.' Give my hunch machine a little more time to grind out something." He was referring then to the problem of finding a way to make the three thousand-dollar pearl grow into a twenty thousand-dollar bankroll.

That was what Ted was most anxious to know.

Sammy took out the red lacquered box from under his pillow, opened it and let a ray of sunlight play upon the satiny blackness of the pear-shaped pearl.

"This is the idea," said Sammy. "This is a three thousand-dollar seed. One o' these days, it's goin' grow into a twenty thousand-dollar idea."

"Singapore," Ted grunted, "what are you driving at?"

"Kid, I'm tellin' you this is a funny country. The longer I live in it, the funnier it gets. Some men, like you, it eats alive. Other men, like me, pick sharks' teeth for a livin'—and get away with it As my old man says, 'A wise man knows the aim of a bottle.'"

"I believe you're running a temperature!"

"Kid, I'm colder than the heart of that guy you're lookin' for! Run along and find him for me. And keep your chin up. One of these days you'll be in South Bend, Indiana; and you'll belong to a country club, and you'll be goin' to the movies every night— and wishin' to hell you were back on the China coast, doin' fool stunts like tryin' to make a three thousand-dollar pearl grow into a twenty thousand-dollar wad!"

"Not much, I'll wish I were back!" Ted snorted.

"Yeah? Well, you find the guy with those eyes."

But Ted did not. In a ricksha that he hired by the day, he

searched Singapore Town from the Jochore River to Pulau Brani, and from Tanjong Ru to the Tanglin Barracks. He not only did not see the man with cobra eyes, but he saw no man who resembled him..

And he did not dare go to the police. The police knew that he and Singapore Sammy were friends; the police knew that Singapore Sammy wanted to find a man who had eyes like a cobra's—and the police wanted Sammy to leave town the moment he was able to travel.

ON THE first day that Singapore Sammy was permitted to dress and walk in the hospital garden, a man from police headquarters dropped in to see him. He was politely skeptical of Sammy's story of the two footpads, and when Sammy mentioned the man with cobra eyes, the police headquarters man looked at him vaguely. And Sammy was forced to conclude that his visitor knew the name of the man with cobra eyes, and was either shielding him or did not want to supply Sammy with the seeds for further trouble. He left Sammy with the blunt statement that the chief of police of Singapore expected Sammy to get out of town as soon as he was able to.

Mr. Halloway, from the American consulate, visited Sammy a day or two later, and repeated the message from the chief of police.

"If you have no money," he said, "we will arrange for your transportation out of the Straits Settlements."

"Where to?" Sammy wanted to know.

"Siam or Indo-China or India."

"Just out of the country?"

"That's all."

"I ought to feel flattered for bein' so important," said the redhead.

"You needn't," the vice-consul assured him. "It's merely that we have enough troubles without you. Don't forget, Mister Shay: you're to leave as soon as you're well enough."

"I'll make a note of it," Sammy promised.

On the day when Singapore Sammy was well enough to leave the hospital, Ted called for him on a double ricksha. Pale and more than a little wabbly, Sammy climbed in beside him.

"Where to?" Ted asked.

"Back to the hotel. My credit's still good there."

But it wasn't. Singapore Sammy was courteously informed that the hotel was crowded, every room taken. The snooty young vice-consul had evidently left no stone unturned.

Ted was staying at a Japanese hotel, and Singapore Sammy joined him there. It was none too clean, but it was cheap.

Some of Sammy's optimism was gone. He was without ideas for helping Ted, and it seemed dubious that he would ever find the man who had stolen his bankroll. Furthermore, at any moment, a man from headquarters or the American consulate might trail him—order him to leave town at once.

The knife wound had left Sammy weak. He should have spent his nights and most of his days in bed, recovering his strength, instead of which he prowled the streets, looking for the man with cobra eyes.

And on his fifth day out of the hospital, he found him.

Singapore and Ted were returning from a ride along the Tanjong Katong in a ricksha. It was almost noon, and the streets were clearing. As their ricksha swung from Beach Road into Brah-Basah Road, a single ricksha passed them, proceeding east along Brah-Basah. And in it, with his snowy sun helmet tilted rakishly, his slender brown hands folded complacently across his lean stomach, his well cut Shantung silk suit fairly glowing in the blistering midday sun, sat the man with cobra eyes.

He did not see Singapore Sammy. And as the rickshas passed, Sammy ducked his head so that his face was concealed by the brim of his helmet, and gripped Ted's arm.

"There," said Sammy in a low, excited voice, "goes my meat!"

"That fellow in that ricksha we just passed?" Ted gulped.

"Yep! Notice his eyes?"

"No. Are you sure, Singapore? He didn't look like a crook."

"I'm dead sure."

Singapore Sammy spoke to the coolie. The coolie stopped, turned and followed the other ricksha.

It turned down North Bridge Road and crossed Middle Road. Halfway down the block it stopped. Its occupant alighted and entered a store. Singapore jumped out and walked slowly past the store. On the window, in gold leaf letters, was the legend:

ARMAND DE SILVIO
DIAMONDS AND PEARLS

Singapore Sammy saw that the man with cobra eyes had gone back of the counter and placed his hat on the shelf. He was now talking to a Chinese clerk.

The redheaded adventurer walked on. At great personal risk, he questioned a Sikh policeman. Yes, that was Mr. Armand de Silvio who had just entered his store. Singapore Sammy tried not to betray his excitement.

"Is it a good store?"

"One of the best in Singapore, sahib."

WELL, THAT was that. Singapore Sammy returned to the ricksha. He climbed in and told the coolie to trot along.

"Singapore, are you sure that's the man?" Ted asked, as they rolled along.

"No question about it," Sammy said cheerfully. He was lighter spirited than he had been since his arrival in Singapore.

"What are you going to do?"

"Ted, it's like a game of chess. There's a dozen moves I can make, but there's only one that'll checkmate him."

"You'll have to hurry," Ted warned. "They'll be ordering you out of town at any moment."

"I know, I know. Let's go down to the waterfront. I want to

look at a horizon and think. It's funny how ideas come sneaking over a horizon if you look at it long enough."

SO THEY went down to the waterfront, dismissed the ricksha and walked down the path to the very tree under which Mr. de Silvio had stood that night and tossed his white cheroot into the water.

Under the date palm they sat down, and Singapore Sammy looked at sailing ships and steamers, at proas and junks and sampans, and smoked innumerable cigarettes, while his active mind played with ideas. Occasionally he grinned. Occasionally he grunted. Occasionally he scowled at the steel-blue horizon where these ideas were coming from.

And suddenly he laughed.

"Buddy," he said to Ted. "I've got it. But it isn't one move. It's two. How much money've you got left?"

"Less than a hundred dollars."

"Have you got any swell clothes?"

"1 have one good suit. I've been saving it."

"Save it no longer! Now, look," said the excited redhead. "You check out of the dump where we're staying, and check in at the Grand Hotel de L'Europe. I want you to put up a million-dollar front. Savvy?"

"No, I don't," said Ted. "What's it all about?"

"On second thought," Sammy said thoughtfully, "I won't tell you. Maybe it's somethin' crooked. You're gonna keep your hands and face clean. You're a puppet in my hands. Get me? A puppet!"

"All right," Ted laughed. "I go to the Grand Hotel de L'Europe, register, and put on my best bib and tucker."

"Right! You mention haughtily that you are Mr. Theodore Varden McAlister, Jr., of South Bend, Indiana—the Agricultural Implement McAlisters. Well, isn't it true?"

"I suppose it is. You want me to make an impression."

"The wealthiest you can, kiddo. And you tell the desk clerk

that you are tremendously interested in pearls. Every pearl dealer in Singapore will know about you inside of half an hour. The desk clerk will see to that—it'll mean cumshaw for him if you do any buying. Follow me?"

"No, Singapore. But go on."

"You put it across strong that you are a millionaire. This afternoon, just before the stores close, you hire a Rolls-Royce for one hour—that'll be twenty-five bucks—and you go down to Armand de Silvio's—with this black pearl!"

"I'm beginning to see the plot," Ted chuckled.

"If you are, kid, you're good, because it has everything in it but a chariot race. You take that pearl into De Silvio, and very haughtily you ask him to appraise it. You tell him you paid five thousand for it, no matter what it's worth."

Ted's eyes clouded.

"Why?" he asked.

"To make him think you're a rich American sucker!"

"And then what?"

"Now we're comin' to the point. You tell him you want to match that pearl. You want to match it exactly, savvy? You tell him you're takin' it home to your mama, and you want to take her a pair. Price is no object. You'll go as high as twenty-five thousand for a mate to this."

"That," said Ted, "is a laugh."

"Why is it? If you had the mate to this, wouldn't the two of them be worth fifty thousand easy? Wouldn't they?"

"Well, what if they would? I haven't twenty-five thousand to buy the mate to it. But he won't have the mate, anyway. You said this pearl was a freak and could never be matched!"

"Kid," said Singapore almost affectionately, "go on up to the head of the class. You tell De Silvio you'll be brokenhearted if you don't find the mate to this pearl. You have him take its measurements, weigh it, study it under a glass—and keep saying that you must find its mate. You tell him you might even go as high as thirty thousand. You are going to break his heart. He will follow you out to the car, tryin' to sell you everything from amethysts to synthetic rubies. You'll tell him you will be at the Europe for a few days. You will wait word from him. Then you go back to the hotel and get rid of that Rolls-Royce before it eats up your bankroll."

"With the pearl?"

"Sure. You keep the pearl."

"Then what?"

"Never mind then what. Make it snappy. Go through with this program and meet me tonight at seven under this tree."

"You seem to like this tree."

"I am superstitious. Any questions?"

"I think not. I'll see you tonight at seven—here."

"Right! And don't let anybody forget that you are the son of the McAlister Agricultural Implement Company, Incorporated! So-long and good luck!"

"Good-by and the same to you, Singapore. I hope we don't both land in jail. I hear it's a lousy jail."

"I've never been in a lousier," said Singapore Sammy.

WHEN TED had gone, Singapore returned to his hotel and went to bed. He lay there all afternoon and thought, checking over his plans, examining them for possible weaknesses. After the evening rice meal he went to the date palm and waited for Ted McAlister.

He came at a little after seven.

"How did it come off?" Singapore Sammy said tensely.

"Okay," Ted grunted. "The hotel people fell all over themselves. The proud old McAlister name worked like magic. I high-hatted them until every servant in the place was tumbling around, doing things. I told the clerk about the pearls. Singapore, you should have seen his expression. No cat that swallowed a canary ever looked smugger!"

"How about De Silvio?"

"He was nearly frantic, Singapore! He had certainly been

posted by that clerk. And I broke his heart when I insisted that I wanted nothing but a mate to the pearl."

"I want to know the details."

"Well, De Silvio transacts his business in a little steel cage in the back of the store. It's like a teller's cage in a bank. It's even enclosed on the top! In back, there's a steel lattice door, with a spring bolt at the top and another near the bottom. He has to unbolt them both to get out of the cage. You talk to him through a window about two feet square, with a little shelf just large enough to rest your elbows on. From that shelf to the floor, it's sheet-steel—or sheet-iron. I suppose, in case there's a holdup, he can drop to the floor and be safe from bullets. And there's a telephone in there, and a safe, and his money drawer. Do you want more details?"

"Those," said Singapore Sammy grimly, "are just the details I want. Go on, kid. Did you notice his eyes?"

"I'll say I did! I never saw wickeder eyes in my life—except in a king cobra's head!"

"You showed him the pearl?"

"Yes. I told him I wanted it matched. He weighed it and looked at it under a magnifying glass—everything! I told him I'd go as high as thirty thousand for its mate. He kept saying, 'It is impossible, monsieur; it is impossible.' But he said he'd try. He said he'd ransack Singapore.

"And you were right. He walked out to the car with me, trying to sell me everything under the sun—emeralds, sapphires, rubies, opals, pearls, diamonds! And I kept saying, haughtily, 'No, Mister de Silvio; I am interested in nothing but the mate to this pearl.' He was almost crying when I left. *Now* what do I do?"

"Nothing," Sammy answered. "You're through. You go back to your hotel. Tomorrow morning you have breakfast in bed—and maybe tiffin. Tomorrow morning, when you wake up, you're sick. Sun fever. You're too sick to leave your room. You stay there all day. How much money have you left?"

"Fifty-seven dollars."

"Let me have it."

Ted took the money from his pocket and gave it to him.

"I'll need this for expenses," Sammy explained. "Your credit will be good at the Europe."

"Won't you tell me what you're going to do?"

"No," said Sammy. "Have you got a telephone in your room?"

"Yes."

"If De Silvio calls you, sound sick. You're too sick to see anybody. Anybody but me. Understand?"

"Yes."

"De Silvio will call," Sammy continued. "He will ask a funny question. He will ask two funny questions. The first will be: will you go higher than thirty thousand for a mate to the pearl. The second will be: have you got the pearl. He will want to know if you are absolutely sure. And you will say, 'Of course, I am sure. I am holding it in my hand at this very moment.' Get that? Where is the pearl, by the way?"

"Here, in my pocket."

"You'd better let me take care of it for you. You're a rich American, and these Singapore wise men may get on your trail."

Ted surrendered the pearl to him and returned to the Europe.

SINGAPORE SAMMY went into the shopping district. In a Chinese paint store he bought a small bottle of mahogany spirit stain.

Leaving the paint store, he wandered over to Jochore Road and spent an hour looking at animals. Singapore was fond of animals. Some day when he got that will from his old man and secured that fortune, he was going to buy a ranch in Arizona, and it would be overrun with animals.

What had really brought Singapore Sammy to the animal stores of Jochore Road was an impulse to play a grim practical joke on Armand de Silvio. Sammy wanted to buy Mr. de Silvio a king cobra. He thought that Mr. de Silvio ought to have a king cobra.

Sammy came to a window in which two large cobras lay coiled. He went into the shop. A plump, smiling Chinese stood behind the counter.

"How much wanchee," Sammy asked, "for one o' them cobras?"

"No can sell," the shopkeeper answered. "Cobras just come, savvy. Cobras still hab got those poison sacs."

Sammy's expression brightened. It had not occurred to him that he could find, in Singapore, a cobra from which the poison sacs had not been removed.

"Me wanchee," he said.

The storekeeper gave him a pained look.

"No can catchum," he said firmly.

"Mebbe," said Sammy, "I catchum. How much wanchee?"

"Flifty dolla."

A spirited dickering began. One hour later Singapore Sammy left the shop not only with a specimen of the deadliest reptile in the world but a beautiful box to carry it in. It was a gilt lacquered box with a mirror on the back. About a foot square, it made a very snug home for the cobra. There was a hinged door on the front of it, with the hinge running along the top. At the bottom was a similar hinge except that it had a long steel pin running through it with a loop at the end. If the loop was pulled, the pin came out.

Singapore Sammy, with the gilded box under his arm and a self-satisfied grin on his lips, went out onto Jochore Road. The cobra had been a piece of reckless extravagance, but he was by no means displeased with himself. His score against Armand de Silvio was a large one, and it would be a lot of fun, if he could somehow arrange it, to see Mr. de Silvio and this cobra together. He would bet on the cobra.

From Jochore Road, he sauntered into the Hindu section and entered a bazaar. He priced turbans, robes and sandals. He wanted a complete Hindu costume. But he did not have enough money, and it was impossible to steal one.

Singapore Sammy returned to the street and waited for an idea to come. It was furnished, ready-made, when he saw a tall, thin Hindu, dark of complexion, in a soiled white turban and dark blue robes. A mean man with a cunning eye. The cunning eye was fixed greedily on the gilt lacquered box.

Sammy stifled a grin and looked at the Hindu stupidly, with mouth agape. The Hindu's expression brightened.

The resourceful redhead now proceeded to put on a performance, for the Hindu's exclusive benefit, of an intoxicated white man. With a lurch, he started off down the street.

The Hindu followed. Sammy staggered a few times and all but fell—and wandered on.

The Hindu, with his eyes on that valuable looking box, kept about twenty feet behind him.

At a dark and sinister looking alley, Sammy turned in. There was a dim light burning at the end of the alley; just enough light to see by if you looked sharp.

When he was well within the alley, Singapore Sammy slowed down and waited for his trailer to catch up with him.

He heard the tall Hindu fumbling along the brick wall. Sammy quickly deposited the gilt box on the pavement, turned about, leaped and wrapped his fingers tightly about the man's throat.

The unfortunate victim of his bright idea squirmed and kicked and clawed; but Sammy held on. When the man was limp, Sammy lowered him gently to the ground. He deftly unwound the turban, removed the robes and took off the sandals.

Rolling these into a bundle, Sammy picked up the gilt box and sauntered out of the alley. A hoarse, gurgling groan from the naked man in the alley caused him to walk a little faster.

SAMMY DID not go to his hotel, because he did not want to be seen. The police or the American vice-consul or both might pay a call upon him at any moment, and demand his instant departure.

By way of dark streets Singapore Sammy went to Tanjong Ru and, with the Hindu's garments for his couch, curled up under a beefwood tree. The rising sun wakened him. With the aid of the mirror on the back of the cobra's box he stained his face mahogany, then his hands and wrists.

In the fresh, warm morning breeze, the stain dried rapidly. When it was dry, Sammy coiled the turban about his head, making sure that no straggling red hairs were exposed. He got into the robes and the sandals, hid his own clothing and the gilt box under a bush, and started forth. He would present the cobra to De Silvio later. That came under the heading of pleasure. Business came first.

He went to De Silvio's. His proposed victim was in the steel cage. He looked to Singapore Sammy as if he had passed a sleepless night, and the redheaded American wondered if he had been trying to match the pearl. The wicked bronzy-silver eyes stared at Singapore Sammy contemptuously.

"Sahib," said Sammy, affecting the accent of a man from the Ganges, "I bring you a pearl."

Armand de Silvio's stare became even colder.

"I am not interested in buying pearls."

"But this one, Sahib, is a pearl among pearls—a black pearl."

"I do not wish to see it," De Silvio snapped.

"If the Sahib will only look!" Sammy begged.

The pearl was in the palm of Sammy's hand. He extended his hand through the window in the steel cage. And then opened his hand.

Armand de Silvio looked, and his thin, arched eyebrows went up. His long, thin fingers reached out like claws and snatched the pearl from Sammy's hand.

"Where did you get this, you dog?"

"Sahib, it was my mother's."

"You lie! You stole this pearl!"

"Sahib, may Allah be my witness, that pearl was my mother's!"

The bronzy-silver eyes were inspecting the pearl. Sammy observed that there was a German automatic pistol on a shelf above a very modern manganese steel safe. His heart began to thump.

De Silvio looked at the pearl under an optician's glass. He placed it on scales and weighed it. His hands were shaking. It was evidently a most exciting moment in Mr. de Silvio's day.

He turned to Sammy with that wicked stare.

"It is not a very good pearl. How much do you want for it?"

"Sahib," said Sammy, "my mother told me at her knee that it was a very fine pearl. My mother would not lie, Sahib. I will sell this pearl for twenty thousand dollars, Sahib."

"You fool!" cried De Silvio. "This pearl is not worth two thousand dollars. I will give you two thousand dollars."

"Sahib," said Sammy in a broken voice, "I was mistaken. The pearl is not for sale."

He picked it out of De Silvio's hand and started for the door.

"Wait!" shouted the pearl merchant. "Come back here!"

Sammy did not return; but he turned.

"I will give you five thousand!"

"No, Sahib; no, no. My mother—"

"Come here!"

"As the Sahib wishes."

The man with cobra eyes had picked up the telephone. "Wait!" he said to Sammy, and in an excited voice called the number of the Grand Hotel de L'Europe. In a moment, he asked for Mr. McAlister.

"Mister McAlister," he said, "this is Armand de Silvio—the jeweler." He waited for Ted's murmur of recognition. Then:

"In regard to that matter that we were discussing last evening—you remember? I believe I can satisfy you. Yes! 1 have not slept a wink. I have exhausted every possibility in Singapore.

And I am glad to say that my efforts have been crowned with success. But the price will be more than you stipulated. It will be thirty-five thousand dollars."

Sammy watched his expression. It was suddenly brightened by a smile.

"Very well, then, Mister McAlister—will you step around to my shop?" A long pause. "Then may I call on you?" A longer pause. Then: "Mister McAlister, are you quite sure you have that pearl?... You are?... Ah! It is in your hand? Very well, monsieur. I will call this evening at five."

He hung up the receiver and turned his cold wicked eyes on Sammy. Sammy looked at him stupidly.

"I have decided," said Armand de Silvio, "to be ten times a bigger fool than you—and pay you ten thousand dollars for that pearl. It happens to take my fancy."

"Sahib," Sammy began, "at my dear mother's knee—"

"Fifteen thousand!"

"Sahib, I have changed my mind. I have decided not to sell the pearl."

De Silvio cursed him in Malay, in Hindustani, in English. But Sammy remained unshaken. In the end, he walked out of the shop with twenty thousand dollars in a compact roll in his hand!

BUT SINGAPORE Sammy's dealings with Mr. de Silvio were by no means ended. He intended to be on hand when the man with cobra eyes discovered he had been tricked; and he wanted to give Mr. de Silvio the present he had bought last night for him on Jochore Road. And he firmly intended to face De Silvio without a disguise and get back the money that man had robbed from him.

But there were certain details to be attended to first. He went into a paint store and bought some turpentine. Then he returned to the beefwood tree on Tanjong Ru, washed off the mahogany stain with the turpentine, changed into his own clothing and, with De Silvio's present under his arm, hailed a passing ricksha.

At the Peninsular and Occidental Steamship offices he purchased a passage and a berth to Hongkong in the name of Mr. Theodore Varden McAlister, Jr. From the P.&O. office he went to the Grand Hotel de L'Europe and to Ted's room.

He knocked on the door. An invalid's voice wanted to know who was there.

Singapore Sammy called through the panel:

"A guy with a ticket to South Bend, Indiana!"

The door was flung open.

"You did it?" Ted exclaimed.

"Here's your change, kid." Sammy tossed the fat roll of money on the bed. "And here's your ticket to Hongkong. How long'll it take you to pack?"

"Two minutes."

"Your steamer is pullin' out in one hour. Now, listen, Ted. I've still got a little business to attend to with that guy. And I want to ask you somethin'. I want you to call Mr. de Silvio right up—"

"And tell him everything?"

"Buddy, will you let a guy finish? I want you to call him up and tell him—tell him you've decided you don't want to match that pearl, after all."

Ted looked at his friend steadily a moment, then burst into laughter. When he could speak again, he said:

"I get you, Sam. You want to be there when I phone, so you can watch him suffer. Is that the size of it?"

"That," Singapore Sammy admitted, "is the idea. Give me six minutes to get there, then phone. Get busy and pack and get to hell out of here. Pay off those damned chits and clear out of China. Promise?"

Ted shot out his hand and grasped Sammy's. He was still laughing.

"Sam," he said, "no man ever had a pal like you. It makes me sick to think we aren't teaming up again and getting ready to look for trouble. What have you got in that flossy gold box?"

"It's just a little something," Singapore Sammy said with casualness, "I picked up down Jochore Road for Mister de Silvio."

"A cobra!"

"Buddy," Sammy said soberly, "you're smart. You're gonna go over big in South Bend. Now, get started packin' and get to hell out of my life."

They shook hands, wished each other "pukka luck," and Singapore Sammy departed. Briskly he walked the short distance to the De Silvio shop.

The telephone began to ring when Singapore Sammy, with a grin on his lips, went in. Mr. de Silvio, back in the steel cage, left off counting a big bunch of banknotes and picked up the receiver. Sammy heard him say:

"Yes, this is Mister de Silvio.... Ah! Yes, Mister McAlister.... I beg your pardon?... What? You don't want the pearl? But, monsieur, I have bought it! I paid an exorbitant price for it! I spent all last night combing this town to find that pearl!" His voice was growing hysterical. "But, monsieur, this is an outrage! You told me to match the pearl—I matched it!"

Unable to restrain himself, Mr. de Silvio broke into a volley of extremely unprintable Malay. His fury rose to towering heights. His voice attained a thin scream of anguish and rage.

And when he hung up the receiver, trembling with fury, Singapore Sammy was at the little window in the steel cage, grinning in at him.

ARMAND DE SILVIO looked at him—and looked again. Those wicked bronzy-silver eyes seemed to bore into the hiddenmost recesses of Singapore Sammy's soul. Then he glanced at the gilt lacquered box on the window ledge. Sammy had his arm about it. His thumb was through the loop at the end of the steel pin. One yank—and that cobra would be Mr. de Silvio's!

And Sammy was sure that a more favorable place for Mr. de Silvio to receive the cobra would be hard to find. The cobra could not escape from the cage, and once the cobra was in it, De Silvio would certainly be too busy to escape! Certainly, he would not have time to unbolt the lock at the top and the lock at the bottom of the door.

The bronzy-silver eyes had returned to Sammy's sparkling blue ones. In an amiable voice, Sammy said:

"Recognize me, brother?"

The wicked eyes narrowed slightly.

"I can't say that I do. No. I never saw you before in my life!"

"Brother," said Sammy, almost affectionately, "you've got a lousy memory. Just about three weeks ago, you borrowed forty-eight hundred dollars from me. You had a couple of friends along. Where are they now, brother?"

"I don't know what you're talking about!"

"No! You don't remember borrowin' that forty-eight hundred? Well, that's just tough. Because I need that money—plus interest. The interest is gonna bring it up to just six thousand dollars. There's more than that in that pile there."

Armand de Silvio acted with alacrity. He reached for the telephone and, with the instrument in his hand, dropped from view. Not even his head was visible. Sammy removed his hungry eyes from the thick pile of bills which De Silvio had left lying in the open money drawer to answer the telephone, and took time to admire Mr. de Silvio's clever steel cage which protected him from holdups.

From the window ledge to the floor, it was sheet-steel. It was a little steel fortress. In case of a holdup, all Mr. De Silvio had to do was to drop to the floor and telephone the police. And by the time a holdup man could get into the cage, the police would be here.

"Clever!" said Sammy.

De Silvio was talking rapidly.

"Police headquarters? This is Armand de Silvio. The American I mentioned is here. As I anticipated, he is trying to hold me up. Send some men here at once!"

There was a little clatter as De Silvio hung up the receiver. His cold voice issued from the floor.

"In five minutes the police will be here. Perhaps your word will be better than mine in court, Mister Shay!"

Sammy was gazing at the wad of bills. He could just reach them.

"Brother," Sammy said, "do you think you are giving me a fair break? Three weeks ago you tried to get the Malobar pearl away from me. Your scheme fell flat—because I happened to have that blue egg parked somewhere else than on the end of that copper wire I used to wear on my neck. But you got my roll anyhow. Be a good sport, will you, and give me back my roll?"

A thin-edged laugh came from the floor of the steel cage.

"You will enjoy the Singapore jail, Mister Shay."

"Listen," Sammy wheedled, "won't you give me back my roll?"

Silence answered him.

"Well," said Sammy in a reluctant tone, "in that case, there is nothin' to do but let nature take its course. Sic 'em, Abdullah!"

He yanked out the steel pin. The maddest snake in Singapore that day leaped out of the gilded box. A writhing, shining black spring of uncoiling cobra shot out into the cage.

Sammy reached through the little square window and leisurely gathered into his hand the thick pile of bills.

Something long and large shot up with a shrill scream from the floor of the cage and clung to the latticelike steel top, with legs drawn up out of harm's way. Then a black steel spring launched itself through the air, and gleaming white fangs missed De Silvio's feet by inches.

The thin scream of terror again rang through the store. An agonized white face turned to Singapore Sammy.

"I'll give you your money!" shrieked de Silvio. "I'll give you all you ask. Run around the counter and open this door."

"Brother," said Sammy, "that idea is sour. That's what it is—sour. I've got the money."

De Silvio shrieked again, as the cobra sprang at him.

Singapore Sammy was leisurely counting the money. There was eighty-five hundred and some odd dollars in the wad.

"My interest rate," he announced to the screaming man, who clung, apelike to the steel, lattice ceiling of the cage, "has gone up."

The screams of De Silvio drowned Sammy's words. Sammy pocketed the money—all of it. For a little longer he watched the most vicious snake in existence trying to reach with its fangs the legs of the unfortunate man who clung to the ceiling.

"Well, Mister de Silvio," Sammy said presently, "I'll have to be running along. I hope you learn to love your little pet. Good luck, brother—good luck! You're gonna need plenty!"

SAMMY SAUNTERED out of the store. The brisk clatter of traffic on Beach Road, the honks and shrieks of automobiles, the shouting of ricksha coolies, completely blotted out DeSilvio's attempts at drawing attention to his unique predicament.

With his score against Armand de Silvio nicely evened, Sammy started off toward his hotel. It was just about time for him to be leaving Singapore for a long, long absence. He was aware that, in spite of the street noises, a crowd was gathering in front of the pearl merchant's shop. A car had driven up. Tall, red-turbaned Sikh policemen, with guns in their hands, were climbing out.

Singapore Sammy walked a little faster. A voice hailed him.

"Just a moment, Mister Shay!"

Sammy turned and looked, with misgivings, into the pale blue eyes of the American vice-consul.

"So here you are!" said Mr. Halloway triumphantly.

"Yeah," Sammy said gloomily, "you guessed it right the very first time. Here I am."

"I've been looking all over Singapore for you. Where have you been?"

"A fair question," Singapore Sammy replied, "deserves a fair answer. I've been buyin' a pet for a friend of mine."

The vice-consul looked at him suspiciously. Over Mr. Halloway's head, Sammy saw that the crowd in front of De Silvio's now extended almost across the street. It was holding up traffic.

"Mister Shay," said Mr. Halloway sternly, "I thought I told you to leave Singapore as soon as you were able to travel."

"I haven't been able," Sammy said, "to leave till right now."

Mr. Halloway snorted.

"You bet you're leaving now! Here's my car. I'm taking you to the Tank Road Station. There's a train for Penang and Bangkok leaving in forty-five minutes. And when that train pulls out, you're going to be on it!"

"If you put it that way," Singapore Sammy said in meek tones, "I guess all I can do is give in and go, Mister Halloway."

The vice-consul softened. He had evidently not expected to find this hardboiled young man so tractable.

"Look here, Mister Shay," he said impulsively. "Aren't you trying to find your father?"

"I certainly am!" Sammy, suddenly interested, declared. "Have you got him?"

Mr. Halloway shook his head indulgently.

"Doesn't he disguise himself in the yellow robes of a Buddhist begging priest—an old man with a long gray beard?"

"That's him!" Sammy exclaimed. "Where is he?"

"The man who supplied me with that information said that your father left Singapore more than a week ago—for Bangkok."

"Can you beat that!" Sammy marveled. "It's always Bangkok. Whenever he slips away on me, he's always just gone to Bangkok!"

Mr. Halloway was gazing at him sympathetically.

"What a pity that he doesn't know that you are trying to find him! Mister Shay, I will confess that when I talked to you before I was not acquainted with this side of your nature. Such—such devotion is beautiful!"

"Yeah," Singapore Sammy agreed. "Sometimes, when I get to thinkin' about it, I cry into my beer about it myself."

The crowd before De Silvio's store had swollen until it had now reached Sammy and Mr. Halloway.

"What's going on?" one man in the crowd asked of another.

And the one addressed answered excitedly, "Armand de Silvio found a cobra in his store!"

"Did it strike him?"

"No one seems to know."

The vice-consul seized Singapore Sammy's arm.

"Let's get out of here!" he said nervously. "One mention of cobra is enough for me!"

"A wise man," Singapore Sammy agreed, "knows the aim of a bottle."

III

SOUTH OF SULU

Singapore Sammy Learns That in the South
China Sea a Man Can Be Shark Bait Only Once

A DANGEROUS MAN was Big Nick Stark, of Shanghai; a bad man from a bad town. Faithless with men and women alike, a bully, a pirate of sorts, a gunman, a card sharp, a blackbirder, a smuggler, a strong arm specialist, he robbed and pilfered and plundered when and where he pleased.

When the need arose, Big Nick could be as smooth as polished jade, as persuasive as gold, as cunning as a *kreit* adder— and as savage as a mad bull elephant.

There was danger in his hawklike blue eyes, in the permanent outthrust of his big, bony jaw, in the slicing edge of his braying laugh. His favorite boast was, "I am the toughest egg south of Shanghai." And he made that boast good.

Big Nick Stark squatted in the bow of the Malay proa which had brought him across the southern bight of the South China Sea from Singapore, and watched the island of Selambang rise out of the bright jade water.

In the swift tropic dusk it took form: a white streak of coral beach, a line of slender palms holding their fuzzy heads against the purple evening sky, a few nipa shacks on their spidery legs, and a compact little cluster of galvanized iron buildings.

From time to time Big Nick shot a glance astern at the brown dorsal sail which, sometime during the night, his proa had overtaken and passed. It was important that he reach Selambang and see Peddy the trader before the man in the proa astern landed.

In the gathering dusk, a jetty took form. Big Nick spoke sharply in Malay to the serang; warned him to change his course slightly. Big Nick knew these waters as he knew the lines of his hand.

The serang altered the course as directed and brought the proa neatly alongside the jetty. Big Nick climbed up on the wooden structure and strode toward the galvanized iron buildings inshore.

A red-faced fat man lay sprawled in a deck chair on the copper-screened veranda of an iron bungalow. He was sipping a long gin rickey. When Big Nick opened the screen door and strode in, Peddy the trader did not rise, or smile, or offer his fat little hand.

The eyes of the fat man were slits of watchful distrust. In a wheezing voice he said, "Stark, I told you never to put your foot on this island again."

Big Nick laughed. He reached into a round tin on the table at the fat man's elbow, helped himself to a cigarette and lighted it. His bold blue eyes seemed to shimmer. His teeth were as large, as yellow as kernels of field corn.

"Peddy," he said, "does ten thousand dollars for a night's easy work interest you?"

"Not," Peddy answered, "if it means doin' business with you."

Big Nick laughed again. He sucked in smoke from his cigarette and expelled it in twin blue jets from his hairy nostrils. He looked down at the table where cards were spread out in an unfinished game of solitaire.

With his hard grin he reached down, gathered up the cards and shuffled them. The movements of his hands were slow and clumsy. It seemed surprising that cards did not spill out of those awkward hands; but no cards fell.

"I will show you a new trick, Peddy."

"I had all I wanted of your tricks."

"But this is a good one. Look! I will deal you a hand, Peddy! I will show you how easy the hand can fool the naked eye. This is a trick worth watching, Peddy. It's the master trick of them all. Look close! These are your cards. I have never had them in my hands before. Would you like a royal flush in diamonds?"

"To hell with your tricks!" Peddy snorted. "What are you doin' on this island?"

"Givin' you a chance to make ten thousand dollars for a night's easy work—maybe only an hour's easy work. You don't want a royal flush in diamonds? Then I will deal you a full house, kings on tens, and myself four aces. Look sharp, Peddy!"

The man from Shanghai dealt the two hands, face up: a full house of kings on tens to Peddy, and the four aces and a deuce to himself!

For a moment a look of amazement: occupied the fat man's red face, then his look hardened into unmitigated distrust again.

Big Nick laughed. "Did you ever," he asked, as he tossed the other cards to the table, "hear of the blue fire pearl o' Malobar? Of course you have, Peddy! Who hasn't? Is it one of the rarest pearls of its kind in the world—or ain't it? You're a pearl expert. I'm askin' you."

"I never saw it," the fat man wheezed.

"But you have heard of it, Peddy."

"Are you peddlin' it?" Peddy snapped.

"Not yet, Peddy," Big Nick laughed, "not yet. Do you know what that pearl is worth, Peddy? It's worth forty thousand dollars if it's worth a florin. On a quick sale it would fetch thirty thousand. Do you want a third interest in that pearl, Peddy? Do you want ten thousand dollars for an easy night's work?"

"You are," stated Peddy, "up to one of your stinkin' rotten schemes. Where is this pearl?"

"Did you ever," the man from Shanghai answered, "hear of a guy they call Singapore Sammy? A redheaded guy he is, a quick guy with his fists, and a quick guy with his brain, too. Look out there," said Big Nick, pointing to rapidly darkening water. "See that sail comin' this way? Singapore Sammy is on that proa—and the blue Malobar pearl is on Singapore Sammy!"

"And then what?" said Peddy sarcastically.

"Ten thousand," said Big Nick, "is your split—for an easy night's work."

"If it's so easy," said Peddy, "why bother with me? Why not go right up to this redheaded guy and take the pearl away from him?"

"You are drunk," Nick answered, "or you would have heard

me tell you that that redheaded guy is quick with his brain. But on two subjects he's as dumb as hell, Peddy. One is the mate to that big blue egg he carries, and the other is his father. He is hipped on findin' the mate to that pearl and he is hipped on findin' his old man. I've been following him for a month now, waiting my chance to get hold of his blue pearl."

"How," Peddy wheezed, "did he get that pearl?"

BIG NICK seated himself on the arm of a chair, puffed at his cigarette and answered.

"Up Malobar way two months ago, hot on the trail of his old man, Singapore Sammy got into a mixup with a maharaja's elephant guards. The maharaja stuck him in jail. There was another American in jail. The maharaja is hipped on boxfightin'. So he staged a ten-round bout between this redheaded guy and the other American. The winner was to get the blue pearl. The loser was to go to the maharaja's pet black leopards for breakfast. Sammy won the bout and got the pearl."

Peddy took a sip of his rickey. The trader's narrowed eyes had not changed expression since Nick had come on the porch, except for that brief moment when the man from Shanghai fumblingly dealt those two amazing poker hands.

"Singapore Sammy got the blue pearl," Big Nick continued with his story, "and went chasing on a new clue after his old man. Well, Peddy, up there in Malobar, Sammy found out that his old man was wearin' a disguise: the yaller robes of a Burmese Buddhist beggin' priest, long gray beard, beggin' bowl and all. Say, you fat slob! What are you grinnin' about?"

"I've been waitin' here," Peddy answered, "for seven days for this redheaded guy to show up. His old man was here. He left a week ago. He's got his own reasons for not wantin' that fightin' redhead to catch up with him."

Big Nick Stark was not laughing now. White lines had appeared along his jaw muscles.

"Yeah?" he said. "Ain't you kind of forgettin' what I came here for?"

"Nope," Peddy the trader chuckled. "You came here to give me ten thousand dollars for a easy night's work."

Big Nick glared at him.

"You knew he was packin' that blue egg around on him?"

Peddy continued to chuckle.

"Cut it out!" Big Nick snapped. "We ain't got any too much time. Do we play or don't we?"

"For a cut of a third? Nick, when was I born?"

"Then," said Nick harshly, "you're out. Get that? This guy is my meat. You lay off—or you'll get that fat belly of yours—"

Peddy the trader hastily interrupted.

"I ain't said I wouldn't play. I'm saying a cut of a third ain't fair."

"It's all you get. Do we do business?"

Peddy the trader turned a little pale under that cold glare. He nodded. "What's your scheme?" he wheezed.

"All you do," Nick answered, "is to stick by me and do what I say."

"We will jump him when he comes ashore," said Peddy practically.

"No," said Nick. "He will be ready for that. You saw my card trick. I have a bag of other tricks just as good. He is smart; I'm goin' to outsmart him."

Peddy shook his head. "The trouble with you, Nick, is that you are too smart. There is only one way to handle this redhead. It is a simple way. Listen, now...."

The big man from Shanghai scowled out into the dusk at the brown dorsal sail and listened. He was not a good listener. He much preferred his own monologues; but on the island of Selambang, Peddy the trader was king.

CHAPTER 11

UNDER THE BROWN dorsal sail that crept toward Selambang, Singapore Sammy crouched, looked, listened and sniffed.

He saw what Big Nick Stark had seen a few minutes before. His attention was occupied principally by the little cluster of galvanized iron buildings at the inshore end of the jetty.

At least one of them was a copra drying shed, or godown, for the hot sticky breeze blowing over the island and on toward Malaya was ripe with the sickening odor.

As the redheaded adventurer wrinkled his nose in this sickly offshore scent, the fingers of one large brown hand were fumbling at a tough copper wire which encircled his neck. Dangling from this strange neckpiece was a small chamois sack.

Singapore Sammy quickly lifted the copper loop over his head. He loosened the cord at the throat of the sack with his strong white teeth. Then, holding up the bottom of the sack and making sure that his serang was not watching him, he shook down into his palm a blue pearl that gathered fire unto itself from all that remained of daylight.

Before landing on Selambang, the redhead wanted one last look at his treasure; for this magnificent pearl was Singapore Sammy's passion. Big Nick Stark had not overestimated his love for the Malobar pearl, or his eagerness to find its twin.

The Malobar blue fire pearl rolled about in the cupped palm of his hand, a bubble of magic flame. As blue as a Chantaboun sapphire, as big around as the end of its owner's forefinger, as full of fire as the eye of a charging leopard, the Malobar pearl was fit to grace the finger or the throat of a princess.

The light of the dying day abruptly departed. Singapore Sammy returned the pearl to the sack, and the wire loop to his neck.

Just then, the serang uttered a sharp cry of *"Makanan!"* which means, "Ready about!" The proa stood into the wind and fell off close-hauled on the starboard tack, its great lateen sail slatting as it banged over. This tack should bring the proa to the jetty.

Now, Selambang is, on even the largest maps, but a tiny freckle on the blue bosom of the South China Sea. No one but pearl and copra buyers goes to Selambang, and Singapore Sammy was certain that he had shaken off the host of crooks and adventurers who had been pursuing him ever since the news of his winning the famous Malobar pearl had been broadcast throughout the Far East. On Selambang, Sammy felt sure, he could, for the first time in a month, find peace.

The brown dorsal sail that he had glimpsed astern the day before and which his excellent eyes had espied far ahead today worried him a little. Perhaps he had not shaken off the pursuit. Perhaps he had. But if he had not, he was prepared to cope with it.

The jetty loomed closer. Tied up beside it, perhaps fifty feet from the outshore end, the white hull of a boat glowed in the semidarkness. A shore light struck glints from bright work. A machinist's hammer, somewhere in the bowels of the white boat, clanged on metal with the measured beat of a temple gong.

The jetty suddenly came out of the blue murk, a black mass of timbers above his head. It was low tide. The serang yelled *"Lekas, tuan!"* Singapore Sammy grasped a projecting timber and swung himself up. He heard a block rattle as the serang paid out his sheet.

For a moment, it seemed to him that the jetty was filled with crowding dark figures, prepared to spring upon him. But this was an illusion, the result of nervous days and sleepless nights. His anxiety over the safety of the blue pearl had almost become an obsession. Where it went, danger followed.

Staring down at the receding proa Sammy called out, in Malay, the formal hope that the serang would make his return journey in the arms of God. Then, turning about to face the beach, he stood perfectly still and listened.

Above the measured banging of the machinist's hammer, Sammy heard nothing but an accordion, the distant babbling of native voices, and the rainlike sound of the trade wind in the palms. The very air of Selambang was sleepy and innocent. Darkness flowed over the island in an inky tide.

Singapore Sammy was certain that he had the pier to himself. So, quickly, he dropped to his knees at the edge of the jetty and explored its under surface with his hands.

He presently found what he was looking for—a nail protruding from a stringer. The nail was about two feet in from the edge. Again assuring himself that he was not under observation, the redhaired young man pulled up over his head the loop of tough copper wire from which dangled the small chamois sack. With shaking hands he draped the loop over the nail, gave it a twist, stood up and brushed flakes of rotten wood from his hands, and waited for his heart to stop thumping.

He softly said "Phew!" Even if he were attacked on Selambang and beaten unconscious, his assailants would not find that chamois sack!

WITH HIS mind at ease, Singapore Sammy—otherwise, Samuel Larkin Shay, American citizen, but for the past six years a wanderer of the Oriental tropics—walked briskly down the jetty. There was so little daylight left, and the starlight was still so feeble, that he could barely distinguish the outlines of the white-hulled boat.

She was a typical inter-island boat, about thirty feet over all, with a roomy cockpit and a hunting cabin in which were the engine and perhaps two bunks. A light burned dimly in the cabin.

This light moved as Singapore Sammy came down the jetty. When he was abreast of the cockpit, the light floated up through the doorway into the cockpit. It was followed by a long, thin white arm, then a long thin white face surmounted by a tangle of red hair.

Singapore came to a dead stop and uttered a grunt of surprise. In that bad light, he might have seen himself coming up out of that cabin. The man on the boat had red hair, and he was tall and blue-eyed. His proportions were close to those of Singapore's; but there the resemblance ceased.

The red-haired stranger looked as Singapore himself might have looked if he had spent the best part of the past six years at the weather end of a whisky bottle.

"Hullo, there!" said the man on the boat in a husky voice. "Who in the hell are you and where did you come from? I thought I was seein' a ghost!"

"I just came over from Singapore," said Sammy.

The man held up the lantern and stared at him.

"You gave me a shock," he muttered. "You gave me a hell of a shock, mister. I thought I was seein' things. For a minute there, I thought I was seein' myself, standin' on that lousy dock. Where you bound for?"

"I'm lookin' for a friend," Singapore replied.

"Well, wait till I douse this lousy light," said the other redhead, "and I'll bear a hand. There's only one place on Selambang to find anybody this time o' night, and that's at Tiger Tom's."

He extinguished the light, placed it on the cockpit floor, and climbed up on the jetty.

Singapore felt a cold, clammy hand fumbling for his in the dark. He accepted it and pressed it firmly in return.

"My name's Wallace—Pete Wallace." He failed to add that on Selambang he was called "Whisky" Wallace.

"Mine's Shay—Sam Shay."

"American, ain't you?"

"Cairo, Illinois," said Sammy. "Where d'you hail from?"

"Portland, Maine," said Mr. Wallace. "I ain't seen an American in four years. I'm skipper for Peddy the trader. He won't trust Malays or Tamils or Arabs around this engine, so I keep it runnin' for him. You must have come in on a proa."

Sammy murmured affirmatively. He was impatient to begin asking questions, but he had learned that, in places like Selambang, it does not pay to be too curious about anything in Malaysia.

They had reached the inshore end of the jetty. "This way," said Pete Wallace.

Bright light streamed from a doorway over which hung a single thickness of white mosquito cloth.

"In there, Mister Shay," said Pete Wallace affably.

Singapore preceded him into a small, low room built entirely of sheets of corrugated iron. The floor was coral sand. A rough pine bar was stretched across the back wall. Behind it on a shelf stood an array of familiar bottles of all shapes, colors, and sizes. There seemed to be no one behind the bar. There were three round tables with rough wooden chairs ranged along each side wall. All of them were crowded with Malays.

Drinks went down on tables and eyes went up to Singapore as he walked up to the bar.

In a shrill voice, Pete Wallace yelled, "Hey, Tom, where the hell are yuh?"

A fat man in white drill appeared behind the bar like a jack-in-a-box. He was half European, half Oriental, with small, ratlike eyes, a fierce black mustache with tapered ends, and a complexion the color of coffee and hot milk. He did not seem pleased when he saw the two redheads. He gave a deep grunt and placed his pudgy brown hands on the bar.

"This," said Wallace, with an airy gesture at Singapore, "is Mister Sam Shay. He just mooched in from Singapore. Mister Shay, this gent is Tiger Tom."

Tiger Tom did not say a word, but turned around, plucked a square black bottle from the shelf and placed it with a whisky glass before the motorboat's engineer-skipper.

Tiger Tom was leering at Singapore Sammy. "Yours, *tuan?*"

"Stengah," said Sammy.

A stengah is a half highball. After such a day as he had spent, under the broiling sun of the equator, Singapore Sammy had found that it paid to drink sparingly.

Tiger Tom placed the stengah before him. Sammy sipped it.

WHISKY WALLACE had tossed off his first drink and was already pouring himself a second. When he had gulped this and poured still another, he looked with brighter eyes at Singapore Sammy and said, in a confidential tone: "Life is hell—on Selambang. Say! Who was it you was lookin' for?"

"I was just lookin' for—a friend," Sammy replied. "It wasn't especially important."

The beachcomber was looking at him acutely. "What's this guy's name?"

"Shay—same as mine."

"Don't happen to be your old man, does it?" Wallace was beginning to grin.

"Well—" Singapore began.

"Listen," Whisky Wallace stopped him. "I know. I know all about it. I spotted you the minute we come into this dump. You're the guy they call Singapore Sammy. You've been huntin' all over the Far East for five, six years for your old man. You get drunk and cry into your beer abo»ut it. He used to be the top bull man with Bartrom and Bradley's circus, back in the States, and you ain't seen him since you was knee-high to a chin-chook. All the clues you got is, he's nuts about pearls and he's nuts about elephants. Ain't that it?"

Singapore nodded. His blue eyes were, at this moment, brighter and more fiery than his Malobar pearl. He answered in a slow drawl:

"That's right, fellow. He's nuts about pearls and he's nuts about elephants. I lost his trail for two years. I picked it up two months ago in Singapore, followed it up to Malobar, and lost it again in Bangkok. I got a hunch and went to Penang. The old boy had doubled back on me. I followed the scent to Kuala Lumpur, to Singapore—and to here."

Whisky Wallace poured and swallowed a fourth drink. Sammy saw Tiger Tom slide a bead on an abacus.

"What's he look like?" the beachcomber asked eagerly.

"He's my size," Sammy said. "Gray beard. Dresses himself up as a Buddhist priest, yellow robes and all. He's a begging priest and he carries a begging bowl. I got that in Malobar."

The beachcomber was grinning at him. "Yeah," he said, and again, "Yeah. Well, he was here!"

"When?"

"A coupla weeks back. He'd heard about the new pearl beds. He come and took a look; then he blew. That must 'a' been a week ago."

"Where did he go?" Sammy snapped.

"Over to Pemanggil."

Sammy seized Whisky Wallace by the shoulders; gripped hard. "You take me there—will you? I'll give you fifty dollars, gold."

"Naw, naw," the other weakly protested. "Now, listen, big boy. If your old man is over on Pemanggil, he'll there tomorrow. Mebbe I'll give you a lift over tomorrow. Maskee! You gotta take things more calm, Singapore. I want to know something. I heard a funny story about you. I heard you went into a boxfight over in Malobar with another American, knocked him kickin', and won a big fire pearl from the maharaja."

"Did you?" Singapore said coldly, and released him.

"Sure, I did! And who do you suppose I heard it from?"

Singapore stared at him dangerously.

"Your old man himself!" cried the beachcomber.

Singapore licked his lips and swallowed. He tilted his glass and finished the stengah. "Another!" he snapped at Tiger Tom.

"Yes, *tuan!*"

Whisky Wallace was looking excitedly at Singapore Sammy. "Well," said the beachcomber, "ain't we friends? Ain't I gonna get a peek at the Malobar pearl?"

"That pearl," said Singapore distinctly, "is parked with De

Silva, the Portuguese jeweler, in Singapore. How much do you
want to take me over to Pemanggil tonight—now?"

"Peddy wouldn't let me."

"A hundred—gold!"

"Naw, naw," said the beachcomber peevishly.

Singapore tossed a gold piece on the bar. He said, "Take 'em
out of this, Tiger."

"Yes, *tuan*."

Singapore turned again to the beachcomber. "What else," he
said in a steady voice to Whisky Wallace, "did my old man tell
you about me?"

"He knows all about how you been huntin' for him."

"He must think it's funny."

"That's right, Singapore. He was havin' a good laugh out o'
tellin' me about it. The last thing he says, was, 'That boy'll have
to grease his heels to catch me.'"

"He said that, did he?"

"I don't see," the beachcomber answered, "why you're wastin'
all this affection on that old fellow."

"Love," said Singapore, "shows itself in funny ways." But he
refrained from adding that the reason he was so anxious to
catch his father was that Shay, Senior, had in his possession a
will—the last will and testament of Sammy's paternal grandfather—leaving to Sammy a large fortune, which Sammy could
not possess without will.

"I'll run you over to Pemanggil tomorrow," Whisky Wallace
was saying—"if Peddy don't mind."

CHAPTER III

WHISKY WALLACE SUDDENLY straightened up and
cleared his throat. Two men in white sun helmets, the extremely white drill of the equator, and mosquito boots, came into the
grogshop. One was short, beefy, and red of face. The other was
lean, powerful looking and darkly tanned. His eyes were as clear

and as piercing as a hawk's. There was a hard recklessness about the carving of his features that made him look dangerous.

The hard brown face was vaguely familiar to Singapore. It was associated with fists, crashing glass, screaming women, overturned .tables.

Singapore remembered. Shanghai! A grand free-for-all in the Café Parisienne on the French bund. The fellow was tall, an inch or two smaller than Singapore, who stood a fair six foot one with boots off. And he had walloped everyone in sight.

And then the beefy, red-faced man caught Singapore's eye. His thick red lips parted, twirked upward at the corners.

"Damn my eyes," he wheezed, "if here ain't another Whisky Wallace—with the 'Whisky' left off! When did you hit Selambang, brother?"

Singapore grinned amiably. "This afternoon," he answered, and was aware that Whisky Wallace was sliding toward the door.

The beefy man snapped, "Hold it, Whisky! Did you get that lousy engine fixed?"

"Yes, sir," the beachcomber said. "She's runnin' like a Swiss watch, Mister Peddy."

The dark man of Shanghai memories was staring at Singapore with intensity. He tilted back his sun helmet and scowled. Then he smiled—a hard smile.

"I've got you!" he declared in a deep, crackling voice. "You're the youngster they call Singapore Sammy. Peddy," he went on excitedly, "get a load of this: Here's the kid we were just talking about—the one who's been burning up the pearl and elephant countries, trying to find his old man."

He seized Sammy by the elbow in a grip of steel and pulled him along the bar.

"Singapore," he roared, "shake hands with Peddy the trader—the biggest scoundrel south of Hongkong. I've seen you before, Singapore. Where!"

"Shanghai—Parisienne—two years ago—a knock-down-

and-drag-out," Sammy mentioned. He knew that this lean brown giant would make a dangerous enemy.

"I'm Nick Stark."

Peddy the trader wheezed, "Big Nick Stark." He was squeezing Singapore's hand, looking into Singapore's face with the eyes of an overfed pig. "Big Nick is a pearl buyer from Cartier's, of Paris. He must have landed about the same time you did. He just got here."

Singapore said nothing. That brown dorsal sail he had seen at intervals during the day must have been on Big Nick Stark's proa. He waited. He was sure that there would now be some reference to the Malobar pearl. But there was not.

In his wheezing, almost guttural voice, Peddy the trader was saying, "This ain't any place to talk, boys. We'll adjourn to my bungalow and have a real chin-chin. Maybe you two don't realize how damned lonesome a white man can get on one of these rotten little islands."

He prodded Singapore in the back. Big Nick Stark sent a sharp glance flashing about the room and then joined Singapore and Peddy on the beach.

The starlight was already bright enough to see the island by. Singapore found his favorite constellation, the Southern Cross, and hoped it would stand by him.

PEDDY THE trader familiarly took Singapore's arm. "This way," he said. Big Nick Stark fell into step on Singapore's other side, and they started up the beach.

Someone fell into step a few paces to the rear; stepped out from the inky shadow of the grogshop, as if his action had been planned and timed to the second. Singapore supposed that the trailer was Whisky Wallace. His heart seemed to give a little jerk, then took up its beating at a quicker tempo. He was walking into a trap—but there was nothing to do about it. Big Nick and Peddy were powerful men—either one of them was certainly a match for Singapore. And Whisky Wallace would have the vicious fighting habits of a *kreit* adder.

In his wheezy, guttural voice, Peddy was talking about Sammy's old man; talking against time; talking until they got well out of earshot of Tiger Tom's.

"He was here disguised as a Buddhist begging priest, and left for Pemanggil less than a week ago. You are hot on his trail, Singapore. I'll send you over to Pemanggil first thing in the morning. And I can put you up for the night in my bungalow. There's room for all."

Singapore Sammy was estimating the distance from where they would turn off the beach to where the launch was tied up. It was his only chance of escape—that launch. He knew gasoline engines, and he knew these waters fairly well. But even if he broke and ran, they would have him before he could cast off the lines and get the engine started.

Peddy had tightened the grip on his arm, as if he had anticipated his designs.

"Are you interested in pearls, Singapore? We have just opened up a rich new bed of high-yield shell right here on Selambang's doorstep, you might say. Right down there in the bay. I'm going to show you some pearls that will knock your eyes out."

They had reached the iron godowns. An overpowering breath of copra came wafting out of a black doorway on Singapore's right.

Big Nick took his arm in his powerful fingers. "Wait a minute," he said.

It was, Singapore Sammy appreciated, nicely planned and timed. Ahead of them the alley between the two godowns came to a blind end, formed by the rear of the bungalow. The other end was blocked by Whisky Wallace.

Singapore promptly acted. He threw himself forward, wrenched both arms free and spun about. He swung his right fist and sank it into the dark blur which was Peddy's face, then addressed himself to Big Nick Stark.

The big man from Shanghai came at Singapore very much

as a leopard charges, crouching low, moving with terrific speed, and flailing out with both long, tough arms as he came.

The tide of battle veered momentarily in Singapore's favor as he rushed to meet this attack and sent up packed knuckles with a crunching crack into the big man's bony jaw.

Big Nick fell backward with a crash against the corrugated iron wall.

Singapore, with his two most dangerous assailants dazed by blows to the jaw, might have escaped then if Whisky Wallace had not been blocking the open end of the alley.

The beachcomber was crouching. Singapore did not see him. As he rushed toward the end of the alley, thin arms were entwined about his knees, and he fell into the sand so heavily that he was almost stunned.

By the time he had recovered himself and was struggling up, Big Nick was on him; his powerful hands were at Singapore's throat.

Singapore felt a rope end drag across his forehead. He supposed that Whisky Wallace had come equipped with it.

With Peddy the trader holding his arms and Whisky Wallace sitting on his legs, Singapore was presently trussed up so that he could not move.

Harshly, Big Nick said to Whisky Wallace, "Bring a light. We'll take him in here."

Singapore heard the soft padding of the beachcomber's feet in the sand as he went away.

"Do you trust that guy?" Big Nick said.

"To the limit," Peddy wheezed. "I've got enough on him to hang him. I trust him with pearls. I trust him with everything but my liquor. He is all right. Don't worry."

Big Nick seized the rope which bound Singapore's legs and dragged him over the sand into the copra drying shed as if Singapore were a bag of grain.

AS THE odor of the decomposing shells assailed his nostrils,

Singapore's resentment was lessened by his discovery that Big Nick, in his haste, had not tied his wrists together as tightly as he might have. Given a little time, he might free himself!

Big Nick tossed Singapore unceremoniously upon a low couch formed of the stinking shells.

A dim yellow light appeared in the doorway. It was an old tin lantern with a dirty chimney. Peddy took it from the beachcomber and hung it on a two-by-four near the door, and shut the door. Then the fat trader dragged a bench over near Singapore, and he and Big Nick sat down and looked at their red-headed prisoner. Whisky Wallace stood back of the bench.

Big Nick lighted a cigarette. The light from the lantern was behind him and it was so feeble that Singapore could see nothing of his face. The spark of the cigarette glowed and waned, glowed and waned again.

"You know what you're up against, kid," he said in his deep, harsh voice.

"We ain't foolin'," put in Peddy the trader.

"No," Big Nick agreed, "this is pretty serious. Where did you hide that pearl? You'd better talk, I'm a tough egg, Singapore. I don't think any more of your life than Peddy does of an oyster's. You carry that pearl in a little sack on the end of a copper wire that you wear around your neck. It ain't around your neck now. And that pearl ain't in any of your pockets. Where is it?"

He struck a match and held it over Singapore's face.

"You're out of luck," said the redhead. "I parked that pearl with De Silva, the jeweler, before I left Singapore. It's locked up in his safe."

"You're a liar, Singapore," Big Nick snapped. "That pearl is cached somewhere on this island. When you left Tanjong Pagan yesterday mornin', that copper wire was around your neck. I saw it. It stuck up in back over the top of your collar. Where's that pearl?"

"In Singapore. It's locked up in De Silva's safe."

"Now, don't get funny, kid. You came ashore from that proa

and you went to Tiger Tom's with Whisky Wallace. Where did you pick him up, Whisky?"

"Right by the *Kingfisher*," said the beachcomber. "He come walkin' inshore along the jetty, and stopped by the boat."

"Then he must have cached it somewhere out on the end of the jetty," said Big Nick.

"No," Whisky objected. "I didn't know who he was then. I led and he followed. He might have stuck it in any of them palms along the beach, or stooped down and buried it in the sand."

"It isn't important," said Big Nick. "We know it's somewhere on this island. Singapore, you know I'm a tough egg. You're not goin' out of here until you tell us where you hid that pearl. Are you goin' to come through—or do you want to be hurt?"

Singapore found that by twisting his left hand, he could almost pull it through the rope loop. Coconut shells were pressing sharply into his back.

Peddy the trader lighted a cigar. When it was going, he bent forward and said: "How would you like to have the hot end of this cigar shoved into your face? If you don't tell us where you hid that pearl, that's what's goin' to happen."

In spite of the heat in the copra go-down, Singapore felt a cold layer of sweat form on his forehead. The glowing cigar butt came closer.

"You gonna talk?" Paddy snapped.

"I tell you I parked that pearl with De Silva."

"Lyin' won't get you anywhere. That pearl is on this island. Where is it?"

Singapore did not answer. The glowing end of the cigar was so close now that it looked as big as the mango moon. He felt the heat of it on the skin between his eyes. He twisted his head sharply, and smelled singed hair.

PEDDY GRASPED a handful of his hair and twisted his head about. Singapore convulsively writhed, twisted; but Peddy hung on. He pulled that handful of red hair until Singapore cursed with fury and pain.

"It's in Singapore!"

"You're a damned liar!" Peddy grunted.

Big Nick coldly advised, "Better come through, Singapore."

The smoldering red moon came close again. Singapore could feel the heat of it. His eyes began to water. A spot between them began to ache. He could feel flesh shrinking from the heat.

"Where is it?"

"In De Silva's safe!" Singapore shouted.

He tried to struggle free. Whisky Wallace now lent a hand. He seated himself on Singapore's stomach and held both his knees. Peddy the trader tightened his grip on Singapore's hair. As the big roound spark came closer and closer, Singapore was sure he could smell scorching flesh. He writhed and struggled and cursed. Big Nick Stark sat on the bench like a judge and coldly watched the performance.

Singapore heard his eyebrows begin to sizzle. He cursed more loudly. There might be help somewhere on Selambang but he doubted it. He was fairly certain that the only help available was the kind that would have willingly coöperated with Big Nick, Peddy the trader and the beachcomber in torturing out of him the whereabouts of the Malobar pearl.

"Gag him," Big Nick instructed, "and cut out that cigar act. We'll leave him here."

Whisky fetched a long piece of burlap. Peddy made a gag of it and bound it into Singapore's mouth. The burlap not only smelled of copra, it tasted of copra.

A gurgle of protest came from the redhead.

"Listen, fellow," said Big Nick. "You're goin' to lay here, just like this, till you feel like tellin' us where you hid that pearl."

"You ain't," added Peddy, "goin' to have a drop to drink or a bite to eat until you kick through. You better make up your mind, you big mule, that we're goin' to get that pearl. You don't get off this island till we do get it. Let's go."

They went, shutting the godown door after them. Singapore Sammy heard their murmurs recede down the alley toward the bungalow. Then he busied himself with the loose loop on his left wrist. It was tighter than he had thought. The rope was old and somewhat frayed. The frayed ends were like tiny needles which pushed into his skin. In a few minutes, his wrists were raw and sore. In a few minutes more, the skin was practically off of the left one.

He continued to struggle. He could almost pull his hand out of the loop. But not quite. It was maddening. And the position in which he was lying, plus the discomfort of the gag, was exhausting him. His indignation continued to rise. But it was his own fault. Why in hell hadn't he parked that pearl with De Silva?

His captors returned in about half an hour. They had been drinking and quarreling. He gathered that from the way they snapped at each other when they came in.

Big Nick struck a match and held it over Singapore Sammy's face. Singapore glared up at him.

"Do you want to tell us where you hid that pearl?"

Singapore, glaring up at him, smelled the fumes of gin *bijt*.

"Let me stick this cigar in his lousy face!" This from Peddy.

"No. Later. Give him a break. We'll give him another hour to come through. If he doesn't then—"

"If you gents would leave me alone with him," Whisky Wallace suggested from the door, "I'll find out inside of five minuntes where he cached that pearl."

"Keep your nose out of this," said Peddy.

"Whisky, you've been a pretty good guy," Big Nick said, "and we won't need you any more tonight. Take this, buy yourself a load of hooch, go on down to your boat and get yourself plastered. And stay there. Get me? Stay there!"

"Why should he stay there?" Peddy demanded suspiciously.

"Because we don't need any help on this job."

"You mean," said the trader, "because you think you can get that pearl and make your getaway off this island. Well, let's see you try it."

"I'm shooting straight with you, Peddy."

The trader snorted. "You call it shootin' straight when all you offer me on the split is a third?"

"Certainly, I call it a fair split. You wouldn't know he'd brought the pearl here if I hadn't told you so."

"And you wouldn't have been as near as this to gettin' it if it wasn't for me. I've got a fifty per cent interest in that pearl."

Big Nick laughed. "Let's get our hands on that pearl before we scrap about it. Let's have another drink."

"All right, let's have another drink."

CHAPTER IV

THEY WENT OUT again. Singapore was reasonably certain that when they returned, they would both be in a nasty mood. Peddy would probably try that cigar trick again—and go through with it this time. They might try the water trick. They might even give him a touch of the bastinado.

As soon as the door closed behind them, Singapore renewed his struggle with the rope. All the skin was gone from his wrist, and the sharp fibers were biting into the raw flesh. He gave a jerk—and sank his teeth into his lower lip at the pain. But the loop slipped up over the heel of his palm. He stretched his fingers out straight—gave another yank.

The loop slipped off his hand!

Singapore worked rapidly. He removed the gag and freed his legs.

And just then he heard someone fumbling at the door.

He sank back on the copra pile and watched the door. It came open slowly, an inch at a time. The greasy lantern light fell on the tangled red hair of Whisky Wallace.

The beachcomber cautiously entered and cautiously closed the door after him. He stopped and listened. From the bungalow came the sounds of a heated argument.

Whisky Wallace's loose wet lips were animated by a grin. He came unsteadily over to the copra pile, fumbled about for the bench, and seated himself.

"Singapore," he said in a low, husky voice, "I'm gonna take off that gag, and you're gonna tell me where you put that pearl. See? And if you think you won't come clean, I'm gonna tell you what I'm gonna do."

He pulled out of his shirt a squat black bottle. Removing the cork, he put the neck into his mouth and drained the bottle. From his hip pocket he now pulled out a machinist's hammer. He struck a sharp blow with the hammer at the base of the bottle. The lower half of the bottle disappeared in glinting fragments, leaving the jagged upper half still in his hand.

Whisky Wallace replaced the hammer in his pocket, gripped the bottle tightly by the neck and bent forward. "I'm gonna shove this into your face and twist it!" he announced. He bent closer.

Singapore Sammy heard him gasp as he made a startling discovery. Two seconds later, Singapore had him by the throat; was kneeling on his chest.

When Sammy saw the beachcomber's eyes begin to bulge, he released him. Whisky Wallace was limp but not quite dead. He began gasping for air.

Singapore fumbled about for the rope, quickly cleared it of knots, and bound up Whisky Wallace. Then he folded the burlap strip into a gag, bound it in place, and arranged his limp victim on the pile of copra as he had been arranged a few minutes earlier.

He went to the door and looked back. In the dim light of the lantern, the man lying on the copra couch might readily have been mistaken for Singapore Sammy!

Singapore opened the door and let himself out. He could

not restrain a triumphant grin. In the bungalow, Peddy the trader and Big Nick Stark were quarreling at a high pitch over the Malobar pearl!

Singapore hastened down the alley. The beach, as far as he could see, was deserted. White light streamed from the doorway of Tiger Tom's, and a babble of native voices issued from there. Singapore glanced out at the jetty. A light glowed in the cabin of the *Kingfisher*. Evidently Whisky Wallace had intended torturing Sammy until Sammy confessed where he had cached the pearl; then the beachcomber could have made his getaway in the launch.

At a quick trot, Singapore went out to the jetty. He found the copper wire and the precious chamois sack where he had left them. As he trotted back along the jetty to the *Kingfisher*, he straightened out the copper wire, hung it about his neck, and tucked the chamois sack under his shirt.

Singapore was hot with excitement. Before climbing aboard the boat, he listened. Peddy and Big Nick were still quarreling in the bungalow. They might quarrel for hours, or the quarrel might stop at any moment, and they would make another trip to the copra shed.

SINGAPORE JUMPED aboard and went down into the cabin. He switched on the ignition, turned on the gas, and spun the flywheel.

The engine only hissed and grunted. Singapore's triumphant grin went away. Grimly he grasped the flywheel and spun it again and again. It took him ten valuable minutes to extract from that stubborn engine its first muffled bark. Then the four cylinders purred.

Singapore did not hear footsteps on the jetty; was not aware of anyone's approach until he felt the boat list slightly. He was starting for the door, with the intention of casting off the lines when the boat moved under the weight of someone coming aboard. And he was in the doorway, with the lantern behind him when he saw Peddy's sun helmet. It was tilted jauntily over one ear, and Peddy's eyes were blurred.

Before Singapore could leap on him, the trader, in his wheezy, guttural voice, said:

"Are ya tunin' up tha' engine, Whisky?"

Singapore's breath whistled in through his teeth. And he realized as long as he could keep his face in shadow, Peddy would remain deceived. He answered, in a very fair imitation of Whisky Wallace's husky voice, "Yes, sir—tunin' her up."

"Tha's good," said Peddy with heavy affability. "That's fine. You drunk?"

"No, sir."

"Well, don't you drink a drop, Whisky. I got a big job for you. I want you to be right on your toes. I'm drunk; but I ain't so drunk I dunno what's what. Drunk as I am, my head's as clear as a bell. Clear'r. I'll tell you what's what. You got plenty gas an' oil?"

"Yes, sir."

"Now, you listen, Whisky. I gotta scheme. It's a pretty one. Where do you s'pose Big Nick is?"

Singapore was certain that Nick was back in the copra shed and would come bounding out the jetty at any moment.

"He's back there in my dining room," said Peddy, flinging out his hand in a loose gesture. "He's puttin' away a loaded drink. D'you begin to see the scheme?"

"No, sir," said Singapore, and smothered the impulse to laugh.

"You're pretty dumb, Whisky," Peddy scoffed. "Now, listen and I'll explain, and you try to follow me. Because I'm countin' on you."

"Yes, sir."

"I loaded up Big Nick's last drink with enough laudanum to make a bull elephant sleep for a week. See? You're to wait right here with that engine runnin' until you hear me whistle. Understand?"

"Yes, sir."

"When I whistle, you come runnin' up to my bungalow, grab Nick and drag him down here. You're to take him to Singapore. I didn't load that drink enough to kill him. We don't want to kill him. But we're makin' a sucker out of the toughest egg south of Shanghai. You sure you got enough gas?"

Singapore squinted through the dark toward the bungalow. He said, "Yes, sir."

Peddy pulled a small, dark, glittering object from his hip pocket. Singapore's heart gave a lurch. It was an automatic pistol.

But the trader was handing it to him butt foremost.

"Take this," said Peddy. "Ya may need it. There's a full clip— and one in the chamber. Don't tell me I don't know what's what! I think of everything. Do I overlook a detail, Whisky?"

Singapore stifled a desire to laugh, and said, "No, sir."

"Now, listen! When Big Nick wakes up, he's gonna be mad enough to murder you. But don't shoot him. Don't kill him, or that gang of his will get us sure. Here's somethin' else to take."

He extracted from a pocket in his coat a small chamois sack very similar to the one attached to the copper wire about Singapore's neck.

"Take these pearls to the usual place and get the cash. After ya buy gas and oil, you ought to have fifteen hundred dollars left. I'll expect ya back with it tomorrow night."

"Yes, sir." Singapore pocketed the pearls and the pistol.

"D'ya know what I'm gonna do now, Whisky?" Peddy chuckled.

"No, sir," said Singapore.

"I'm gonna have a li'l party. As soon as Nick's outa the way, I'm goin' out to that copra shed. I'm gonna light a cigar and sit down and smoke it part way. Then I'm gonna say, 'Singapore, where is that pearl?' I'm gonna count five. At five, if he don't come clean, I'm gonna shove that cigar in his eye! Right in his eye! If that don't make him talk, I'm gonna boil some lard and pour boilin' lard on him!"

"That'll make him talk," Singapore warmly agreed. "Don't you think you'd better keep an eye on Big Nick, Mister Peddy?"

"Nope," the trader chuckled. "I'll give that drink time to take effect. And when you get back from S'pore, I'll have a blue pearl to show you that'll sell in N'York for forty thousand gold. And if I can find the mate to it, I'll sell the pair to some fat American millionaire for a hundred and fifty thousand. And I'll find it, because the mate to that pearl is somewhere. Now, do you understand my scheme, Whisky?"

"Yes, sir," Singapore answered.

Then Peddy the trader climbed unsteadily onto the jetty.

"Now, you wait," the fat man cautioned Singapore. "And come when I whistle."

SINGAPORE WATCHED Peddy waddle away, chuckling. But not until Singapore had cast off the lines and let in the clutch did he begin to chuckle himself. The humor of the situation appealed to Singapore, And then suddenly he heard, above the throbbing exhaust and chattering tappets, the hard hammering of feet on the jetty beside him. Someone was coming, and coming fast!

The redhead threw the wheel hard over. The *kingfisher* nosed out from the jetty. A long, lean figure in white flashed through the air and landed in a squatting position in the cockpit.

Big Nick Stark was grinning. As the man from Shanghai straightened up, Singapore let him have it with both fists square on the grin—one, two!

The toughest egg south of Shanghai lurched back from the impact of the two clean, hard punches, steadied himself with a groping hand against a stanchion behind him, kicked back with his foot, and catapulted himself at Singapore Sammy.

Singapore abandoned the *Kingfisher* to fate and met the big man's attack with head low, chin covered and fists pumping in and out like pistons. A bony fist glanced off his red-haired skull.

Singapore closed and began driving a terrific rapid-fire volley of punches into Nick's midsection.

Big Nick wilted under them as an advancing company of troops wilts under accurate machine gun fire. He dropped his big hands to protect his stomach. Singapore lashed out twice for Nick's big bony chin, and felt the satisfaction of bone crashing upon bone.

The big, tough man from Shanghai sat down heavily on the cockpit seat and yelled, "Lay off, you wildcat. I've had plenty!"

He looked it, too. Blood was trickling from his mouth, and from a cut on his chin.

Singapore backed away from him, panting. "You're goin' back where you came from," he stated.

And just then a hail came from the jetty. Singapore couldn't put back. He let in the clutch and advanced the throttle.

As Big Nick started to arise, Sammy, with his left hand on the wheel, quickly drew out of his pocket the automatic pistol.

"You sit there," he ordered. "Maybe you don't know how this thing is itchin' to pour trouble into you, tough egg."

And Big Nick said, in a soothing voice, "Put it away, kid. I've had all the trouble I need. I'm with you, not against you."

Singapore grinned. Big Nick went on:

"A little stabbard helm wouldn't do any harm. You're headin' straight for a sandbar. Why not let me take her? I know these waters like a book."

"Take her," said Singapore. "If you put her aground, one second later your backbone's gonna think an elephant's takin' a walk on it. Snappy!"

He held the gun on Nick until the big man took the wheel; then Singapore ran his hands over the other's pockets and other likely hiding places for guns and knives. Finding none, he sat down.

"Listen, kid," Big Nick said amiably, "I came to talk business. To hell with that pearl."

"Listen, tough egg," Singapore mocked him, "for the pure pleasure of it, I could turn you into curry of lead."

"Cool down, redhead, I know how you feel. But if you'll give me the break a guy would give a dying cobra—"

"You said plenty," Singapore stopped him. "Don't forget how willin' I am to turn you into so much shark bait. We're goin' to Pemanggil. Know where Pemanggil is? Know what the course is?"

"Sure, I do, buddy. And I don't care where we go as long as we have a chin-chin. You see, buddy, I know how clever you are. I know it as well as you do. What I come leapin' aboard to tell you was that I've had my eyes peeled for a smart kid like you for I don't know how many years. The fact is, redhead, I've got some ideas for makin' the two of us richer than the Maharaja of Johor."

"Horse feathers!" said Singapore.

"Oh, yeah? Well, when you cool off, we'll have that chin-chin. I know how you feel. You foxed us all, and your pride is hurt because I doped it all out just one jump behind you. You wanted to have this boat alone, so you could have a good sleep, because you didn't sleep a wink last night. And you want to be free to look for your old man. Am I right, or am I wrong?"

"When you put all that together," Singapore coldly answered, "what is it supposed to spell?"

The man at the wheel chuckled. "Great minds use the same channels, kid. You made a pretty getaway. I hand it to you."

CHAPTER V

SINGAPORE SAID NOTHING, as they made their way safely out of the harbor. He was still mad enough to shoot Big Nick Stark. Singapore wished that he had as little conscience as Big Nick had. The light in the cockpit glinted on an object slicing through the water close alongside. It was the dorsal fin of a big shark. Sammy looked at that slicing dorsal, then he looked at the gun in his hand, and then he looked at Big Nick's broad back. The sharks in these waters were arrogant and ruthless. Shark bait!

"If I don't get him," Singapore reflected, "he's goin' to get me. I'm shark bait. The minute I started to carry this pearl, I turned into shark bait!"

As if he had read his thoughts, Big Nick burst out laughing again. He said presently: "Kid, I'll tell you where you made your mistake. You should have parked that pearl with the Société Anonyme Belge, up in Bangkok, that day you had them appraise it."

"What," Sammy coldly asked, "are you tryin' to sell now, tough egg?"

"I'm givin' you the tip-off, bo, on what a mistake you made to tote that blue egg around. When you got that pearl for winnin' that fight up Malobar way, you made a news item that went from lip to ear all over Malaya, up the China Coast, and well over into India. That pearl made you anybody's victim."

"I've still got it."

"Sure, and you're gonna keep it. And I'm gonna see that you lock it up with De Silva."

"*You're* gonna see!"

"You heard me, Singapore. Believe it or not, we're gonna pal up. And once you get it into that red head that I'm with you and not against you, we'll commence gettin' somewhere."

"Save it," said the redhead.

"Take a nap," Nick said amiably, "and you'll feel better. Take a long nap and get wise to yourself. You put a fast one over on Peddy—and so did I. He slipped enough dope into a drink he mixed for me to paralyze a steamboat. Then he come down and talked to you, thinkin' you were that beachcomber."

"This monologue," said Singapore, "ain't gettin' you anywhere, tough egg. Stow it!"

Big Nick smiled patiently. "While he was down here pala-verin' with you, I was out in that shed, findin' out what a fast worker you are. You're clever, kid, you're clever! Right there and then I says to myself, 'Nick,' I says, 'you and this kid are born buddies. Don't waste time teamin' up with him. So I made one flyin' rush to catch your shirt-tails."

He paused. "It was kinda tough about Peddy. Maybe you think Peddy is out in that shed now, shoving hot cigar ends into that redhead, Wallace. Well, he ain't."

Big Nick paused again. He peered ahead, glanced at the binnacle, and gave the wheel a little twist.

"You got to watch out for these reefs," he said. "The natives think they're haunted. They are—with old wrecks." He lighted a cigarette and puffed at it leisurely. Singapore watched him intently, and fingered the trigger of the pistol.

"No," the big man went on in a drawl, "Peddy ain't back there in that shed—unless he has nine lives. I left him stretched out on the beach. I guess he's still lyin' there. The big crabs ought to be collectin' on him soon. It seems he ran onto my knife. It stuck and I was in too big a hurry to pull it out. Say! Run on along and take your nap."

Singapore was grinning. "You're gettin' tougher every minute," he said. "Well, I'm not sleepy." The fact was, he was so sleepy he could hardly keep his eyes open. His head fell forward. He jerked it up and shook it.

"I wonder," Big Nick said, "if there's any water aboard."

"I'll take the wheel," Singapore answered, "while you look."

Big Nick turned, looked at him and began to laugh again.

"Kid," he said, "you are one hard guy to convince. All right, take her. I'll see what's aboard. How would you like a nice thick juicy beefsteak smothered in onions and a bottle of that good brown Japanese beer?"

Chuckling, he went into the cabin, while Singapore took the wheel. Nick returned presently with a gallon glass jug in one hand and a thick wad of greasy old playing cards in the other.

"This seems to be distilled water," he said. "That burlap gag ought to have made you thirsty, kid. Drink hearty!"

Singapore drank a pint of the distilled water, and Nick consumed most of what was left.

"There's no food aboard," Big Nick said, "not even a tin of biscuit." His eyes had hard lights of mirth in them. "Ever play solitaire, Singapore? It's a good game to keep you awake. Your eyes look like burned holes in a blanket, kid."

SINGAPORE TOOK the thick wad of cards and discovered that there were two decks. The backs were the same shade of red and identically the same in design, so that the task of sorting them into two decks was a long one.

When he had sorted the cards, Singapore began to play poker solitaire.

Big Nick divided his time between observing the game and watching the compass. He said presently: "Sam, you're too sleepy even to play solitaire. Go on down there and saw some wood."

Singapore put down a queen that filled a royal flush in clubs and said to himself: "Why am I lettin' this guy live? He made a sap out of me once, and by lettin' him live, I'm givin' him an engraved invitation to make a sap out of me again."

"Maybe you don't realize," Nick broke into his thoughts, "how far a couple of clever birds like you and me could go on this coast. The world is full of suckers. I've got a gang organized in Singapore, and another gang in Rangoon. If you'll team up with me, we'll organize Shanghai and Yokohama. I've doped out rackets that'll make us rich. Are you interested?"

"Nope."

"Goin' to stay that way?"

"Yep."

"You wouldn't be interested in anything I could say—is that the size of it? My ideas leave you cold, eh?"

Singapore grinned. "As cold as a shark's heart, Nick."

The big man turned quickly about from the wheel. He was

no longer laughing. His eyes were narrow and they glittered metallically And his mouth was a hard red line.

"Nothin' I can say would interest you?"

"That's right."

"How about pearls?"

"My only interest in them," said Singapore, "is to find the twin to the one I've got."

Big Nick's eyes had narrowed still more.

"You sure you've got it, kid?"

Singapore's hand mechanically flew the hard round ball in the sack at his throat. "I'm sure," he said.

But the queer, hard light remained in Big Nick's eyes.

"Maybe it was switched on you, kid," he said. "Maybe what you've got in that sack is a marble—or a steel ball bearing."

Singapore's grin became uncertain. He knew that Big Nick Stark was dangerous and clever—probably the most dangerous and the most clever man he had ever encountered. The automatic pistol lay beside Singapore's elbow. He could reach it two seconds sooner than Nick could.

"What's your game?" he asked.

"Maybe I'm leading up to a proposition. You're sure that ball-shaped thing in that little sack is the Malobar pearl? That's what I want to know."

"Yeah," said Sammy. "I'm dead sure."

"All right, kid. Now I'll show you somethin'. But first, where's the mate to that pearl? You know there's a mate. But who's got it?"

"The chief of a Moosar tribe in northern Siam."

Big Nick's eyes were glowing like a cat's. "You're sayin' that the mate to your pearl is just about two thousand miles due north of where we are?"

"More or less."

"All right, bo. Now watch me close. Remember: the hand is quicker than the naked eye!"

Big Nick plunged his big brown fist into his pants pocket and brought out a round dark-brown lump about an inch and a half in diameter. He held the lump, delicately balanced, on his fingertips.

"Know what this stuff is?" the big man asked Singapore.

"Opium gum."

"That's right. Know what comes out of opium gum?" Big Nick was twisting the gum slowly about on the tips of his fingers. "Watch close, kid! You're gonna see as fancy a dream as ever came out of opium, cooked or raw!"

With his two powerful brown thumbs, Big Nick split the lump of gum into two halves. And in the center of one of the halves lay embedded a round, fiery blue ball!

Singapore Sammy, with one swift movement, reached for the automatic. With his other hand, he snatched the loop of copper wire over his head.

LOUNGING AGAINST the cabin wall, Big Nick watched him and grinned. Then he began to laugh.

Singapore loosened the cord at the throat of the chamois sack with his teeth. Then, holding the bottom of the sack in his teeth, he shook down into his palm the blue pearl.

From the pearl in his hand, Singapore looked at the half revealed pearl in the lump of opium gum. His bushy red eyebrows slid upward on his forehead and back into place. His eyes were filled with a dancing light.

"Do they match?" he said eagerly. On two subjects, Singapore could not be rational: his old man and blue pearls. He was so excited now that he was unaware of the slyly satisfied expression in Big Nick's eyes.

"If they don't match, size for size, color for color and fire for fire," said Nick, "you can open up on me with that gun. That's how sure I am! But see for yourself."

He forced the pearl out of the gum and indifferently gave it to Singapore.

"It's dirty from bein' in this gum," Nick said. "You have to consider that. But when it's cleaned up, it shines like hell's fire."

Singapore was eagerly comparing the pearls, size for size, color for color, fire for fire.

"Mine's dirty from the gum," Nick repeated, "and this is a lousy light—but are they twins or ain't they?"

"You bet they are!" Singapore exclaimed.

"Let's have mine back," Nick drawled. "I'm just as nervous when it gets out of my hands as you are with yours."

Reluctantly, Singapore surrendered the blue Malobar's pearl's twin. He hated to see them separated. Entirely aside from the tremendous monetary value of these two pearls was the thrill of seeing them together again—after how many years!

"Where'd you get it?" he excitedly asked.

Nick jerked his dark head backward, toward the bow of the boat. "From the head priest of that Moosar tribe, kid." He was pressing the pearl into the gum again. Almost in panic, Singapore watched it disappear into the brown substance. "But don't ask me how."

Singapore Sammy's search for the mate to the Malobar pearl was at an end. But what was he going to do about it?

Big Nick, with narrowed eyes, was regarding Singapore's flushed face, his eagerly sparkling eyes, his excited grin.

"Well, kid, my cards are on the table just like those cards there. Nobody in the world but you knows that I've got this pearl, because I didn't get all the free advertisin' that went with yours! What are we gonna do, Singapore? Do we pal up, or don't we? With these two pearls between us, we're four to five times richer than we were separated, with a pearl apiece. United, we're rich; divided, we're suckers. Do we pal up?"

He was still molding the lump of gum in his fingers. Singapore wrenched his fascinated eyes from it and stared at Big Nick. He came momentarily to his senses.

"No," he said.

Big Nick's smile vanished. "For cryin' out loud, aren't you

ever gonna show some brains? Why did I follow you all the way to Selambang? To steal that pearl! Sure! And I fell down on it, didn't I? You got me where you wanted me, didn't you? I come clean. I admit you outsmarted me. You've got the drop on me. Now I make you a friendly proposition. You're the kind of guy who wouldn't buy genuine five-dollar gold pieces for a nickel apiece! Will you listen to my proposition, or won't you? I say: let's take these pearls to New York and sell 'em. We get the cash and we split it. Do we do business?"

Singapore wanted that pearl as he had never wanted anything in his life; but the rational part of his brain that was still functioning warned him. Hadn't Big Nick already committed two known murders in the sacred interest of this pair of pearls?

"No," he said.

"You don't trust me."

"Not any farther than I could throw this boat by her rudder!"

Big Nick's complexion seemed to turn black. He glanced at the automatic at Singapore's elbow.

"All right," he said, "we'll settle it some other way. You don't want me, but you do want this pearl. I want you; I still want to team up with you; and I want that blue pearl if I can get it. Do I deny it? Hell, no! You won't sell out for a reasonable price, and you haven't the money to buy me out. How'll we settle it? How bad do you want this pearl of mine?"

The fanatical light had returned to Singapore's clear blue eyes. He wanted that pearl so badly that he would almost commit murder to get it—almost!

"Will you gamble?" Big Nick growled. "You play poker and so do I."

He reached down for the pack of cards nearest him. Singapore, misconstruing him, snatched up the automatic.

Big Nick grunted. "To hell with that! Will you play a cold hand to see who gets 'em both—or won't you?"

Singapore hesitated. His eyes were burning much more brightly than the two blue fire pearls. Common sense warned

him not to enter into any kind of transaction with this man;
but the desire to possess the Malobar pearl's twin overrode
caution.

BIG NICK was clumsily shuffling the deck. It was obvious to
Singapore that he had had little card playing experience. Some
of the cards spilled, and Big Nick stooped over and picked them
up. In a voice that was hardly more than a husky whisper, Singapore said: "All right. A cold hand. Deal 'em!"

Big Nick dealt slowly and clumsily. Singapore saw, for the
first time, that these hands, while they looked long, had short,
square-ended fingers and thick, blunt thumbs.

Singapore picked up his cards. His hands were trembling so
violently that he almost dropped the cards. His eyes, blurry
with excitement, stared at the five oblongs of pasteboard which
would decide whether he would be independently rich—or
almost broke.

But his expression did not change when he saw three jacks,
a ten of hearts, a seven of spades.

"What have you got?" Singapore asked.

Big Nick drawled, "Maybe you got me licked, buddy; but I
seem to have a pretty strong hand. What've you got?"

"Three jacks!"

"Well, can you tie that! I've got three fours—and a pair of
deuces!"

"Show me!"

Big Nick displayed his hand. He tossed the cards onto the
cockpit seat.

"Tough luck, kid?"

"Am I yellin'?" Singapore asked. He removed the loop of
tough copper wire from his neck, loosened the cord at the throat
of the little chamois sack, dumped the blue pearl into his hand,
and gave it to the man from Shanghai. He handed it over as
indifferently as though it had been a clay marble.

Nick's blunt fingers engulfed the Malobar pearl. He placed it in his pocket carelessly.

"Kid," he said, glancing for a brief moment at the automatic pistol, "I'm sorry. No foolin', I'm sorry to see you lose that egg. I know what it means to you."

"Lay off the crocodile stuff," Singapore said tersely.

"No, I mean it, kid," Nick persisted. "You're a good game kid, and I like you."

"Want to play some more?" Singapore asked. "How about another cold hand? I've got some more pearls." He fished out the sack that Peddy had given him and spilled its contents into his hand. There was one pair of fairly large matched white ones, and an assortment of a dozen smaller ones, some white, some black, some round, some pear shaped.

"Peddy's pearls!" Big Nick laughed. "Kiddo, you keep on bein' cleverer all the time!"

"Yeah? These pearls are worth two thousand, Mex."

"Sure, they are! Every florin of it!"

"Got that much cash on you?"

"Sure, I have! I always carry plenty of cash." Big Nick withdrew from his pocket a thick roll of bills; counted out twenty hundred-dollar-notes on the Bank of Hongkong and said, "Here's your two thousand."

"They ain't for sale," Singapore said. "Deal another cold hand."

"Kid, why do it? Maybe your luck ain't so good tonight. I've got a feelin' my luck is awful good."

"Deal 'em," Singapore said coldly. He was willing to risk Peddy's pearls to see Big Nick shuffle and deal again. If he was dealing off the bottom, or employing any other trick, there was going to be a murder on board in less than one minute!

Big Nick picked up the cards and shuffled them. As clumsily as before, he shuffled. And much more sharply than before, Singapore watched. Never in all his years of poker playing had he seen a man so clumsy with cards.

And the moment Singapore saw the hand that had been dealt him, he knew that all that remained of his fortune was lost. Yet he had seen Nick employ no tricks—unless that clumsiness was the trick. Sammy's high card was a ten of diamonds. There was not a pair in his hand.

Big Nick won Peddy's pearls with a pair of queens.

"Tough luck, kid, tough luck!"

"Save it," said Singapore coldly. "Now, I am going to take a nap."

The eyes of the man from Shanghai flickered again to the automatic pistol.

"That's the idea, old feller," he said in a sympathetic voice. "Hit the flax. And don't let the future look too black. Those brains of yours are worth a pile of jack to me. Tie up with me, redhead! You wouldn't have to stop lookin' for your old man. With my gang behind you, you'd find him quicker. Say, are we still headin' for Pemanggil?"

"Yeah, tough egg. And listen. When I sleep, I snore like hell—but the touch of a feather wakes me up. Savvy? I'm gonna sleep with this gun in my hand. If anything heavier than a feather touches me, this gun is goin' to begin goin' off."

Big Nick looked at him with well assumed amazement.

"Why, what's bitin' you, redhead?"

Singapore picked up the two decks of cards and placed one deck in each hip pocket.

"If I find out that you foxed me with these cards, you're gonna smell brimstone. Hold a course for Pemanggil, fellow."

Big Nick grinned at him. "Sweet dreams, redhead."

Singapore went into the cabin and threw himself down on the starboard bunk. For perhaps a minute he lay awake, while sleep seemed to rush at him like a black torrent from every direction. He was certain that Big Nick had cheated with those cards. But how could he prove it?

CHAPTER VI

BIG NICK HELD the *Kingfisher* on her course until a glance into the cabin assured him that his latest victim had fallen asleep; then he twisted the wheel sharply and changed his course to southwest by west—for Singapore! When that redhead was sleeping sound enough, he would go down there and take his pistol away.

A self-satisfied grin flickered over Big Nick's hard red lips. Leisurely, he removed from his pocket the lump of opium gum. His grin widened. With his strong thumbs, he pried the lump open and removed the pearl with which he had so ingeniously fooled that redhead. He placed the pearl in his mouth, sucked it with his tongue, removed it, and spat out a stream of saliva stained faintly blue.

The Malobar's twin was now white. It was a pearl—an excellent pearl. It had cost Nick three thousand ticals, and a hundred more for that remarkable layer of fiery blue stain. A Jap in Bangkok had disguised the pearl and had guaranteed that the stain would not injure the pearl, would wash off in water. The Jap had seen the Malobar pearl when Singapore took it to the Bangkok jeweler's to be appraised. He had secured its measurements, helped Nick to find a white one of identical size and shape, and then stained it with water color.

Big Nick restored the pearl to his pocket and lit a cigarette. His nerves were badly shaken. He needed a smoke. That redhead had been a tough customer, alert, suspicious and dangerous to the very last. Until the minute he had gone down there to sleep, Big Nick had been afraid the boy would see through the clever drama he had staged to obtain that pearl, even at the point of a gun; afraid Sammy would use that gun.

But Nick wasn't afraid of anything now. For a while he gloated over the magnificent Malobar pearl. He was at peace with the world until, by habit, he chanced to glance up at the heavens.

What he saw caused Big Nick to open the *Kingfisher's* throttle to the last notch.

CHAPTER VII

SINGAPORE SAMMY'S RETURN to wakefulness was accomplished so violently that he was almost knocked senseless. He came awake to the startling discovery that he had been hurled out of the bunk and to the floor.

For a moment he lay sprawled out, while his sleep-drugged brain gradually informed him where he was and what was taking place.

Big Nick must have been shouting at him, for he angrily shouted now, "Singapore! Singapore!" And there was in his voice a brittle edge.

The engine was no longer running. Singapore discovered that he was lying in several inches of water. Dazedly, he wondered what had happened. The floor was perfectly dry when he turned in.

As he started to his feet, the floor of the cabin gave way under him. The redheaded adventurer went sprawling into the bunk on the port side and struck his forehead so smartly against an oak rib that the remnants of sleep scattered.

Now, clearly, he began hearing the wash and roar of heavy waves, the hiss of rain on the deck, and the rising scream of the wind.

The *Kingfisher* was plunging, pitching and rolling heavily. He heard a wave thunder down on the stern. White foam floating on black water descended into the cockpit and came slopping down into the cabin.

Singapore lurched out of the bunk as the boat staggered under a larger wave. He felt the water jacket of the engine. It was so hot that it scorched his fingers. He clambered up into the cockpit.

Big Nick, soaked to the skin, with water streaming in long

filaments from his nose and chin, was spinning the wheel this way and that, evidently trying to head into the wind. His hair in black clumps snapped in the wind.

"You can't," Singapore calmly pointed out, "steer her when you haven't got steerageway."

"I ought to have some steerageway," the big man snarled. "That lousy engine didn't lay down until twenty seconds ago!"

"These high bows always swing around and bring the stern into the wind," Sammy informed him. "We'll have to rig up a sea anchor. How long've I been asleep?"

"Not more'n ten minutes. This squall came down on us like a screeching devil out of hell. One minute, it was as calm as noon. Next, this wind was blowing blue blazes. Then that damned old engine had to stop!"

"Run up and take a look at that gas tank," Singapore suggested.

And Big Nick snarled at him. "What're ya gonna make a sea anchor out of? There ain't a toothpick of spare wood on this lousy boat. The bunks are galvanized iron, ain't they? Do you know where this squall is blowin' us? Right into those Pemanggil reefs!"

He plunged into the cabin to inspect the gas tank, and while he was gone Singapore looked for a pump. He found an old sheet iron bilge pump and a length of old fire hose. He lifted a hatch cover out of the cockpit floor, lowered the suction end of the pump into the *Kingfisher's* bilges, connected the hose to the ejection elbow, and began to pump.

Big Nick came out of the cabin wearing a grin that seemed to be caused by the wind tugging at his lips.

"Dry as a bone! Not a lousy drop!"

"Take this pump," Singapore directed, "while I look for a bucket."

Another wave came over the poop and flooded the cockpit. Big Nick began energetically to pump.

Singapore found a collapsible canvas bucket in the cabin. He began to bail. As the position of the *Kingfisher* shifted, waves began smashing aboard over the weather rail.

Big Nick pumped until he was exhausted, then he bailed while Singapore pumped.

It was impossible to maintain a footing for many seconds at a time. A wave would crash against the *Kingfisher,* and she would stagger or lurch or rise or fall. Singapore would let go the pump handle and make a flying grab at tarpaulin stanchions or cabin wall.

IN SPITE of their efforts, the water perceptibly gained. Swirling and gurgling about their feet, it was lukewarm and aglimmer with phosphorescent flashes. At times, the stream of water gushing overboard from the pump was a stream of liquid green fire.

Above the shouting wind Big Nick yelled that they were getting nearer and nearer the reefs.

"This wind is blowin' us right on 'em. They're sharper than *parangs,* these reefs. They'll rip the bottom out of her."

Shortly after he had spoken, the *Kingfisher* smashed against one of the invisible reefs. She shuddered and staggered on. Both men were thrown to the floor.

"These waters," Big Nick said as they scrambled to their feet, "are lousy with sharks. Sharks breed here. You could walk ashore on their backs."

"What shore?" Singapore wanted to know.

"Pemanggil! Where else do you suppose this wind and current are drivin' us?"

"Maybe we'll wash up on the beach!"

"Not a chance. We'll never live through these reefs."

They spoke as men will, when united by a common necessity. Pearls and personal hatreds were, for the time being, put aside. Shoulder to shoulder, they worked to save the *Kingfisher* from foundering.

The lantern went out. The sudden blackness was startling.

Wave crests, glimmering green, came hurtling at them. Once Singapore saw, not a dozen feet away, a comber break over saw-toothed fangs. And the *Kingfisher* drifted on.

The squall died, as South China Sea squalls have a habit of doing, with the same alarming suddenness with which it had sprung up. A stiff breeze from the southwest followed, and the motor boat continued to drift

Shortly before dawn, the *Kingfisher* came to a harsh, grating rest on a rock or coral ledge. A tremendous wave picked her up and carried her farther up on the ledge.

THE FIRST rosy rays of dawn found the two men, utterly exhausted, staring toward the northeast, where Pemanggil should lie—staring and simultaneously bursting into the profanity of exultant relief.

Less than one hundred feet from the flat coral ledge on which the *Kingfisher* had come to rest was the dark impressive wall of a jungle!

"Kiddo, we're safe!" Big Nick jubilantly exclaimed. "That's Pemanggil! You see that little white strip between the water and the jungle? Buddy, that's a beach! That beach is an easy twelve-mile walk into the *kampong!* Are we clever or ain't we? We made our way, without power, in the black o' night, through the Pemanggil reefs to a moorin' without losin' an eyebrow! It's an easy swim to shore. But maybe we won't have to swim. Maybe when the tide comes up, we'll float off."

"It's high tide now," Singapore pointed out.

"Let's swim!"

Singapore was staring at the narrow stretch of water between the boat and the white beach.

"Lousy," he said, "with sharks. Look at 'em! Just look at 'em!"

The brightening light showed them a squadron of a half dozen slicing dorsals. And as the light increased, they saw that the passage was fairly alive with sharks; big fellows, the tigers of the southern seas; always starved, always rapacious.

"Talk to 'em," said Singapore. "You ought to talk their language, tough egg."

And thus their old footing was restored. But Big Nick preferred to ignore this.

"Maybe it ain't high tide," he argued. "Maybe it's just makin'. Let's pump some more."

He seized the pump and Sammy picked up the bucket. They pumped and bailed. The water went down perceptibly. Then Singapore discovered why.

"The tide's on the ebb," he announced.

Big Nick stopped pumping and stared at the beach.

"We'll wait," he said. "It'll come in again."

"Just look at those damned sharks!"

The passage was churning with the flashings of the long dark bodies.

"It's shallow," Nick said. "At low tide, it'll be dry enough to walk across."

"We wouldn't need much of a raft to float ashore," said Singapore.

They abandoned the pump and the bucket and looked for materials with which to fashion a raft. But there was no loose planking from which even a small raft could be built. And there was no ax or crowbar with which deck or cabin planking could be pried off. The cabin and deck were of dowel-fastened teak, as was also the hull.

The two men divided the drinking water that remained in the glass jug and waited for the tide to go out. And the more the water receded, the deeper, it seemed, became the narrow stretch between ledge and shore.

While Singapore waited, he occupied himself with examining both the decks of cards. One after another, he carefully inspected every card in each desk, but he found no markings of any kind. He began to play poker solitaire.

The sun slid higher and poured down heat that soon made of the cockpit a furnace.

"The natives think it's haunted here," Big Nick said. "And they never come within miles of here in their boats, on account of them bad reefs. Kid, you're clever. Tell me how we're gonna get out of this. I'm thirsty enough already to drink sea water. There ain't a scrap of food aboard. We can't make a raft to get ashore. My God," he shouted, "it's so close you could almost jump it!"

Nick began to curse again, and Singapore continued to play poker solitaire.

CHAPTER VIII

HOURS PASSED. THE tide went to dead ebb, and commenced flowing in again. And not once since daylight first revealed them, had that stretch of water between the shipwrecked launch and the beach been free of shining dorsals.

"If a fellow took a runnin' dive from the cabin roof," Nick said presently, "and swam like hell, he might scare 'em enough to make shore before they turned on him."

"Yeah?" said Singapore. "Watch!"

He picked up their empty water bottle and hurled it into the sea. The instant the bottle struck the water, slicing dorsals came to the surface in a boiling rush. At least a dozen sharks reached the big glass bubble simultaneously.

"Well," said Nick, "what're we gonna do, Singapore?"

"You're a smarter man than I am," said the redhead, as he discarded a king of clubs. "You make some suggestions."

"You got that other deck on you?" Nick asked.

"Sure! Think we can build a bridge with it?" Singapore gave him the other deck and watched the big man clumsily shuffle them.

"If I don't do somethin'," said Nick, "I'll go nuts."

He began playing poker solitaire beside Sammy.

"Kid," he said suddenly, "there's only one way out of this jam—and you know it. One of us has got to take the chance and swim ashore!"

"Go ahead," Singapore said amiably, "and do it."

"The question is," said Nick, "who will be?"

"You win on the first ballot."

"Now, listen, kid. This ain't anything to wisecrack about. If we stay here, we croak. As sure as you live, we croak. If we don't go nuts with heat and thirst and jump overboard, we die of starvation."

Sammy looked at the slicing dorsals and his eyes narrowed.

"It's a good idea," he said, "providin' you do it. I'm too young, Nick. All my life's ahead of me. I've got too much to live for. You—you're a has-been. Go on and jump and fetch me some help."

But Nick did not grin. He remained grim.

"All right, buddy. If you've got some better suggestions, make 'em. I'll meet you halfway."

"Don't you think somebody might come by lookin' for wreckage?"

"Not a chance. Nobody ever comes by here. Look here, kid. One of us might get through those sharks and make the shore. It's worth tryin'. I'm willin'—if you are."

Singapore looked at him intently. "How do you mean, big boy, you're willin'?"

"I'll gamble if you will."

"You mean—with these cards?" Singapore asked.

"Is anything wrong with 'em?" Big Nick snapped.

"Nope."

"Well," Big Nick stated, "if one of us don't swim, what do we do? We're both burnin' up for water. I've got good eyesight and all I can see starin' us in the face is slow music. What do we do?"

"Just what we did last night. You're goin' to deal us each a cold hand. Low hand wins. Don't use that deck. Use mine."

Singapore had returned the deck he had been using to his right hip pocket where the pistol was. He tossed the cards on the seat and said, "Go ahead and shuffle and deal."

If there was a trick, with the aid of the glaring noon sunlight, he would see it. Singapore was willing to risk his life with those sharks to discover how the man from Shanghai worked that trick.

BIG NICK was clumsily shuffling the cards. Singapore watched them. It was amazing to him that, if there was a trick, it should be concealed behind that awkward shuffling.

"One thing," said Nick: "They kill you fast, those babies. It's better than sittin' here and goin' nuts with heat and thirst."

Singapore did not once remove his eyes from those clumsy hands. Big Nick dealt.

The redhead picked up his hand. A pair of tens, a pair of sixes and a jack of hearts.

He was staring at them when Big Nick growled, "Well, what have you got, buddy?"

Singapore laid down his hand.

Big Nick grunted, "Tough luck, buddy. I guess you swim." And laid down four aces.

The red-headed adventurer glanced from them to Nick's face. Singapore's expression was one of begrudged admiration.

"How in hell," he asked, "do you do it? Is it a gift?"

"Kid, it was luck."

"Horse feathers! Well, if I could 'a' found out just once that it wasn't luck—"

"Ain't welchin', are you, redhead?"

"You know I ain't, tough egg. I'll swim in. I mean, if I don't give those sharks their lunch. I'll swim in. And if I make it, I'll go and fetch somebody in a boat to take you off. That was the bargain."

"Yeah, that was the bargain; but there wasn't anything in the bargain about your settin' on your fanny there and gassin' for a coupla hours. Button up your lip, redhead, and get into your swimmin' clothes."

"I'm workin' on an idea," said Singapore. He was taking off his soiled white drill pants. "Did you ever hear that sharks don't ever attack natives?"

"What country," Nick asked contemptuously, "are you a native of?"

"Use your lamps, tough egg," Singapore answered with a hard grin, "and maybe you'll learn a new trick."

Singapore quickly removed all of his clothes. Naked, he went into the cabin, and, with a handful of waste, mopped black grease and oil from the engine and smeared himself with it liberally, until he was a brownish-black from forehead to toes. Nick, grasping the idea, smeared the places on Singapore's back the redhead couldn't reach.

"Maybe," said Nick, as he concluded this task, "I could sit here and knock off a few sharks with that gun of yours while you was swimmin' in."

"And maybe," Singapore said, "I can use that rod myself when I get ashore. Is there anything else of mine you haven't got you'd like to have?"

"Can the sarcasm, buddy. It's a case of sink or swim for both of us. You might take a runnin' dive off the cabin roof. And if you don't land swimmin' fast, it's a cinch you won't swim far. These sharks would just as soon make a meal off a native of Greaseland as anybody."

Singapore Sammy had decided to roll up his clothes in a bundle with the automatic pistol at the center to give it weight. This bundle he could throw ashore. And when he reached the beach—if he reached the beach—he would have dry clothes to put on.

He said as he picked up the pants: "Nick, I don't know how you foxed me, but I know you did. You crooked me out of that blue pearl. You crooked me out of Peddy's pearls. And you crooked me on this last deal."

"Go ahead and prove it, guy!"

"If I get through those sharks, I'm goin' to spend the rest of my life finding out how that card gag is worked. And when I find out, I'm gonna look you up."

"Yeah? Well, redhead, I'm home to guys who're gonna turn me into curry of lead every Friday afternoon from two to four."

Singapore looked at him thoughtfully and ran his hand into the right hand hip pocket of his pants with the intention of taking out the pistol and rolling it into the center of the bundle. His fingers encountered not only the warm steel of the pistol but a shiny rectangular piece of paste board. In pulling out the deck of cards which Nick had used in dealing that last cold hand, he had evidently left one card behind.

He pulled out the card and looked at it. It was the ace of spades. From it he glanced at the four aces which Nick had dealt to himself.

CHAPTER IX

THE MAN FROM Shanghai was lounging against a stanchion with a cigarette dangling from a corner of his hard red mouth. He looked sharply at the card in Singapore's hand. With a sweep of his hand he knocked the cigarette out of his mouth.

Singapore dropped the card and plunged his hand into the hip pocket. The automatic pistol flashed out. Big Nick made a lunge for it; struck it with the palm of his hand. The pistol flew out of Singapore's grasp and fell into the deep water alongside.

The force of his rush sent Singapore backward, jamming his back against the steering wheel. Big Nick followed up that rush. With his eyes narrowed, his lips drawn back from his yellow teeth, he attacked.

Singapore, still somewhat stunned by the discovery he had

made, tried to slip aside. The toughest egg south of Shanghai spat out, "Now, you fresh ape, we'll settle this!"

His body crashed against Singapore's. The sharp corner of the companion hatch grating dug into Singapore's naked back. Big Nick's powerful hands closed on his throat. He brought up his knee; but the redhead, twisting, interposed a hip.

Singapore bent backwards, bent forwards and ducked down. His neck, slippery with oil and sweat, slipped out of the big man's grasp. Singapore brought down the heel of his fist on Big Nick's mouth. Nick threw his loglike arms about Singapore's upper body and clawed for a hold, but the slippery black coating of oil and sweat again cheated him.

Once more free, the angry redhead resorted to the tactics he had employed with such good results when Big Nick came aboard the previous night. He drove his right fist into Nick's stomach. The toughest egg south of Shanghai uttered a grunt. Singapore followed that right hand punch with a left.

Nick dropped his elbows to protect his middle, and when he did so, Singapore drove a left and a right into his face.

Big Nick staggered back, now decidedly on the defensive. His hawklike eyes were blazing with wrath. But they blinked when a fist hammered into his nose.

"That," Singapore panted, "is for that first cold hand!"

He sent in a staggering blow to Nick's jaw.

"And that," the redhead informed him, "is for that second cold hand."

Another smashing left to the nose was followed by another comment. "And that is for those five aces, you lousy crook!"

The big man tried to fight back. As far as brute strength went, he far outmatched the redheaded American; but Singapore had spent some time in the ring. He knew where punches hurt the most, and how to inflict damage.

He inflicted it now unsparingly. With a fury born of his discovery, he battered the toughest egg south of Shanghai almost into insensibility. He closed one eye. He started blood to flowing freely from the big man's nose and mouth. He knocked him down, taunted him to his feet, and knocked him down again.

A blow in the jaw that would have fractured a normal jawbone sent Big Nick down to stay down. With dazed eyes he lay on the cockpit floor and cursed.

STANDING OVER him, a shining black figure of vengeance, the redhead panted, "You had enough, tough egg?"

And Big Nick weakly snarled, "This ain't the end of this, you redheaded bum!"

"Stand up!" Singapore snapped.

The big man slowly obeyed. He could hardly stand.

"Come across with my blue pearl—and let me have a look at its mate," Singapore ordered.

With a curse, Big Nick surrendered the Malobar pearl, and then the white one he had faked Sammy with.

"You fooled me plenty with that dyed pearl, you big cheat," Singapore said. "Your game's up now, though. Hand over Peddy's pearls and the cash!"

"You know what'll come your way for this!" Big Nick grunted. But he disgorged Peddy's pearls and two thousand in cash.

"You lost the bet on the swim, too," Singapore said. "But I ain't gonna take a chance of your swimmm' to shore and sendin' help to me. I've sort of lost my confidence in you, tough egg. I'm goin' overboard now. And the only way you're goin' to get off this boat is to swim off."

Big Nick was getting his breath back.

"Don't worry," he snarled, "about me gettin' ashore. You better begin worryin' about what's gonna happen to you the next time we run together."

Singapore grinned at him. He was finishing rolling up his belongings, with the pearls and money in the center. The blue Malobar pearl he restored to the chamois sack at his throat.

When the bundle suited him, he went up on the cabin and

heaved it ashore. It landed on the beach and rolled under a mangrove root. Then Singapore went into the cabin for a screwdriver. He found a long sharp one and placed it between his teeth. It might serve as a dagger.

He returned to the cabin top. Big Nick followed him. His face was swollen.

"I just want to tell you, redhead," he said huskily, "in case it didn't register, that you had better make fast time out o' these parts. The next time you and me meet, you ain't gonna come off the way you did this time. I'm gonna get you and I'm gonna get you good!"

Singapore Sammy said nothing. With the screwdriver between his teeth, he backed to the extreme edge of the cabin top. He gathered himself together, took three hard, fast strides, and dived off.

That swim to the beach, Singapore Sammy would always remember as the most realistic nightmare, asleep or awake, he had ever experienced.

Suddenly he was among the sharks. A dark body, as rough as the coarsest sandpaper, brushed past the calf of his left leg— and ground off the skin as if Singapore had held his leg against a spinning emery wheel.

A yellow-pink mouth yawned ahead of him. It was full of shining white teeth. Singapore drove the screwdriver into that maw—and thrashed on.

Then, suddenly, his knees were barking on coral. His hands came down on hard white sand. He scrambled up into shallower water, sprang up and looked back, panting.

Big Nick was still standing on the cabin top. He was lighting a cigarette and looking down at the sharks. Slowly, he began to divest himself of his clothing. He presently was naked. Even at that distance, his white body, in the glaring sun of the tropical noon, looked gigantic.

Singapore found his bundle under the mangrove root. He

unrolled it and began swabbing off the coat of oil with handfuls of waste which he had rolled into the bundle.

AS HE wiped off the black layer of grease he watched Big Nick. The tough man from Shanghai had wrapped the fingers of one hand about the short mast at the forward end of the cabin. With the cigarette dangling from his lower lip, his other hand on his hip, he stood and considered the water.

Singapore shouted, "You better swab some oil on, big boy!"

And Big Nick cordially yelled back, "I can get along without advice from you, you slob!"

The redhead grinned. "Goin' to throw your stuff ashore, tough egg? I'll catch it."

"You'll catch somethin' heavier than my stuff one of these days!"

"Yeah?"

Sammy suspended the operation of cleansing himself. Big Nick was preparing to dive. His clothing he had rolled into a tight bundle. This, with a length of cord, he was tying on his head.

Singapore yelled, "Hey, tough egg; that bundle's goin' to cramp your style. You better heave it ashore."

"And you walk off with it, and leave me stripped and strapped!"

"I wouldn't play a lousy trick like that even on you!"

"Yeah? Ain't it too bad I didn't graduate from your Sunday school, you red-headed bum!"

Singapore said no more. He waited and watched. Big Nick finished tying the bundle on his head. Then he flicked the cigarette away. He stepped backward, as Sammy had done; took three short, quick strides and dived.

He came to the surface in a smother of foam. His long, powerful white arms flashed out. With narrowing eyes, Singapore watched the dorsal fins converge along that precarious line of travel. They came from every direction, slicing down on the thrashing white man like black sails. Singapore counted eleven of them.

He saw a shark ten feet long gracefully roll over and show its white belly; saw its pinkish-yellow mouth open.

The water in the immediate vicinity of Big Nick Stark was lashed to a white froth.

And suddenly the man from Shanghai vanished. In going, he made no sound.

Now, only the white froth remained. Not a dorsal remained above the green water.

And as Singapore watched, the white froth turned pink, then red. The red was like a cloud. It spread until the bubbling surface for twenty feet in all directions was crimson.

Singapore finished mopping off the black oil. He dressed.

Late that afternoon, the red-headed adventurer reached the *kampong* at the northern extremity of Pemanggil, to find that his father—or the begging Buddhist who he was sure was his father—had left for Bangkok on a trading schooner the morning before!

IV

THE PINK ELEPHANT

One Big Drink of Whisky and Singapore
Sammy's War Elephant Was the Equal of
All the Warriors of the King of Siam

THE THIN, HIGH squeal, as if some beast were in mortal terror, sounded again!

Singapore Sammy had halted his caravan of elephants in a small clearing in the dense Siamese jungle, and now was listening with head cocked to the left, carrot-colored brows bent down, blue eyes squinting.

Heat devils danced in the air. Sweat ran from under Singapore's mushroom-shaped khaki sun helmet and trickled down his face.

The jungle mocked the red-headed white man with its silence. The twenty elephants in Singapore's caravan murmured uneasily in their throats—that squeal had made them all restless. Trunks were waving wildly. Great gray masses of flesh were doing little dancelike shuffles.

The trail to Paknam Po led to the left, but the sound that had arrested Singapore Sammy and caused him to order a halt had come from the right. Now, the captain and the nineteen brown-skinned soldiers of the bodyguard which Prince Poot Alla had placed at Sammy's disposal, all stared at the red-headed white man inquiringly.

Singapore Sammy lifted his eyebrows and sent a glance in the direction of Captain San Nyun, an olive-skinned man of thirty in a uniform as red and as elegant as the body of a scarlet tanager. In passable Siamese, Sammy asked: "Captain, what do

you make of it? Is it a
leopard in a trap or a
jaguar howling for its
dinner?"

"Master, it is," the red-
uniformed officer respect-
fully answered, "a pig in
distress."

"A *pig?*"

"A baby elephant,
Master."

"What would be his
trouble?"

The lean shoulders
under Captain San Nyun's
bright uniform rose and
fell with a shrug. "Buddha
in his great comprehension alone knows, Master."

The red-headed white man lit a cigarette and pondered. The
question was: could he spare the time to investigate that agonized squeal? Why should any baby elephant be so alarmed?

Singapore Sammy—otherwise, Samuel Larkin Shay, American born, but for the past six years a wanderer of the Far
East—remained absolutely motionless, waiting for that squeal
to occur once more. He and his great war elephant might have
been carved from a single granite boulder.

For six hard, weary years, Singapore Sammy had been
hunting for a man. For six years, in every manner of conveyance,
from ox cart to lady liner, from Malay proa to airplane, he had
followed the tortuous trail; losing it, picking it up again. It had
taken him from Pekin to the Punjab, from Ceylon to the
Celebes and far beyond.

The man was Singapore Sammy's father—a rascal if ever
there was one, who had deserted Sammy and his mother when
Sammy was an infant of two; who had suddenly and without

warning answered the siren call of the Far East—and been answering it ever since.

Singapore Sammy had several accounts to settle with this old man. And in this strangest of all lands, it was the strangest of manhunts: this elephant caravan pursuing through the steaming swamps and upland jungles of Siam an old man who carried the gourd and wore the *kaban,* or girdle, and the yellow robes of a Buddhist begging priest.

From Bangkok to Ayuthia to Chengmei and so to Pyuhakiri, the trail had led across Siam. In Pyuhakiri, the day before, Sammy had acquired his impressive consort. Pyuhakiri was the capital of a principality in the northern part of the Kingdom of Siam. In this picturesque and barbaric jungle capital, with its golden temples, its poisonous snakes, its jade gods, its scorpions and its Oriental magnificence, the red-haired American had scraped the acquaintance of a modern and carefree young monarch, Prince Poot Alla.

Prince Poot Alla had ordered the visiting stranger to be brought into the royal presence. The prince was an inquisitive

young man with a great sense of humor, a fine sense of justice
and a passion for gambling.

In his halting Siamese Sammy told the prince his story—the
story of his heartbreaking six-year search for the old rascal who
had so wronged him and his mother. Prince Poot Alla was
amazed and sympathetic. He organized an investigation, and
the investigators duly reported that such an old graybeard in
the robes of a mendicant priest had passed through Pyuhakiri
only the day before. He had made sly inquiries concerning a
rumor of a *phoouk,* or off-colored elephant, that was reported
to have been seen somewhere along the middle reaches of the
Menam River. And he had gone on toward Paknam Po.

The investigators completed their report by saying that the
old man was riding a half-wild Afghan pony, of a color ap-
proaching yellowish red, like a mango coming to ripeness.

NOW, A *phoouk,* or off-colored elephant, be he white or tan
or red, is a four-legged treasure in Siam and will make his finder
rich and renowned beyond an opium smoker's wildest dreams.
The *phoouk* is a rare beast, so rare that the Siamese believe him
to be the abiding place of a god. As such, he is worshipped. As
such, when a *phoouk* is found, he is transported amidst much
ceremony and rejoicing to the City of Brilliant Flashing Diamonds, as Bangkok is called in the poetic Siamese tongue, and
placed with due honor in a handsome teak temple.

Singapore Sammy knew that it was his father's lifelong ambition to find a *phoouk.* That and the perfect pearl. For old Bill
Shay was mad about pearls and he was mad about elephants.

All of this and other details Sammy told to the inquisitive
Prince Poot Alla; and the prince was so taken with the story,
so outraged at the unfairness which had been done Sammy,
that he forthwith declared his intention of furnishing the likable
American with an escort of his most experienced soldiery under
command of a captain who knew these jungles as Sammy knew
the lines of his right hand.

So it came about that Singapore Sammy, rover, adventurer

and pearl hunter, came into the possession for an unlimited time of an elephant caravan.

Sitting motionless on his elephant, patiently waiting, Sammy thrust out his jaw. Before tonight, if luck was on his side, he might come upon that old rogue, his father!

Through the high yellow grass on the right came again that sound for which Singapore and his armed escorts were listening—a squeal of mortal terror.

"We will find out what it is," Sammy said to Captain San Nyun.

Thus did destiny in an amazing form: take a hand in the adventure.

The grass became higher and greener. That meant swamp. As the caravan, with Sammy in the lead, neared the swamp, a new sound came waiting to him. Soft, low and mysterious, it resembled the purring of a gigantic cat.

P'r̄r̄r̄r̄'t!

Now came again the agonized squeal. And once more, the rough, loud purring.

Eyes wide with wonder and expectation, the red-headed young American penetrated the last of the grass and came out on the edge of the swamp. Black swamp it was, steaming and bubbling like a cauldron in the terrific midday jungle heat.

Not more than a hundred yards away, where black mud met black quagmire, a graybearded man in yellow monk robes sat astride a pony the color of an almost ripe mango!

With his heart thumping, for a moment Sammy could only stare. His six-year quest was over at last! As a man will under such dramatic circumstances, Sammy went weak and white. The fact was almost too tremendous to grasp. After six heartbreaking years he had finally caught up with his father!

Horse and horseman were looking out over the black swamp at what appeared to be a dark bubble a hundred feet from shore. It tossed and moved about mysteriously. It uttered a squeal, and the old man on the mango-colored horse answered with that remarkable purring sound.

Singapore Sammy felt a tide of exultant triumph sweep over him. He had caught the old rascal at last!

He let out a shout. The old man seemed to leap into the air. The Afghan pony lifted its forelegs from the mud and, pivoting on its hind legs, wheeled sharply about to face the long array of war elephants.

"Don't kill him!" Sammy shouted. "Catch him!"

He caught a glimpse of fiery opaque blue eyes over a long tangled gray beard. Then the horse and horseman flashed from sight. At least, that was Singapore Sammy's impression. It was amazing. Not merely mystifying, it was magical. The mango-colored horse crossed the mud flat in tremendous bounds. It was as if there were springs on his hoofs.

And before the red-headed manhunter could do anything about it, horse and horseman had vanished into the elephant grass!

"After him!" shouted Captain San Nyun. The tropical noon thundered in response to the trampling feet of war elephants.

Sammy headed the chase. He followed the trail through the high grass. Lost it and could not find it again. He returned to the clearing and searched it for tracks. He found none. Captain San Nyun found tracks and followed them to a bog; lost them. Could not find them again!

While a dozen men searched the jungles, Sammy and the others returned to the black swamp. The redhead wanted to investigate that black bubble. An amazing suspicion was forming in his mind.

The black bubble was still there, still agitated.

The red-haired man now observed that the tossing bubble was the center of a mysterious arrangement of four slime-coated logs. With the black bubble as an axis, they pointed outward, as do the four points of a compass.

One of the logs moved. A hideous mouth yawned wide,

revealing rows of yellow fangs and a pinkish yellow maw that looked as large as a rain barrel.

Another snout opened, and the midday calm was disturbed by a long and sinister hiss. And in all the world there is no hiss that can compare in downright malignance to that of a crocodile preparing to attack.

Now the bubble took on a new form. A long, tapering tentacle dripping with mud shot out from it. It waved about. Again came the piteous squeal.

Bogged down in that swamp and surrounded by swift and horrible death in the form of four savage "crocs" was a baby elephant. After the manner of their kind, the crocodiles were lazily preparing to attack.

Sammy supposed that the little elephant's mother was dead; that it had strayed into the swamp, got bogged down, and become helpless with terror. And now—peril in this new and awful form.

SAMMY WENT quickly into action. He slipped out of its scabbard his Winchester carbine. As fast as he could pull trigger and yank lever, he fired and loaded and fired again.

One crocodile he missed, and the reptile got away, diving down into the mud. The other three shots were direct hits. And while the three crocodiles were struggling in their death throes, the baby elephant decided to make a break for liberty. Its mud-coated head and trunk surged up, and, squealing, it started for shore.

Sammy could see its eyes now. They peered out from the mud covering its face. As the baby elephant stared dolefully, Sammy burst into roars of laughter. Never, on any face, animal or human, had he seen such self-pity.

The little pig whimpered and came floundering in. It waved its small trunk and squealed. With terrific effort it dragged itself through the thick black mud.

Halfway to shore, the baby elephant sat down and refused to go farther.

Sammy ordered the soldiers to go into the swamp and bring the little "pig" ashore. They hesitated. That swamp looked dangerous. Sammy's elephant now took charge of the affair. Sammy called him "Bozo." His true and complete name was Maung Ho Danyubu Mat Than Lwyin, which is Siamese for "Old Man Yonder Who Sleeps All the Time And Has a Voice Like Little Cymbals." All of which was a downright lie. Bozo seldom slept, was aways on hand when wanted, and had a voice like a war horn. He weighed three tons, was approximately as old as the hills, and was every inch as clever, as understanding and as wise as the Buddhas of his native land look.

Back in the Fifties, Bozo had been a war elephant, distinguishing himself in battles against the wily Laos of the north. Since then he had been looked upon as the dean of the elephants in the Pyuhakiri *kraal.* He was a war lord, a master of elephants, a king.

Bozo had only two bad habits, his method of swimming and his thirst for strong liquor. In swimming a river he swam so deep—holding only the tip of his trunk above the surface—that it was necessary for his rider to stand erect on his back. And in the crocodile infested rivers of Siam, that was far from a pleasant experience.

Each night when Bozo was fed he expected a half pint of whisky, gin or rum—it made no difference which. He was not a connoisseur; what he enjoyed was the kick. If Bozo did not get that nightly drink, his eyes began to smolder. Presently he began to roar and to grow belligerent. If the drink was not forthcoming, he declared war on every elephant in the *kraal.*

But if, on the other hand, Bozo was given his nightcap, he became as gentle as a lamb. If he was given more than the usual portion, he became affectionate. If it can be said that an elephant becomes sentimental, then Bozo became maudlin. He wanted to wrap his trunk gently and lovingly about any human within reach, and croon to him. He would stare at the object of his affections with his cold, inquiring, disillusioned yellow eyes and make small, loving sounds deep in his majestic throat.

Bozo was, in short, an elephant among elephants. He had an amazing, human understanding of what was wanted of him. His forehead was high, massive and domelike. His chin was long and pointed and hairy, and fitted so close to his trunk that at times he looked like a man with a weak chin and a silly smile.

His feet were huge and flat, and he walked with a laugh-provoking precision, moving the foreleg and hindleg on the same side together, so that he actually looked like two men walking along in an elephant costume.

Sammy had taken a great fancy to Bozo, and the three-ton mountain of gray flesh had developed a strange and striking affection for the white man.

Bozo was now softly trumpeting. The baby pig squealed in answer. Bozo trumpeted again, impatiently. The baby uttered a whimpering sound. The big bull trumpeted angrily. Bozo seemed to be losing his royal temper. His trumpeting sounded like oaths.

The little pig stared at Bozo, waved its small trunk, and squealed. It was not accustomed to being ordered about. That squeal was an insult! Bozo roared and began a curious dancing shuffle with his forefeet. Singapore Sammy laughed until he was weak. Bozo, in his fury, was like a choleric old man giving commands to a stupid, stubborn, silly child.

Waving his great trunk and roaring elephantine oaths, Bozo started cautiously into the swamp to complete the work of rescue. The little pig stood still and stared piteously at him. Deeper and deeper in the black mud went Bozo. He was almost shoulder deep in the yielding mire when he got within reaching distance of the pig. His trunk shot out, wrapped itself about the stubborn one's neck—and yanked.

With a strangled squawk of dismay, the little elephant came shooting out of the mud with a pop like that of a gigantic cork being pulled from a bottle. Muttering deeply in his throat, Bozo dragged the kicking, choking infant ashore and stood it on its feet. But the fun was not yet over. With the feel of substantial ground underfoot, the little pig bolted for the jungle.

With a roar of fury, Bozo followed. At the very edge of the jungle, the chase ended. The little elephant wheeled about defiantly. Bozo lifted his loglike trunk and brought it down with a hard, loud smack on the pig's rump. The pig squealed with pain, but Bozo did not stop until he had administered what he considered to be a sound spanking.

Singapore Sammy was now so weak from laughter that he was in danger of falling off his perch.

BUT SUDDENLY Sammy stopped laughing. He wiped tears from his eyes and looked. And his eyes went wide with excitement. His suspicions were confirmed! Where Bozo's trunk had spanked the little elephant mud had been slapped away and wide strips of hide were revealed. But this hide was not the usual elephant gray. It was decidedly unusual. Not gray at all. It was, in fact, the color of human flesh—pink!

Members of Prince Pout Alla's guard made the exciting discovery simultaneously.

"Phoouk!" they clamored. They slid to the ground. The little elephant eyed them apprehensively, but he dared not move. Sammy excitedly scraped and scooped mud off the pig with his hands, uncovering portions of the trunk, the legs and the belly. And all of the hide thus exposed was the same astonishing, rare color—pink!

"By the green-toed Buddha," Sammy said devoutly, "you *are* a *phoouk!*"

Undeniably it was true—a pink elephant! Sammy had found a four-legged treasure worth his weight, if not in gold, at least in silver, honor and glory. Or had he found it? Hadn't these men, representing Prince Poot Alla, found it?

Sammy thereupon made a decision that was destined to cause him a vast amount of trouble and discomfort. He loudly proclaimed: "In the name of his majesty King Rama, ruler of all Siam, I claim this *phoouk* as my own!"

Sammy had done some fast thinking. The soldiers growled. Others, abandoning the hopeless search for the graybeard on the horse crowded about and muttered. The *phoouk* was rightfully the property of Prince Poot Alla. Had it not been discovered on his principality? Had not the prince's own elephant, Maung Ho Danyubu Mat Than Lwyin, actually done the discovering?

"But who saved the *phoouk's* sacred life from those hungry crocodiles?" Sammy countered.

Captain San Nyun was coldly polite. He had received orders to obey the red-headed American's commands unquestioningly. And the American's proclamation partook of the nature of a command, did it not?

But, by Buddha, what a find it was!

"Master," said the captain, "how about the old man? Do we continue the search? Do we proceed to Paknam Po? Or to Pyuhakiri?"

In Siamese equivalents, Sammy answered that, for all he cared, the old man could take a big running jump for himself into nowhere—and not return!

"Not Pyuhakiri," Sammy said shrewdly. For he knew that if he once let Prince Poot Alla clap his royal eyes on the pink elephant, the pink elephant would quickly change ownership.

And what was his father compared to a pink elephant? Sammy could find the old rascal some other time. As a matter of fact, he was certain that the pink elephant would act as an irresistible lure, a magnet which would draw the old man.

Sammy chuckled. This was revenge indeed! Snatching out from under his father's clutching, greedy hands this prize of which he had all his life dreamed! A genuine, intact pink elephant! And "Pinky" was far handsomer than the sacred elephants now in the king's temples in Bangkok. They were *phoouks*, but they were not pink. Common elephants they were, compared to Pinky.

Sammy's grin widened. He saw that weary trek back across

Siam to Bangkok as a triumphal march, with villages all along
the way turning out to do him honor. There would be feasts,
holidays, dancing girls! Priests would kiss his feet. Princes would
lavish gifts upon him. The world was Sammy's.

The red-headed adventurer's eyes became vague with dreams.
He saw himself being escorted to King Rama's marble palace
in Bangkok. Saw himself being decorated with the Order of
the Elephant and receiving rich gifts—Chantaboon sapphires,
Ceylonese emeralds, matchless pearls. He chuckled again. Elephants and pearls! How furious his father would be!

The soldiers of Prince Poot Alla were marveling over the
perfection, the beauty, of the little elephant. Instead of common
black-and-white toenails, Pinky had solid black ones. And
Pinky was further distinguished by an intact tail. Most wild
elephants because of their quarrelsome nature, have their tails
bitten off at an extremely tender age.

"Bozo," Sammy solemnly addressed his mount, "You're gonna
get a quart of gin tonight. You've done a good day's work."

Bozo seemed to understand. He placed his great trunk about
Sammy's shoulders, gave him a gentle hug, and murmured sweet
nothings in his royal throat.

Captain San Nyun said coldly: "Whither, master?"

"Paknam Po," said Sammy.

CHAPTER II

ACROSS THE Menam River, the village of Paknam Po
drowsed in the smothering heat of mid-afternoon. Gilded
temple spires rose mightily above giant mahogany and tamarind
trees and poked holes in the fierce blue sky. The fragrance of
pepper trees drifted across the jungle stream. The Menam here
was narrow, but deep and fast.

Sammy ordered Bozo to start across. The big bull drove the
little pink prize ahead of him down the bank and followed him
into the swirling, brown flood. Bozo discarded his customary

swimming habits. He swam with head above water and great broad back awash, so that he could keep a watchful eye on his protégé.

Behind Bozo and Pinky came the rest of the caravan— twenty elephants supporting twenty men, silent and glum in various stages of envy and resentment. Each soldier was thinking: "By Buddha! If only I had had the boldness to proclaim that the *phoouk* was my discovery! I would be, by tomorrow, a national hero and a wealthy man!"

But Captain San Nyun had other equally bilious thoughts. What would His Highness, Prince Poot Alla, say? The prince would be furious! Permitting a white devil to snatch away a prize of such great value!

That swim through the rapid water accomplished at least one happy result. It radically affected the state of Pinky's cleanliness. When the baby elephant emerged and started up the bank he was as free of mud as if newly born; was shiningly clean and pink. He was gaunt and thin from that horrible experience in the swamp, but he was undeniably a sleek and handsome little beast.

A drowsing boy caught sight of the pink elephant, and shouted and awoke the village. Men, women and children came swarming out of nipa-thatched houses. In a few minutes, Pinky was the center of dense, babbling mob. They crowded about to touch him reverently. The little pink prize squealed in dismay, but when he tried to escape, Bozo laid his great trunk hintingly upon him.

Pinky's little pale-colored trunk was patted, his ears were scratched, his toenails were examined, his mouth opened and searched. Even his fatty little tail was stroked and admired. For to these little brown people he was a sacred beast.

The soldiers of Prince Poot Alla looked on enviously.

A thousand hilariously happy Siamese escorted Sammy and Pinky to the kraal at the end of the village. Adjoining the kraal was the *sala*—the comfortable, airy house which is a feature of every Siamese village and is intended for transient guests.

Fruits, boiled rice, fish, live and cooked fowl and wines were brought in abundance for Sammy. Pinky received boiled rice, goat's milk and the tenderest of green grass and bamboo shoots. The little beast ate as if he were starved. Certainly, there was nothing sacred about his capacity for food, but the villagers hung about him and laughed and encouraged him like so many children. He gorged himself until he could eat no more; gorged himself until his belly was as round and hard as a Karen temple drum.

Men left Paknam Po on muleback and in dugouts, up and down river, to spread the word that the most perfect of all pink elephants had been found.

Sammy saw to it that one courier left promptly for Bangkok with a verbal message for King Rama. This was by way of recording his claim to the gold mine that Pinky represented, and it would spike any attempt Prince Poot Alla or any one else might make to steal the pink pig and claim the rewards and honors.

"Tell His Majesty of Siam," Sammy said to the courier, "that the Little One has blue eyes, red hair, ears like silver shields, a tread like the sound of thunder and an expression meditative and tender. Tell him that the little one's toenails are as black as a raven's wing, that his tail is as straight and beautiful as a Lao arrow, that his trunk is divinely formed, and that a man named Shay requests His Majesty to send a delegation to take possession of this rare and exquisite animal. Tell him I will start south in a few days, as soon as the *phoouk* is able to travel, and that I wish to be met at least halfway."

There again Sammy was shrewdly showing that he knew his East; knew the depths of knavery of which some of its people were capable.

SAMMY INTENDED to spend no more than a few days in Paknam Po, but long after Pinky had recovered his strength and was able to travel, the American's stubbornness made him linger.

Overnight Paknam Po had become a Mecca. People came from as far as the Karen Hills to see the pink treasure. They came afoot, by dugout, on muleback; the richest came by elephant—thousands of them to pay homage to this most perfect of pink elephants. Sammy himself became an object of worship, but he soon tired of having his feet kissed and old men with lice in their hair clasping him rapturously in their arms.

There was an ominous silence on the part of his recent friend, Prince Poot Alla. Disturbing rumors reached Sammy. Shortly after the return to Pyuhakiri of Captain San Nyun and the soldiers, a man told Sammy that the prince was jealous and resentful; that the prince would grasp the first opportunity to take revenge; that if Sammy stepped foot in Pyuhakiri, the reception given him would be a very warm one indeed!

There was more to all this, Sammy learned, than showed on the surface. Prince Poot Alla had recently incurred the King of Siam's disfavor. There was scandalous talk that the prince had diverted for his personal use certain tax funds which were supposed to have gone into the king's coffers. The prince had made other mistakes. The prince was, in short, in wrong with the king. And it could be readily seen that Prince Poot Alla would welcome such an opportunity as the pink elephant presented to reinstate himself in the king's good graces!

All in all, Sammy clearly saw the advisability of steering a wide course of Pyuhakiri whenever he was in that neighborhood. He would not take Pinky through Pyuhakiri on his journey to Bangkok. Yet he longed to see Bozo once again. Pinky was sadly in need of Bozo. All the attention, the worship, the praise and, above all, the tidbits he was receiving, were spoiling the little pink treasure. The baby elephant was a peevish, greedy, selfish little beast at best. And he deserved and needed the stern discipline that only Bozo, in his vast wisdom, could administer.

While great throngs of pilgrims came and worshipped and departed, Sammy watched tirelessly for a certain graybeard who carried the gourd and wore the *kaban* and the yellow robes of a mendicant priest. Priests came. They came by the ox-cartload. But none of them was the priest in whom Sammy was interested.

So, stubbornly, he waited. He hoped that his father would try to take revenge for the theft of the baby elephant—for the old man had certainly been in the act of acquiring Pinky and the rewards that went with Pinky when Sammy came upon him that morning.

A week passed, but Sammy's father did not appear.

The day that marked the end of Pinky's second week as a sacred elephant brought to Paknam Po a white hunter's caravan from the northern wilderness. It was an impressive entourage— almost as impressive as the entourage Prince Poot Alla had lent Singapore Sammy. It consisted of a dozen hunting elephants, and twenty beaters and gun bearers.

The excitement of their arrival occurred at midday. Sammy was in the *sala* taking a siesta. A village priest who had become Sammy's slave awakened Sammy; told him that a great white hunter wished to see him. And in the *sala* compound, in the shade of gently waving bamboos, Sammy met the white hunter—a tall, distinguished, elderly man with keen blue eyes who wheezingly introduced himself as Sir Lester Preece.

Sir Lester wore a monocle, the crisp mustache so popular with British generals, an enormous brown sun helmet, a khaki singlet and khaki shorts. Snake boots completed this sporting costume. Sir Lester's complexion was beef-red from myriads of tiny ruptured veins, and the tip of his large nose was faintly a telltale purple.

Sir Lester wheezingly announced that he had seen the sacred elephant and wished to congratulate its lucky finder and owner.

"By jove," Sir Lester wheezed, "I never saw such an extraord'n'ry specimen. I was up Kong-Kai-Lai way lookin' for big cats when the word came that a young feller had trapped a pink pig. I do congratulate you most heartily, my dear feller. American, aren't you?"

"Yeah—Amurrican," Sammy said. "How long were you up in that country?"

"Let me see. Three months. And I've bagged some extraord'n'ry specimens, Mister Shay."

"Where'd you outfit?"

"Pnom-Ponh. I wanted Cambodian lions, and I hoped to get a shot at the Cambodian pygmies—they're just like monkeys, you know. But the pygmies were too shy—I didn't get a shot; and the French administrator of reconstruction at Angkor convinced me the big cats over here were bettah sport. Get me to tell you the story sometime of the black leopard that almost did me in. Ferocious beasts, those black leopards."

"I suppose," Sammy said, "you've been up and down and around this country considerably in the past few months."

Sir Lester adjusted his monocle and gazed at Sammy benevolently.

"I've seen Siam—particularly the Lao—as few white men have seen it, my dear feller."

"I was wonderin'," Sammy said, "if you'd happened to run across a man of about fifty who dresses up as a beggin' priest. He looks like an Irriwaddy Burmese, but a good look wouldn't fool you. He wears a beard like Moses'. Most of those upcountry Burmese are pretty smoothfaced."

Sir Lester was thoughtfully rubbing his mustache between a thumb and forefinger while a frown rode between his keen blue eyes.

"It seems to me," he said, "that I did see such a feller just a few days ago. Was it in Chum Seng or Payan or Raribanga? I'll buzz my Numbah One boy."

Sir Lester roared. His Number One boy, like a sentinel who has been on guard, stepped out from a great hibiscus bush and walked across the compound. Singapore Sammy looked at him with sudden interest. The Number One boy was a man of about Sammy's own age. He was a halfcaste. Yet he lacked the usual Eurasian characteristics. He was fashioned on the lines of a gorilla, with tremendous shoulders, long, hairy arms and hands several sizes too large for him. His brow was low, his eyes were small, deep and close-set; and the color of his skin was a deep cream.

His manner was somehow belligerent, antagonistic. Perhaps it was the way he parried his big hands, in half fists, as if he were preperad to give battle at the slightest provocation.

"This," Sir Lester said to Sammy, "is Maung Lat. Maung Lat, this is Maung Shay."

THE INTRODUCTION was made in very bad pidgin Siamese. And in the trade tongue, Sir Lester questioned Maung Lat. Sammy, with a fair command of Siamese, took the matter out of his hands.

Had Maung Lat seen such and such an old man, wearing the *dugot,* the *kowut,* the *thinbaing* and the *kaban* of a begging holy man?

"Aüe, master. It was in Chum Seng three days ago."

"Whither was he going?"

"Master, I know not."

That was sufficiently that. Sir Lester looked at Sammy with shrewd eyes.

"Are you, by chance, a government agent looking for this old beggar? Is he a criminal?"

Sammy answered: "No, Sir Lester. He is my father. When I was two years old he deserted my mother and me and beat it off to the Far East. For the past six years I've been trailing him, and two weeks ago, for the first time, I found him. It was the day I found the pink elephant. But he got away."

"He must be clevah."

"He is as smart as a fox. My main reason for wanting to find him is that he took a will of my grandfather's that leaves me a pretty big fortune back in the States."

"By jove! You can't get the estate without the will!"

"Worse than that, Sir Lester. The lawyer who drew the will told me that it says than in case of my death, my father is to inherit the estate."

"How extraord'n'ry! Fancy that! Would he do you in if he saw you first? Is that what you mean, Mister Shay?"

"He is a rat," Sammy said. "He knows I'll half murder him when I lay hands on him. So he is keepin' out o' my way. And I'll tell the world he's good at it. He used to be top elephant man with Bartrom and Bradley's circus, and he's nuts about pearls and he's nuts about elephants."

"Pos'tively incredible, by jove!"

"I know," Sammy went on, "that it's been his lifelong ambition to lay hands on a real *phoouk*."

"*Phoouk?*"

"An elephant enough off-color," Sammy explained, "to get into the sacred elephant temples in Bangkok. Well, I've found his *phoouk*. And I'm sure he's somewhere around. I thought this *phoouk* would draw him into the open. But I'm tired of waitin'. Tomorrow morning I head for Bangkok."

"How will you travel?"

"I will buy or borrow an elephant and lead or drive the *phoouk*."

"Isn't that rather a risk?"

Sammy looked quickly in Sir Lester's eyes; saw something there that he did not like.

"You mean, somebody might get Pinky away from me?"

"Why not? Every native of this barbaric country is jealous of your ownership of that elephant. In case you should die en route, the man who inherits Pinky is the man who kills you. Let me make a suggestion. Let me put my elephants and men at your disposal while you deliver Pinky to the king."

The greedy gleam in Sir Lester's eyes had not departed.

"No, thanks," Sammy said.

"But have you sufficient money?"

"Plenty."

"You wouldn't consider selling Pinky to me at any price, I suppose."

"Nope. He ain't for sale."

Sir Lester sighed. The gleam departed. He said: "I envy your reception in Bangkok. It will be barbaric and splendid—like a scene from the Arabian Nights. Supposing we stroll over to my camp and drink your health and continued good fortune. I have some excellent whisky in my kit. Irish. There is no whisky like Irish."

He slipped his arm through Sammy's and began discoursing on the merits of this whisky and that. Sammy did not need this to know that Sir Lester was a connoisseur. One glimpse of the Englishman's nose had told him that Sir Lester knew his whiskies.

He was a little suspicious of Sir Lester. Obviously, the big game hunter was a man accustomed to getting what he wanted. And Sir Lester wanted Pinky.

And Sammy was a little suspicious of Sir Lester's Number One boy. Maung Lat had too watchful an air.

The hand companionably grasping Sammy's arms was as hard as iron. Maung Lat walked on Sammy's other side. The two men were keeping in step with Sammy. He didn't like that, either. But what, after all, could Sir Lester do? In that message to the king, Sammy had staked his claim. Still, he felt uncomfortable. There was trouble in the air. Sammy had been in too much trouble not to sense its presence.

The Englishman's camp had been pitched in a clearing between road and river a quarter of a mile below the village.

Sir Lester's tent was a luxurious affair, with a wooden floor and mosquito bar front and back; a collapsible cot, folding chairs.

As the area before Sir Lester's tent was in shade and there were no insects about, the hunter had Maung Lat bring two chairs and a table out of the tent and set them up.

Squarely in front of the tent door and about ten feet from it a post had been driven into the ground. The post was about six inches in diameter and stripped of bark. Sammy, in taking stock of the encampment, carelessly noticed this post. It stood out of the ground some five or six feet.

One chair was placed by Maung Lat with its back to this post; the other chair Maung Lat placed facing it.

"Do sit down," said the Englishman, indicating the chair with back to post.

Sammy again glanced at the post, wondered indifferently what its purpose was, and seated himself. Sir Lester took the other chair. The table was thus between them.

Maung Lat fetched a black square bottle, glasses and—luxury of luxuries!—bottles of charged water.

The two white men poured and mixed their drinks. Sir Lester lifted his glass. And Sammy, who had been wondering about the post said, "Sir Lester, what's the idea of the post back of me?"

The Englishman revealed strong yellow teeth in a flashing smile. "It's an old Siamese custom," he explained. "I picked up the idea in the Lao. It is supposed to keep devils away and bring good luck. The Laos are *ngat* worshippers, you know."

He looked at Sammy with sparkling blue eyes above the rim of his glass.

"Mister Shay, I'm going to propose a toast. I drink to your health, your continued good fortune—and the early and successful termination of your six-year manhunt! When you find that errant father of yours, give him a punch on his bally old nose for me, won't you? Cheerio! Bottoms up!"

At that moment, in the dark green thickness of the mahogany trees over their heads, a *tha-thong* burst into song. Now, the first few beats in the song of the *tha-thong*—"bird-that-beats-on-gold"—always surprise and delight the visitor to Siam. The sound is amazingly like the rich hollow clang that would result if a golden vessel were struck sharply with a leather-padded stick. But the song of the *tha-thong* will almost drive the listener mad if it persists. It always persists. The *clang-clang-clang!* finally wears down a man's nerves until, with rifle or shotgun, he grimly sets out to murder his tormentor.

There came a short lull in the *tha-thong's* clanging. It was filled by Sir Lester in a manner that caused Sammy to look up with astonishment. In the purest of Siamese, the Englishman said, "Now, Maung Lat! Do it quickly!"

MAUNG LAT had, for some minutes, been invisible to Sammy. Now the Eurasian's presence was manifested by the sudden sharp pressure of a rope across Sammy's chest. The rope barked his arm, sent what remained of his drink flying to the ground; it tightened, binding him and the back of the chair to the post. Another coil looped down about him and tightened; another and another.

Realization exploded upon Singapore Sammy. His heart gave a terrible thump. The moisture seemed suddenly to dry up in his mouth. The blue-eyed "Englishman" who called himself "Sir Lester" was Sammy's evasive father!

The redhead threw himself with a furious summoning of every ounce of strength he possessed against the strands of that giant spider's web. Veins stood out in knots on his temples. His eyes seemed to bulge out of their sockets. Sweat burst out of every pore. He strained and kicked.

The rope held.

In a harsh strangling voice Singapore Sammy screamed at the self-styled "Sir Lester," "you're my father!" His voice got jammed in his throat, he gasped, then panted, "You're Bill Shay!"

"Smart boy!" the big blue-eyed man jeered. "All you needed to find it out was a moving picture and a full set of directions!"

Singapore Sammy cursed and fumed and threw himself against the rope again. He strained until his face went purple, until his eyes threatened to leave their sockets, until it seemed that a blood vessel must burst. The rope held.

Old Bill Shay watched his red-headed son's agonies with a mockingly grave and sympathetic interest. One corner of his hard mouth began to twitch, then the other corner. Suddenly he laughed; great, booming laughter.

Sammy stopped struggling. With teeth bared, he glared at his father. Waited.

The laughter stopped. Old Bill Shay, elephant man, pearl man, Buddhist priest, master of trickery, vagabond extraordinary, bent forward and contemplated his offspring with shimmering blue eyes.

He shook his head. Sadly he said: "I thought you were hard and smart and clever and wise! They told me how you fought your way out of the Maharaja of Malobar's jail—and got away with a fine blue-fire pearl. They told me how you threw a cobra into a crooked jeweler's cage in Singapore and got away with all his jack. That must 'a' been a load of applesauce."

"Damn you!" Sammy panted. "Take off this rope!"

"They told me how you swam through a nest of tiger sharks in Pemanngil Passage and outsmarted the toughest crook south of Shanghai. That must 'a' been another mess o' boloney."

"Yeah? Who's tryin' to compete with a guy who runs out on his sick wife and baby?"

Old Bill Shay's hard blue eyes momentarily narrowed. "They told me," he continued, "that you were one dangerous guy to cross. Hell," he said with scorn, "you ain't hard. You ain't smart. You're just a sucker. I was almost gettin' proud of you—and then you have to up and pull this sap stunt. You sucker!"

Sammy made another violent attack on the rope. It did not give an inch. His father grinned at him contemptuously.

"What did I tell you in that letter I sent when you were in the Singapore Hospital? 'The hand is faster than the naked eye. A wise man knows the aim of a bottle!' I warned you. You're just dumb."

"You've double-crossed me, damn you!" Sammy panted.

"Let's take that up," his father said calmly. "Did you think for a minute, you boob, I was goin' to let you get away with that pink elephant? Why don't you do some travelin' and broaden your mind? All my life I wanted to lay hands on a real *phoouk.* You knew it. You knew what it meant to me. And you thought I was goin' to let you take this one right out from under my nose! You simp, what do you suppose I've been doin' up in these jungles the past three months—if I haven't been trackin' down every rumor of that *phoouk?* D'you think I've been afraid of *you?*"

"Listen, big shot," Sammy interrupted, "I don't like your looks, I don't like the way your brain works, and I don't like the sound of your voice. Everything about you is poison. You've outsmarted me. You've beat me to the gun. All right. Let's get it over with. You've got that will of my grandfather's, and you've got me where you want me. The quicker you have one of these mahouts run a spear into me, the better off we'll all be."

Bill Shay looked at his son incredulously. "Kill you!" he said in a marveling voice. "You big boob, why should I kill you?"

"To get that jack—you wife beater!"

Bill Shay grinned. "I don't need that jack—yet. There'll always be time to get that jack. If I killed you, what fun would be left? Nothin' but pearls and elephants! Why, half the fun I've had these past six years you gave me—chasin' me all over this part of the world!"

The old elephant man's shimmering blue eyes roved over his son's face.

"That's the idea," Sammy snarled. "Help yourself to an eyeful of the guy who's some day gonna make you drink your own blood. I'll do it. I've sworn to do it. And I will."

Bill Shay burst into roars of Gargantuan laughter. "All right, Sam," he said. "That's a bet. The next time we meet, you make me drink my own blood. And next time—be smarter. Now I'm afraid you'll have to excuse me. The king of Siam is waiting for a pink elephant to be delivered by a man named Shay! Happy idea that one was, Sammy. A man named Shay! Of course, you meant your dear father, didn't you? I thought so. It was mighty kind and considerate of you, Sammy. Now, I'm goin' to leave you sittin' here nice and comfy, with Maung Lat to look after you. And to show you I'm not a bad sport, I'm goin' to leave you a few bottles of this whisky. You're like your old man, Sammy—you appreciate good liquor."

Bill Shay paused and grinned at his son. "Just to punish you a little for talkin' so disrespectfully to your dear, gray-haired old father, you're goin' to sit right here all night. And Maung Lat and that *tha-thong* will keep you from gettin' lonesome."

The old elephant man backed away.

"And while you're settin' here, Sammy, you can just think of me, takin' that little pink pig of mine down to Bangkok. Ah-h-h, just think of it, Sammy!"

There was no irony, no scorn, in this. The eyes of the old elephant man were glowing now.

"Think of me, Sammy! Think of the royal reception they're goin' to give me! Think of the attention your father is goin' to get! Aren't you proud? Think of all the pints of sapphires, diamonds, emeralds, pearls the king is goin' to pour into my hands! Think of the banquets, the parades! Just like a scene from the Arabian Nights, Sammy! It's just too bad I can't give you an invitation to look on; but I can't, Sammy. By the time you get to Bangkok, it'll be all over—and I'll be somewhere else, spendin' some of it, havin' me a time!"

"Yeah," snapped his son; "tomorrow is a long day."

"Not," said Bill Shay quickly, "to the man who knows how to enjoy himself! Well, Sam—" Bill Shay lifted his drink; there was still an inch of the amber fluid left—"here's to that day when you make me drink my own blood!"

He tossed off the drink; got up, began roaring orders.

Above Sammy, in the mahogany tree, the *tha-thong*, "the bird-that-beats-on-gold," resumed its metallic melody.

In Siamese and in profane circus American, old Bill Shay ordered his camp broken and loaded on the elephants. Mahouts, gun bearers, beaters ran about, executing his orders.

The tent behind Sammy was struck, folded, packed, loaded. In an amazingly short time, nothing of that elaborate camp remained but the chair on which Sammy was sitting.

With the elephants loaded and prepared to start, Bill Shay came over to his son. Reaching down, he took off Sammy's moneybelt and pocketed it.

"Now, let's see," he said to Sammy. "Is everything done? Elephants loaded, you here, with Maung Lat to keep the tigers off of you, four quarts of good old Irish whisky to drown your sorrows tomorrow when Maung Lat lets you go. Have I forgotten anything? Have I punished you enough for being so—so unfilial?"

"The worst punishment I can get," Sammy said, "is to have you standin' there where I can look at you. What a break I got when I drew you for a father! Why weren't you a plain, honest, decent burglar?"

Bill Shay chuckled. "One thing you got from me, sucker—a sense of humor. You'll need it tonight. Yes, Sam, you sure will need a sense of humor before tomorrow this time. Just laugh it all off, Sam—that's what you want to do. Laugh it off!"

The word seemed to be contagious. Throwing back his head, Bill Shay opened his mouth and laughed in hard, harsh barks. Laughing, he strode away.

CHAPTER III

BUT THE WORD was certainly not contagious as far as Sammy was concerned. Grimly, he sat there and watched the tall, lean, muscular man who was his father stride away. And the last he saw of Bill Shay was when that jocular spirit lightly swung himself up to the back of a kneeling elephant, and vanished down the lane of trees.

Then the *tha-thong* began to clang. Sammy compressed his lips and gritted his teeth.

"Just feature this," Sammy went on with his glum meditations. "He hasn't laid eyes on me for twenty-two years—not, since I was old enough to wobble around. "When a guy's old man, who hasn't seen him in twenty-two years, leaves him tied to a post for tigers to eat—this world ain't fit to live in. It's a lousy world! Damn everything in this lousy world!"

Singapore Sammy, tough, hard, world-wise, found himself blinking tears out of his eyes. Curiously, his mind went flashing to the black swamp from which he had extricated Pinky. He recalled that expression of self-pity on the little pink elephant's face as it wallowed shoreward. Sammy's tears promptly dried up.

He had simply underestimated the cleverness, the deadliness of his father, Bill Shay. He'd be wiser next time.

Next time? Only one feature of the whole catastrophe interested Sammy now. The pink elephant. Somehow he must contrive, if it was his last act on earth, to prevent Bill Shay from reaching the king's palace in Bangkok with the pink elephant. Accomplishing that would hurt his father more than any punishment he could devise.

How could he get Pinky away from him? First of all, he must free himself.

"Maung Lat!" he called.

The Eurasian, with gorilla arms dangling, came from behind the post.

"Yes, Master?"

"How long were you ordered to keep me here like this?"

"Until this time tomorrow, Master."

"Where is your home, Maung Lat?"

"Kong-Kai-Lai, master."

"What do you do there?"

"I am a hunter."

"Are you a poor man?"

"Poorest of the poor, master."

"How would you like," Sammy eagerly asked, "to be the richest man in your village?"

"What man would not like to be the richest in his village, master?"

"Maung Lat, you can get rich quick. Listen! Take off this rope. I will make you the richest man in Kong-Kai-Lai! For you and I will get the *phoouk* away from that old man of mine."

The Eurasian shook his head. "No, Master. I have given my promise to the old man, your father. The men of Kong-Kai-Lai do not break promises. Besides, you could not steal the *phoouk*. That old man is smarter than Min-Magayi, the king of *ngats*."

Sammy perceived the uselessness of persuasion. He growled, this time in English: "You yellow snake, tomorrow when you take this rope off—just wait till I get my hands on you! I'm gonna knock your head off I'm gonna—"

Maung Lat surprised him.

"Master," the Eurasian interrupted, in English, "I will not be here to remove this rope. Someone else can have the pleasure. I will be ten *ri* away!"

Sammy had nothing more to say. He tried to calm himself. He was seething with fury, and of all forms of fury there is none fiercer than that born of humiliation. The bird-that-beats-on-gold was contributing nothing to his peace of mind. It played harsh tunes on his raw nerves.

The afternoon passed. Swift tropic dusk descended. Night. And with the velvety blackness of the great upland jungle night came the insects. Not singly or in pairs or dozens or even legions. They came in a dense whining fog. As if thirsting for vengeance, they settled on Sammy's face, neck, hands. They bored through his shirt and undershirt.

Maung Lat, proving that he fostered no hard feelings, draped a mosquito net about the cursing prisoner; started a smudge to drive the insects away. Sammy blew mosquitoes out of his nose and shook them out of his ears. The smudge acted as an anesthetic.

His arms, gripped by the rope, had gone to sleep early in the afternoon. Then his feet and legs went to sleep. Now Sammy went to sleep.

HE AWOKE once during the night with a red glare on his eyelids. Opening his eyes he saw Maung Lat throwing logs on a great fire. Some distance away, a growl occurred. It sent the wind up Sammy's spine. Beyond that fire a leopard or a tiger was no doubt regarding him with drooling jowls.

But the blazing fire kept the great cat away. And soon Sammy went back to sleep.

When Singapore Sammy awoke again it was dawn. The insect hordes had vanished. Maung Lat gave him water to drink and cold boiled rice to eat. With the first rays of the sun, the *tha-thong* started its infernal song. Sammy suffered. The hours dragged by. He pictured the pleasure it would give him to climb that mahogany tree like a monkey, seize that *tha-thong* and slowly, a little at a time, wring its damned neck.

"Clang! Clang! Clang!" said the bird-that-beats-on-gold.

Maung Lat gave him lunch of cold boiled rice—fed it to Sammy with a stick of wood; at the American's request opened one of the four bottles of Irish whisky that Bill Shay had left behind and poured some down his throat.

At about two in the afternoon, Maung Lat vanished without a word. Maung Chi, the village priest who had been Sammy's slave during the reign of Pinky, came to him.

When the rope was removed, Sammy tried to stand up but could not. The nerves in his legs were temporarily paralyzed.

Maung Chi vigorously massaged them. The paralysis left but was replaced by an exquisite ache. Millions of needles began to run marathons in Sammy's legs. But he could walk after a fashion.

With the four bottles of whisky under one arm, and leaning

heavily on the friend of his past popularity with the other, Sammy managed, limping on both legs, to reach the village.

The road was empty. The village looked deserted.

The modern Rip Van Winkle could hardly believe his eyes. Only yesterday that road had trembled and shook to the tread of pilgrims' feet, and the village had been a babble of voices. Word had gone forth by Siamese grapevine that the *phoouk* was gone. Now—silence and desertion.

Not far away was the heavily timbered kraal where Pinky had been honored and grossly overfed. Empty, of course.

"You had better begone, my son," the priest was saying. "The great white hunter, before he departed with the *phoouk*, declared that you are a thief."

"What else," Sammy grimly inquired, "did the great white hunter say?"

"That you stole the *phoouk* from him, and a sum of money. He said that you deserved the bastinado at least, and he recommended to our headmen that you be driven out of Paknam Po with sticks and stones."

Sammy shook each leg in turn. Needles now seemed to be pouring out of his toes. In a restrained voice, he said, "What else, holy man, what else?"

"He said that only the fact that your guardianship of the *phoouk* entitled you to a little merit prevented him from calling upon the headmen to kill you outright. The headmen agreed that you should be punished. All the men are hunting for the tiger that killed Maung Gung's bullock last night. In an hour they will return. My advice is begone—quickly begone!"

Sammy grimly nodded. His father had certainly left no stone unturned.

The yellow forehead of the old priest became furrowed with lines of puzzlement.

"Perhaps, my son, you can tell me," Maung Chi said, "why it was that, upon leaving, the great hunter burst into wild barks of laughing?"

"He was seeing himself," Sammy replied, "being decorated with the Order of the Elephant by King Rama."

"What are your plans, my son? What is to become of thee?"

And in classical Siamese Sammy made reply, "Buddha, in his vast wisdom, alone knows."

With his legs finally awake and devoid of needles, and with the four quarts of good Irish whisky under his arm, Singapore Sammy trudged off down the road toward Bangkok. A man could not proceed afoot to Bangkok. There were swamps, jungles bristling with numerous forms of death, rivers, to consider.

There was only one thought in his mind: somehow to regain possession of the pink elephant. How? How? How?

It must be accomplished cleverly, quickly and by force. Who in all Siam would believe his story? Who, indeed, but the soldiers of Prince Poot Alla? And how slim were his chances of getting their aid! Not even slim—non-existant!

Trudging down the old road, putting Paknam Po behind him, Singapore Sammy considered and rejected this plan and that. How could he surprise his father, who was a master of surprise? Lay in ambush and shoot him? What with? Sammy had no gun, no money with which to purchase one. His father had even taken away his carbine.

Smoldering with plans of reprisal, testing this one and that with the flint of his worldly wise young mind, Singapore Sammy plodded on. A mile down the road he came to a settlement. Men were at work on the river's edge, hewing square timbers from mahogany logs.

To avoid them, he left the road, waded knee-deep through paddy fields. When he returned to the road, a man saw him. The man was young, bronzed, built on the lines of a gladiator. With an adze, he was putting the finishing touches on a canoe hollowed out of a breadfruit log.

The young Siamese was alarmed; perhaps he had never seen a white man before. At all events, he evidently decided that Sammy was an enemy and must be obliterated.

Grasping the adze in both hands, he charged. Sammy, weakened by trials and tribulations, was for a moment too dazed to act. Then he acted with his customary quickness. He placed the four black bottles on the ground; wrapped the fingers of his right hand firmly about the neck of one bottle; stood up—and hurled it.

The speeding bottle caught the boat builder in the nose and mouth. The adze flew out of his hands, and the bottle, rebounding, fell to the ground, unbroken.

Sammy followed that surprise counter-offensive with a right-hand punch to the belly and a lefthand punch to the jaw.

The boat builder fell heavily, rolled over and over and clasped both hands to his midsection.

CHAPTER IV

SAMMY LOADED HIS whisky into the dugout, pushed it into the water, selected a paddle from a pile, climbed aboard and pushed off.

The current in the Menam was dangerously swift, but Sammy had handled dugouts before. With a dig of the paddle, he sent this one into the swiftest current and went flying south.

For some miles, he paddled with all his strength—paddled until his strength gave out. His muscles were weary, but his eyes were bright. He fanned his wet face with his sun helmet, and his eyes grew brighter and brighter. He presently emitted a bark of laughter.

He looked downriver. He looked at the square black bottles in the bottom of the canoe. An idea had come at last!

"Bozo!" said Sammy aloud, and picked up the paddle again.

Darkness came swiftly, but Sammy paddled on. A sliver of moon rose in the east and faintly etched out the black masses of jungle growth on either bank.

The moon was riding high when the spiderlike riverfront shacks of Pyuhakiri came into view around a bend. The moon

sent beads of silver dripping down the gold spires of Prince
Poot Alla's temples.

The village seemed asleep. So quiet was the riverfront that
Sammy heard distinctly the voice of a sentry at the palace
grounds a half mile away.

He beached the canoe and walked ashore with the greatest
caution, carrying the whisky under each arm.

Heart thumping, eyes alert, ears attuned to the most delicate
sound, Sammy made his way down the muddy waterfront lane,
through a grove of tamarinds and so to the great elephant kraals.
There were several of these. One contained young elephants
under training; another sick elephants; another work elephants;
still another, the war elephants.

In the black shadow cast by a sago palm, Sammy waited,
looked, listened. Nothing reached his senses to alarm him. With
the stealth of a spider he tiptoed toward the war elephant kraal.

Would they trumpet? Squeal?

A sleeping man lay in the black shadow within the great
teakwood gate. A guard! To open that gate it would be necessary for Sammy to slip the thonged peg from its notch, swing
the gate inward.

Sammy pushed the four bottles through holes between the
massive teakwood posts. He climbed to the top. Through some
mischance he had selected a loose post to climb. It gave out a
rumbling sound.

Poised on top of the kraal, Sammy looked down and into
the gleaming eyes of the waking guard. A sound like a moan
floated up from the amazed guard. Then the guard made prep-
arations to repel this invader. His hand plunged into the folds
of his *panung* and promptly displayed a curved knife with a
blade ten inches long.

The guard seized the blade with the obvious intention of
throwing it at the easy target above him.

Sammy anticipated him by leaping. With arms outspread so
that he resembled a flying squirrel, he landed on his knees on

the guard's shoulders and carried him with a crash to the ground. Fortunately for Sammy, the guard's body absorbed the concussion. While the guard lay gasping for breath, Sammy secured the fallen knife, used it to slit strips of cloth from the man's *panung*. With these he deftly gagged and bound his victim.

Free once more to pursue his whims, he recovered the whisky and tiptoed about the enclosure, looking for a mountain of flesh named Maung Ho Danyubu Mat Than Lwyin, *alias* Bozo. It was dangerous business. War elephants are not selected for their docility or good manners; some are sullen and vicious.

In a far corner, with his rump against the timber wall, Bozo stood. Sammy approached his old friend warily. Bozo's small, disillusioned eyes, in the dim light of the crescent moon, held forth little encouragement.

The old war elephant regarded him, with trunk uplifted and slowly moving from side to side, making no murmur of recognition or pleasure at Sammy's appearance.

Sammy drew the cork from one of the bottles. It made a soft pop. So that Bozo might fully understand, Sammy let a little of the whisky gurgle out onto the ground.

Bozo made a soft sound in his throat, and Sammy went nearer. The redhead was now so close to that death-dealing trunk that, had he wished, Bozo could have killed him in an instant.

But Bozo was evidently not in a murdering mood, not, at least, since hearing the pop, the gurgle and smelling the familiar and beloved fragrance.

"Bozo," said Sammy, somewhat under the spell of those coldly inquiring eyes, "you're my pal, and I'm your pal. Let's not forget that. What's mine is yours, kid. Hey! Don't look at me like that! Don't you know me? It's your old pal! Sure, it is! Your old pal and a lot of first-class liquor!"

Singapore held the bottle a little closer to the big elephant.

"Take it, old pal," he urged. "Take it all. Every drop is yours—and there's more where it came from!"

The powerful, sensitive trunk of the old war elephant shot out. Daintily it wrapped itself about the bottle. Abruptly, the bottle left Sammy's coldly perspiring hand.

Bozo spilled scarcely a drop of the rare liquid. Cleverly up-ending the bottle, he swiftly lowered the neck into his mouth.

There followed a sound of gurgling. The gurgling presently ceased. The great trunk tossed the empty bottle to the ground.

A comfortable murmuring sound now arose from the interior of the three-ton mass of gray flesh. Bozo heaved a great sigh.

"You're right, kid," Sammy said. "That liquor. How do you feel now, eh? Better? Attaboy! No! Hey! Lay off me, you big boloney! Wait a while. The night's young yet."

Bozo had mischievously snatched at another bottle. He was, in defeat, gracious. He took a step toward Sammy and laid his trunk across the young man's shoulders.

He gave him what corresponded to an elephant's idea of a hug. It almost broke Sammy's back; but Bozo meant no harm. A low crooning came from him.

Sammy waited a little longer. Waited until every doubt had scampered from Bozo's remarkable brain; waited until that quart of prime Irish was sending a mellow glow through every ounce of Bozo's three tons of elephant being. Then he said: "Big Boy, how'd you like to take little walk with papa—huh? You big stiff, quit neckin' me, willya?"

Bozo's affections were growing. The crooning came forth louder and louder. Since he had been a young warrior, it is doubtful if Bozo had ever taken so much to drink in one gulp. And, as Bozo was the most demonstrative of elephants when in his cups, he hugged Sammy and crooned to Sammy until the exhausted young man wondered if he could ever make the old fool see reason.

And it presently did reach Bozo's whirling center of thought

that this charming and delightful friend of his wanted something. Thereupon he relaxed and awaited orders.

SAMMY QUICKLY grasped the end of the elephant's trunk,
gave it a gentle tug and started for the gate.

Staggering slightly, Bozo followed. Judged by the way he
carried his feet, they must have seemed as light as thistledown.
Gayly, he stepped over the writhing form of the guard. Gayly,
with little mincing steps, he followed the lovable young man
who had given him these delightful sensations.

Crooning, swaying a little, he followed Sammy. If Bozo had
been able to talk, he would have been saying, "Whither thou
goest, I will go. Let's go places! Let's make whoopee!"

Sammy was beginning to feel concerned. The old fool was
likely to burst into carefree drunken squeals at any moment;
liable to begin expressing his joy by pushing over houses or
pulling up trees by the roots. Or he was apt to become more
maudlin, develop a crying jag, and insist on stopping and talking
over his sorrows with Sammy for hours. An elephant as drunk
as Bozo was rapidly becoming was a unique problem. He might
suddenly lie down and go to sleep.

On the outskirts of Pyuhakiri, Sammy indicated that he
wished Bozo to kneel. Bozo refused. Playfully, he slapped
Sammy so hard with his trunk that Sammy was propelled at a
fast, stumbling run at least twenty feet.

Returning, coldly asweat, the nervous American tried it again
and again. But Bozo wanted to play, and play rough.

It finally dawned on Bozo that his old pal wanted him to
kneel. Crooning, he knelt, and Sammy boarded him.

"Now, travel!"

The big elephant seemed to understand perfectly. With long
strides, he started south.

Sammy began to feel better. Equipped now with a ten-inch
knife and a three-ton elephant, he might get somewhere. The
three remaining quarts of Irish he was certain would hold Bozo's
devotion until he was through with him.

With brief rests, the man and the borrowed elephant traveled all night. Shortly after sunrise they entered the village of Gong-Kan, where Sammy obtained the electrifying information that the white hunter's caravan had passed through Lemkala, a few miles to the east, at noon yesterday. His father was traveling like the wind, but would stop in Chung Wan tonight. Chung Wan was only a day's travel.

What corresponded to a hangover must have laid its burning hand on Bozo's brow shortly after they put Gong-Kan behind them. He seemed peevish and resentful. Sammy gave him a half pint of whisky as an eye opener, and they went on.

They reached Chung Wan at dusk. The Menam here was full of canoes containing pilgrims, and all roads leading into Chung Wan were dark with them. The village was ablaze with torches.

Sammy proceeded cautiously. Just north of the village he descried a gigantic raft made of mahogany logs roped together. The raft was big enough to float a house. Its assembly had evidently been completed this afternoon, and it would probably be sent into the swift current first thing in the morning. A stout rope at each inshore corner held it against the bank.

Sammy waited for night to come, then smeared his face with mud, and rode into town on his big war elephant. He rode past the kraal where the mob was thickest and glanced into the *sala*, but he did not see his father.

With his heart beating fast with nervous anticipation he returned to the outskirts and waited. By the time the moon was up, the town was quiet. By midnight, it was asleep. The torches had died down.

Sammy prepared to attack. He gave Bozo a pint of Irish and told him just what he had in mind. And Bozo, with his vast understanding, may have understood.

"There won't be time for snoopin' around," Sammy said to the intelligent animal. "We'll charge the kraal gate and smash it down. We'll dash in there, and you'll grab that little pink brat—and we'll run like hell to that raft over there. Once we're

on that raft, we're safe. Do you follow me, big boy? Knock down
the kraal gate, grab Pinky, run to the raft—and away we go!"

He paused and stroked Bozo's trunk. The cold yellow elephant eyes looked at him with human understanding.

"Are you my pal, or ain't you?" Sammy asked. Bozo made a
crooning sound. "All right, then! Let's go!"

CHAPTER V

THANKS FOR THE successful carrying off of that preposterous and audacious idea were due to Singapore Sammy's deep
understanding and knowledge of elephants, and to Bozo's deep
understanding and knowledge of men.

When the order came to charge that kraal gate, Bozo charged.
The order to pick up and carry off the petted pink pig Bozo
could not be expected to understand; yet the old war elephant
understood roughly what was wanted.

The little pink elephant was drowsing. He came awake with
a squeal of terror when the big trunk of Bozo was laid with a
hard smack on his little pink rump.

Overindulgence in rich food may have been giving Pinky
nightmares. When he blinked open his mean little eyes and
saw that gray mountain towering over him, he yelped and fled.

Out of the kraal. Down the street of the sleeping village.
Bozo thundering after, dealing out giant slaps to direct Pinky,
as Sammy, perched high on the big elephant's back, was direct-
ing him with a pointed stick.

At the raft, Pinky rebelled. Bozo fairly knocked him aboard
with one blow of his trunk.

Then came complications. Behind, in the village, an uproar
was rising. And Bozo, with elephantine caution, was refusing
to board the raft. It looked too uncertain. He tested one log
with a forefoot. It sank. Water gurgled. He tested a stouter log.
It, too, gave way.

Sammy could have deserted Bozo. He no longer needed

Bozo. The old war elephant had fulfilled the purpose for which Sammy had stolen him. But the man had developed a great fondness for this almost human friend; he couldn't leave Bozo.

Bozo tested other logs; found a group of yard-thick trunks; got aboard. A man flew past Sammy in the semidarkness.

Sammy hacked through one rope; ran to the other end of the raft; hacked through the other. He held his breath. Had the great weight of Bozo grounded the raft?

He dashed sweat out of his eyes; with pulses racing, watched, hoped, silently implored the raft to leave the shore.

It began to move. One end, caught by the swift current inched out. The raft began to move more rapidly.

Sammy held his breath.

The raft was free! Like a great liner starting off, its progress was at first almost imperceptible. Then trees, spiderlike huts, temples began to drift astern. They moved faster and faster.

On the shore, torches appeared. But, so far, the disappearance of the raft had not been noticed.

Sammy thanked his stars for a cloud that covered the new moon. A glare of radiance rose into the trees. Shouts and cries came to him. Men with torches were running into the jungles, running down all roads that led from Chung Wan.

Magically, the raft did not go aground. And not, for another hour, did the moon reappear.

The audacious and preposterous plan had worked. Sammy, Bozo, Pinky and the raft were safely slipping down the river— to riches, renown and glory!

But the future is a fog which no eye, elephant or human, can penetrate.

CHAPTER VI

THEY REACHED THE town of Ang Tor early in the morning, and there, more or less conveniently, the raft struck a shoal and would not dislodge itself. Sammy would have preferred to float down all the way to Bangkok, or at least Ayuthia. But fate had other ideas.

The people of Ang Tor had been apprised of the coming of the little *phoouk*. Strange and conflicting rumors had come to them. Yet no one caviled at the manner of the pink treasure's arrival.

That day was one that Sammy would never forget. He was received as a visiting prince. The people of Paknam Po had been poor; but Ang Tor was in a rich section. Gifts of gold and hammered silver were lavished upon Sammy. But the most valuable gift of all was a pair of matched pink pearls. They repaid him for all of the suffering he had undergone. Their value, he knew, would exceed ten thousand dollars in the Singapore market—in Paris, fifteen thousand.

Most of that day he spent in the kraal. He was worried about Pinky. Since his rescue from the black swamp, the little pink pig had adjusted himself to his exalted position in life too well, he was so fat from gorging on rich food that he could hardly stand. He was so spoiled he would permit hardly anyone to go near him. He needed dieting and he needed several spankings. His mean little eyes had lost their brightness.

Sammy longed for the moment when the little brat would be turned over forever to the priests in charge of the elephant temples in Bangkok. They would put him on a strict diet, and they would discipline him.

That day proved to be one of the most eventful that Sammy had ever experienced. At noon, runners came and reported that a royal delegation, headed by a brother of the king, was making fast time from Ayuthia, and would arrive by midafternoon.

Sammy fervently hoped so. If old Bill Shay arrived on the scene before the king's brother did, there would be trouble. Then a rumor spread like wildfire through Ang Tor that Prince Poot Alla, of Pyuhakiri, was headed for Ang Tor with forty men and forty war elephants, on the trail of a white man who had stolen his wisest and oldest elephant.

The adventurer saw his plans toppling. If Prince Poot Alla meant trouble, that was the end of everything! Poot Alla's word would certainly outweigh Sammy's with the king's brother. And the punishment for borrowing Bozo would be serious.

Sammy, in his growing anxiety, realizing that he had a tiger by the tail, began to wish that he had never seen Pinky. Pinky had brought him nothing but trouble—if the pair of perfect matched pearls were excepted.

Then a courier arrived from Chung Wan with more trouble. Last night, he declared, a white man with red hair had boldly entered the kraal at Chung Wan and stolen the *phoouk* and a great mahogany raft!

The tide, which had set so vigorously against Sammy, gained in momentum. A runner entered the village and spread the disquieting news that the king of Siam had given orders to his brother to arrest the red-haired American and bring him back in irons to Bangkok to answer to sundry charges of misconduct in the upland jungles.

Sammy sought out this runner and learned the truth from the man's betel-swollen lips.

Every word of it was true—and more! The king was furious. Sammy had obtained no one's consent to go hunting in the Siamese jungles. The king had heard of his dealings with Prince Poot Alla. And the king had heard of other previous doings which had aroused his royal wrath.

Sammy listened to the runner's story, knew that every word of it was true; became indignant and then furious. He had thought the king would be so grateful that he would forgive certain little incidents of the past.

He walked down to the waterfront where he had left Bozo in the cool shade. He wanted to make sure that, in case of dire need, he could make a quick getaway. Bozo crooned to him.

The final blows fell just when the vanguard of the king's brother's caravan was entering Ang Tor.

Sammy was startled to hear the voice of Maung Chi, the old

priest of Paknam Po who had befriended him and been virtu-
ally his slave.

The old man was breathless. He had followed Sammy down
the Menam in a dugout, hoping that with his own testimony
he might convince the king that the *phoouk* was Sammy's and
not the white hunter's. But it was too late for that now. It was
too late for anything but flight.

"My son, if you value your life, you will fly," Maung Chi
advised the redheaded white man. "Prince Poot Alla claims you
stole this war elephant from his *kraal!* He claims that you stole
the *phoouk* from his men! He is coming here with forty men
and forty elephants to arrest you! Even if you go to Bangkok,
he will follow you with his claims!"

"Yeah?" said Sammy. "Well, his royal majesty had beat him
to it. The king's brother has orders to put me in irons and drag
me back to Bangkok."

"Fly, my son, fly!" Maung Chi reiterated. "You two white
men have caused too much trouble already among these simple
people. The great white hunter is saying he will shoot you on
sight. He swears the *phoouk* is his own. He will fight for the
phoouk with his life—and through all the lawcourts in the land!
What chance have you against him? What chance have you
against Prince Poot Alla and his band of soldiers? What chance
have you against His Royal Majesty of Siam?"

"I suppose," Sammy said bitterly, "I'd better vamoose."

"My son, take my counsel," urged Maung Chi. "Do not
hesitate. Never, in a hundred years, can this confusion be set
right in the eyes of His Royal Majesty. You would be imprisoned
for years while it was being straightened out. It will never be
straightened out. Prince Poot Alla will fight the great white
hunter. They will appeal to the king. In his wrath, the king may
imprison both of them. It is a hopeless situation, my son. And
your very life is in danger. You will be ground between the upper
and nether millstones. Fly, my son, fly!"

Sammy glanced up the street. He saw gold sparkling on the

rich harness of an elephant caravan. Evidently the king's brother was entering Ang Tor. Prince Poot Alla would soon be entering the village from the east. Sammy's father and his caravan would soon be entering the village from the north.

Westward lay his line of escape. Westward lay Burma.

Sammy crisply ordered Bozo to kneel. He said farewell to the old priest and climbed aboard the old war elephant.

Bozo, under his direction, started up the street toward the kraal where the sacred baby elephant was staying. And before the horrified eyes of the villagers, Bozo lay his great trunk on Pinky's flanks. The spoiled baby squealed but obeyed. A roar went up from the assembled elephant worshippers.

But before steps could be taken to stop him, Sammy had acted. Pinky, with Bozo close behind him, bolted out of the kraal.

The crowds in the streets scattered. At a lope, Bozo drove the pink treasure out of Ang Tor and into the jungles to the west. They traveled fast. Pursuit would be certain—but not immediate. And Bozo needed only a little start. The old war elephant seemed to realize the urgency of the situation.

Not until an hour had passed was Sammy at all certain that his audacious scheme would work. And not until then did he relax.

"Old pal," he said, "they didn't give us an even break. They rubbed our fur the wrong way. As for you," he addressed the scampering pink pig on the trail ahead, "you won't ever become a royal elephant. Over in Burma where you're goin', they don't think a pink elephant is any better than a gray one. Somebody may try to steal you and sell you to the King of Siam, but the chances are you'll spend your days where you belong—in a teak yard, workin' hard and earnin' an honest livin'."

V

OCTOPUS

With a Golden Treasure Thirty Fathoms Down, Singapore Sammy Could Laugh at the Dangers from Pirates and an Octopus!

CHAPTER I

SINGAPORE FRAME-UP

THE BLACKJACK GAME in progress in Un Gung's hop joint was as crooked as a cobra track, and Singapore Sammy was reasonably sure that knives would flash, fists and bottles would fly and furniture would be wrecked in a matter of minutes.

Having due and proper regard for the value of his skin, Singapore's first impulse was to walk in an orderly manner to the nearest exit and let himself out into the comparative safety of the Malayan night.

The redheaded American was not sitting in the game; was merely an interested onlooker. He had dropped into Un Gung's on the off chance that a man he was looking for might be there. He had investigated the bar, the smokers' stalls and the fantan and roulette layouts, and had paused idly, on his way out, to watch the blackjack players, of whom there were four—four human promises, as he saw now, of sizzling trouble: one yellow man, one yellow-hearted white man, and two young Americans of the type generally found in the merchant marine.

Un Gung was, himself, banking the game. Un Gung was a flat-faced Cantonese, with eyes like over-ripe blueberries, mouth like a four-inch length of wet red string, and with all the human warmth and loving kindliness of a man-eating shark.

His presence in the game meant rich pickings, else he would not have abandoned his customary post at the bar. And this guess was upheld by the neat stacks of winnings at his elbow. There were bills and coins of many nationalities: Straits dollars,

Javanese guilders, Siamese ticals, Indian rupees, and American greenbacks, eagles and double-eagles.

Somebody had been digging deep into a money belt to bring forth all that assorted currency! Singapore estimated that ten thousand dollars, in terms of American gold, was cuddled there beside Un

Gung's elbow. Rich pickings, indeed!

Of the other three players, Singapore was slightly familiar with the face and the reputation of but one. Pierre Lauzanno, a short, thickset, thick-lipped man of thirty-five, with coldly malignant, pale eyes, the arms of a gorilla, and the hairy, powerful, inhuman hands of a strangler. American born, of Portuguese ancestry and Oriental upbringing, Pierre Lauzanno was down in Singapore's mental catalogue as a human octopus; a man who would indulge in any form of murder to accomplish an object; clever to plot, swift to strike, a wanton genius at crime and the evasion of laws.

Knowing his Far East and the habits of such gentry as Un Gung and Pierre Lauzanno, Singapore guessed that Lauzanno had somehow inveigled the two young Americans into the game and would receive, for his services, *cumshaw*—a split of the takings.

He wondered if they knew they were being ribbed and were making the best of a dangerous situation. They looked world-wise. Both were clean-cut and clean-shaven. Both wore "shore-going clothes" of white duck. One was black-haired and looked like a buccaneer. His brown complexion, with the sun wrinkles about his eyes, stamped him as a man who knew his way about the sea. The other was a fair-haired lad, much younger, with the thin lips, high coloring and murky blue eyes which generally go with a hair-trigger nature. He looked like a Viking.

A buccaneer and a Viking—at the mercy of a shark and an octopus, not to mention two tough-looking Eurasians and a number of Chinese and Malays who were backed against the walls, watching the game. The room was thick with tobacco and opium smoke, the reek of stale booze, and it hummed with conversation from the adjoining rooms.

Singapore abandoned his plan to slip peacefully out of this danger zone when the man who reminded him of a buccaneer glanced at him and, after taking Singapore in, went through a strange pantomime. Holding Singapore's eyes with his, he reached behind him carelessly and tapped himself on the ap-proximate location of his right hip pocket. At the same time, he slightly raised his right eyebrow.

Singapore promptly translated the pantomime into the ques-tion, "Have you got a gun on your hip?"

THE ANSWER was no. Singapore did not pack a gun in the Straits Settlements. He was unpopular enough with the au-thorities, and it went hard with Americans upon whose persons firearms were found.

So he shook his head. The fair-haired lad looked up now and noticed him; ran his murky blue eyes up to Singapore's flaming red hair and pushed out a lower lip. There was no question that here was a young man thirsting for trouble. Drunk, a heavy loser, he was in a nasty mood. Singapore saw the wisdom of getting the lad out of this robbers' roost quickly.

"What's that," the Viking jeered, staring at Singapore's hair—"a bonfire?"

Singapore saw an opportunity. "Let's go outside and put it out."

The Viking glared at him. "Maybe you think I couldn't!"

"That's what I think," Singapore taunted.

For a moment longer, the drunken Viking glared at him. Then, with one of those quick changes of mood common to drunks, he said, "My name is Kelvin Broome. I'll settle with you later. My pal here is Captain Lucifer Jones. They call him Lucky. What do they call you?"

"The name is Shay," Singapore responded. "Sam Shay."

"American?"

"Go to the head of the class, Buster."

"You're hard, ain't you, fellow?"

"Yeah," Lauzanno drawled. "They call him Singapore, he's so hard."

"I thought," the Viking said insultingly, "they saved that name to call the lousiest town in the Far East. I guess they use it on anything too tough to call anything else. I guess they save it for big, redheaded gorillas like you."

"Pipe down," Captain Lucifer Jones barked at him.

"I won't pipe down. That big red-headed gorilla insulted me."

"Come outside," Singapore urged, "and make me like it. And bring your pal along."

Lucky Jones flicked a narrow-eyed glance at him; grasped the drift of Singapore's intentions and said to the Viking, "Let's go out with him, kid, and teach the guy manners."

But Kelvin Broome was perverse.

"Later," he said.

Singapore walked around and stood behind them, placing a hand on each of their chairbacks. The pale, malignant eyes of Pierre Lauzanno searched his face. His uneven teeth were bared in a loose-lipped grin. As Singapore looked at him, one of the pale eyes fluttered in a wink.

Singapore let his eyes travel to Un Gung's flat face. The Chinese was staring at him with coldly, inquiring eyes. You couldn't fool these Chinks. Un Gung didn't say, "What thing wanchee?" But he would.

"Kid," Lucky Jones said to the Viking, "we're cleaned. Let's blow."

"Not me," said the Viking grimly. "I'm out seven thousand bucks and I'm gonna get it back."

Singapore wondered how. Un Gung was dealing. He flipped the cards off the pack with clever, yellow fingers. The Viking lifted his; Singapore saw an ace of spades. The Viking tilted a green bottle, spilled two inches of straw-colored liquid into a glass; tossed it down.

He cleared his throat; said harshly, "I want to bet more cash on this card than I've got. Un Gung, get a load of this."

He reached into his coat pocket. As he did so, Lucky Jones' hand flashed out like a striking snake and gripped the elbow. "Let it be!"

The Viking jerked free and snarled, "Stop trying to wet nurse me!"

"You're drunk," Lucky Jones said.

"Yeah?" the blond jeered. "Well, I'm smarter drunk than you are sober. Kick that around till you lose it!"

Lucky Jones desisted. "It's your funeral, kid," he said.

The Viking reached into his pocket and brought forth a tobacco sack. Untying the yellow string at the throat, he rolled out onto the table a silky sphere of creamy white. It seemed alive. It danced and shimmered. It drew sparks of light from the single *dong* that burned overhead and gayly threw them back.

SINGAPORE, WHO knew pearls, let out his breath in a grunt of sheer amazement. It was one of the most beautiful pearls he had ever seen. It must have weighed eight carats.

The long, yellow fingers of Un Gong reached out for the pearl, but Pierre Lauzanno anticipated him. His strangler's hand shot out and scooped up the gleaming white bubble.

"Where'd you get this, kid?"

The Viking laughed. "Paumotus. Know what it's worth?"

"Too much," Singapore said, "to carry around loose in this man's town."

"Pay my look see," Un Gung grunted.

Pierre Lauzanno compressed the pearl against a thumbnail with his index finger, as a boy holds a "glassie" in playing marbles, and deftly shot the pearl along the table to the Cantonese.

Un Gung delicately picked it up and poised it on the tips of four yellow fingers. The dirty, clawlike fingernails enclosed it in a mounting that reminded Singapore of fish scales.

"Velly pukka."

"How much?" the boy snapped.

"How much wanchee?"

"Ten thousand—gold."

Un Gung replaced the pearl on the table as if it burned his fingers.

"No can do. Mebbe five can do. Ten—maskee!"

"All right. Give her back!"

"Seventy-five hundred can do."

Lucky Jones was looking up at Singapore. "Can you beat it?" he asked. "It's all the poor sap's got."

"Give me the seventy-five hundred!"

Un Gung counted out the money and pocketed the pearl. The Viking slapped the wad of money on the card before him.

"You ain't bettin' all that jack," Lucky Jones protested, "on that card, are you, kid?"

"Yep."

"Snap out of it! That pearl's worth ten thousand in Paris. If you lose that, you're back where you were two years ago. How about that kid sister of yours? Come on, Kel, do some thinkin'."

"I've done my thinkin'. I'm gonna win now. My luck's due to turn. I can feel it."

Singapore felt something else, and by no stretch of the imagination could it be called luck. He felt something resting lightly on his back, on the left side. It might be an elbow, a hand—or a knife.

There was no question that the atmosphere in the blackjack room was tightening up. Lauzanno had the look now of a man who expected action. His eyes were sliding from side to side like marbles in slots.

Singapore moved slightly and glanced behind him. The pressure against his back eased. A pair of ink-black eyes stared into his. They were twin black threats. It was one of the Eurasians. At his side stood one of the Chinese. He was glancing obliquely at Singapore with an idiotic grin, but his eyes were like gravel. Behind the Chinese and slightly to his left stood a Malay, with teeth bared in a fixed grimace, eyes narrowed. He would be handy with a knife.

The redhead drew a deep breath and wished that that damned kid hadn't tossed that pearl into the pot. A virgin pearl to this pack was a rabbit to starved wolves.

Evidently, by some subtle eye message, Un Gung had signaled these three to "take care" of Singapore in the event of trouble.

Lucky Jones laid one Straits dollar—a dirty bill—on his card with a hand that visibly trembled. Singapore noted that Lucky's ears were pale. Apparently the only man in the room who did not sense that trouble was ripe for the plucking was Kelvin Broome. He did not realize that Un Gung, with Lauzanno on the other end of the whipsaw, had cleaned him out systematically; that this attempt to recoup with the turn of one card his entire evening's losses meant danger.

Singapore would have warned him, if it had not been for those three human watchdogs behind him.

The drunken Viking was watching Un Gung's hand eagerly.

"Let's have that card!" he growled.

The slim, yellow hands seemed to fumble the deck. Perhaps the tension had affected Un Gung's cast iron nerves. Perhaps a card was sticky. At all events, the trick was done so clumsily that a man much drunker than the Viking would have detected it.

SOMETHING INSIDE Singapore said, "Come on, Trouble!" He bent down and said rapidly in Lucky Jones' nearest ear, "Grab the money, try for the pearl, and get this kid out of here! I'll take care of the light and Lauzanno. Meet me outside!"

He saw Lauzanno rising from his chair inch by inch with

Lucky Jones. It was like the most fantastic of slow moving pictures.

The Viking's swift wrath exploded. "You lousy Chink rat!" he shouted. "You dealt that card off the bottom! You dirty, cold-decking—"

Singapore waited for no more. Veteran of countless waterfront free-for-alls, he struck backwards with one heel with the swiftness and accuracy of a Kreit viper. An Oriental knee gave way with a snap. He snatched up the chair Lucky Jones had vacated, brought it up and back over one shoulder and felt it crunch on a skull, then up in a wild arc to obliterate the *dong*. That was one uninterrupted flow of movement. His next was a belly-dive across the table in the darkness; a lunge with swooping, clutching hands for any available area of Pierre Lauzanno's anatomy.

True to his deep sea protoype which can, with one flip of its gill plumes, retreat one hundred feet in a split second, the human octopus was—elsewhere.

Singapore sprawled on the table, clutching at emptiness. He floundered, kicked out and snatched at the spot where Un Gung had last been seen. No one there either!

This seriously complicated matters. He was dealing with experts at this sort of thing.

He now heard, in the bedlam of howls, fists thudding on hard flesh or bone accompanied by deep sea cursing, and knew that Lucky Jones was finding an outlet for stored up resentment.

Singapore went on over the table like a snake; struck the floor on one shoulder and reached out, finding a bare calf. As neither of his new friends had been without pants when last seen, Singapore jerked the leg. A volume of Oriental profanity struck the floor beside him with a crash and Singapore, finding in the darkness a jawbone, snapped his free fist into it. A gobblet of blood struck Singapore between the eyes and his unseen enemy went limp.

He scrambled to his feet and shouted, "Lucky Jones! Where are you?"

That was, of course, a mistake. The pack of alien bodies about him formed a crude wedge and carried him along at amazing speed through darkness into which light from torches was just beginning to filter. A flaming brand danced in a doorway. Over tossing shoulders the redheaded adventurer saw the buccaneer profile of Lucky Jones, hemmed in, wielding a whisky bottle.

Then Singapore was being pushed, elbowed, beaten and kicked down a long hall. Fists, feet and harder objects rained on him like the attack of a horde of giant gnats.

He was struck on the back of the head. A club or a foot caught him as he spun and knocked most of the wind out of him. Gasping for breath in the foul air of the dive, he was brought up hard against an iron door which gave. Then a breath of cool, flower-scented air chilled the sweat that streamed with the blood down his battered face.

The iron door clanged shut behind him. How he had managed to escape with his life was a mystery that would puzzle him for some time to come.

The last shove sent him toppling out across a lane paved with wet and slimy flagstones. He plunged, tripping, to hands and knees, with his head hanging down like that of a stricken gladiator. Here, fortunately, there were no starving lions to finish him off. He was evidently to be punished no further for interfering in the affairs of Un Gung.

CHAPTER II

THE ALLEY

A PULSE THROBBED on Singapore's neck. His lungs felt full of liquid fire.

He coughed and tried to lift his head. It felt as though the universe were piled upon it. He drew in deep lungfuls of tropical night; and heard, far away, the mooing of a steamer in the roadstead.

The breeze cooled him off. Vitality began flowing into bruised muscles. His head became clearer, but he was as weak as a half-drowned cat. Resentful fury made him shiver.

A weak, gasping voice inquired, "Who's that—the guy they call Singapore?"

Singapore dropped back on his haunches and managed to lift his head. He swept sweat and blood out of his eyes with the back of his fist.

A dim white figure squatted against a date palm across the flagging.

"Who are you?" Singapore panted.

"Lucky Jones."

"Hurt?"

"They knocked the calking out of me," Lucky Jones gasped.

"Where's your pal?"

"I don't know. I think he got out all right."

"Did you get the pearl?"

"No."

"The money?"

"Nary a dime. I've heard tell that Singapore is the toughest town east of Suez. Now I can qualify as an expert on it. I have been in waterfront brawls from Ceylon to Rarotonga, but this is faster work than I even went up against."

SINGAPORE SUMMONED all his strength and crawled over and squatted down beside the black-haired young man under the palm, A limp hand met his and two new friends, tossed together by a capricious fate, tried to grin through the bloodsmear on their faces.

"Much obliged, Singapore," the buccaneer said.

"I should have been the entire United States Marine Corps," Singapore said bitterly. "How's for getting out of here and looking up your pal?"

"I couldn't walk a step," Lucky Jones answered, "if they offered me the Malay Peninsula. I suppose you think I am a sucker for letting Pierre Lauzanno and his Chinese friends take me and Kel for a cleaning. Do I look as if I was born this morning just before lunch?"

"No," Singapore said. "As soon as we can navigate we will circle around and look up your partner. It ain't so safe here. We are pickings for the first footpad to come along. Those vultures would steal the shroud off a dead man."

"Do you know the lay of the land?"

"Yeah. This lane runs around into Beach Road. There are half a dozen exits from Un Gung's place here and on another alley. When you catch your wind, we had better smell around."

"I can't move yet," Lucky Jones answered. "I want to explain to you that I am not the sucker I seem. We took this Lauzanno aboard my schooner when we stopped in for water in the Flores. He had been shipwrecked there and was so glad to get off he almost kissed my hands."

"They call him the Octopus," Singapore mentioned.

"Yeah? They should. I got him pretty quick, but the kid thought he was hot stuff. The Octopus kept tellin' him what a wild time we would have when we hit Singapore. I blame myself for giving the kid his head. I have had him in hand for two years, and tonight is the first time I ever gave him an inch. We hadn't seen any civilization in four months, and I won't say I wasn't rarin' to go myself. But Lauzanno smelled bad. I should have knocked Kel's block off, as I have done before, and made him go my way."

"You been pearling?" Singapore interrupted.

"You might call it that if you don't know pearling. What we got was tumbler's luck. I picked up two diving outfits from a stranded Jap in New Zealand and we tried 'em out in the Paumotus. I found a coupla little fellers and Kel found that cantalope, and we called it even. I used mine to pay off the balance I owed on the *Blue Goose*—"

"Your schooner?"

"Yeah."

"How is your wind now?" Singapore asked. "I am worrying about that partner of yours."

"You needn't," Lucky Jones answered. "He used to be the light heavyweight champion of California, and we have been in jams before. When you fight him, you think he is tossing cannonballs at you. I lick him when we scrap because I out-think him. I sort of dread finding him right now. He is goin' to be in a much worse state of mind than he was two years ago when I picked him up off the beach at Tutuila. He was tryin' to knock out his brains on a piece of coral rock then, because he wasn't fit to shoot, so he said. This time, when he sobers up, it will be terrible. I think I might walk now."

WITH A groan, he came to his feet. He wavered, took one staggering step, and cursed.

Singapore grasped him firmly by the elbow and slowly helped him down the damp flagging toward Beach Road.

"He was blacksandin' down there in Tutuila," the tired voice of Lucky Jones went on. "I took him aboard the *Blue Goose*. He was a pukka handful. He has a weakness for women, a weakness for every known brand of liquor, and a weakness for every game of chance that has ever been invented. There was a dame in Tahiti with eyes like Javanese grapes and a smile like a saber-toothed tiger who had him runnin' in circles. There was only one thing to do in a case like that—sock him into a state of unconsciousness, take him aboard and get under way, which is what I did."

"He looks," Singapore said, "like a good kid."

"That's the trouble," Lucky Jones agreed. "He is a good kid. His father and mother sound like fine people. They are runnin' an irrigation farm, tryin' to grow oranges, just outside Phoenix, Arizona, but it is a losin' game, accordin' to letters the kid got from them. With land at two thousand an acre, your trees would have to bear solid gold oranges to pay the mortgage money.

There is a kid sister who needs a musical education. Some old hound in Phoenix, a pipsqueak lawyer, has a yen for the girl and is yappin' after her to marry him. Kel wanted to raise enough jack down in the Islands to help out her and his paw and maw. You see? It puts Kel in a spot. That was the thing he told me that night I found him tryin' to knock out his brains with that coral rock, and it sort of got me. So I took him in hand and I've been tryin' to help him pile up a stake to go home with."

"And the stake," Singapore guessed, "all went into Un Gung's pocket tonight."

"Yeah. I made Kel a sort of a partner. We did some tradin' and we did this pearlin' I mentioned. In two years, he ran up a stake of seven thousand, not counting the pearl. He kept writin' his kid sister to hold the old hound off and saying he would be home soon and blow her to a fancy musical career. The letters he got from her made tears come into my eyes. You can figure out the present situation for yourself. It makes me kind of sick to think of that kid sister of Kel's."

Singapore was staring down the dark lane. Just around the bend was Beach Road. They had passed three of the iron doors which served as exits from Un Gung's, and he was growing worried. He knew Un Gung much better than Lucky Jones did; knew how miraculous it was that the two of them had escaped with nothing worse than beatings.

"Don't get me wrong," the buccaneer was saying. "Kel is a game little guy—a great little guy. He is a fine pal. It is my fault that he ran hog wild tonight. I brought him here to catch a P & O for Europe. He was going to stop off in Paris and sell the pearl, then go straight home. What's this? Another drunk?"

In the shadowed gutter ahead and to their left a man was lying. He appeared to be lying face down. Arms and legs were asprawl.

Lucky Jones suddenly shouted, "Kel!" in a strangled voice. He broke free from Singapore's supporting arm and lunged ahead. He knelt down beside the sprawling figure in the gutter and struck a match.

The flaring flame told a concise and horrible story. It confirmed the identity of the man in the gutter and sparkled on the haft of the dagger which protruded from a round red stain in the back of the Viking's white coat.

Lucky Jones rolled him part way over; held the match flame to the open and glazing eyes until it expired. Singapore heard the hiss of the still-hot ember as the match fell to the wet flagging.

"Strike a match!" Lucky snapped.

Singapore found one; struck it. Lucky rolled the dead man over on his back and, in the flickering light, plunged his hand inside the Viking's bloodstained shirt. It came out of the shirt with fingertips glistening red.

"They got the chart!" he gasped.

SINGAPORE STRUCK another match. Lucky Jones was wiping his hands on a handkerchief, and staring at him with wildly dilated eyes. They seemed all whites.

"They got the chart!" he repeated, and began to curse. Singapore sympathetically stood by.

"You better take a good look, Lucky," he suggested.

Lucky Jones hastily complied. He ransacked pockets. At length he declared in a voice shaking with fury, "Nope. It's gone. They got it!" He began to curse again."

"Listen," he said savagely, "is there an American battlewagon in this lousy port?"

"There isn't a U.S. gunboat nearer than Hongkong," Singapore answered. "Why?"

"I'd get every gob on board," Lucky panted, "and clean out this joint. I wouldn't stop there. I'd clean out this lousy town. I'll clean out this joint, one-handed. You stay here. You watch him. I'll show the lousy rats!"

Singapore grabbed his arms. "Steady!" he growled. "It was

nothin' but fools' luck that saved us from what he got. Keep cool. What was this chart?"

Lucky Jones freed himself by savagely twisting his arms. He started for Beach Road, where the main entrance to Un Gung's was.

Singapore grabbed him again. In the random ray of a distant street light the wild, dilated eyes of Lucky Jones glared at him. His swinging fist would have struck Singapore down if he had not swiftly ducked.

"Cut that out!" he snapped. "Go back there and you'll get a knife in the back. Where this one came from there are plenty more."

"To hell with you! Get out of my way! I'm gonna tear this dump apart with my hands!"

"Steady," Singapore repeated. "What are you gonna do with this kid? Are you goin' to leave him here to rot?"

The questions had the calming influence that Singapore hoped for. Lucky Jones dropped his hands to his sides. It was unfortunate, perhaps, that at that moment a Chinese came padding down the lane. He may have been a cutthroat; he may have been an honest laborer. Before Singapore could do anything about it, Lucky Jones sprang on the unsuspecting wayfarer with bellowed curses, struck savagely at him with his fists. The Oriental went down as if he had been shot.

Lucky Jones stood over him with chest heaving. Then, before Singapore could act to prevent him, he wheeled about and ran down the lane toward Beach Road and vanished around the corner. Lucky Jones was going to take his revenge if they killed him!

Singapore had seen Malays run amok. They generally went about their maniac business with a *parang*—ugliest of swords. Lucky Jones was amok with bare fists. And if Singapore did not do something drastic, the dead man's maddened pal would certainly be stabbed.

He reached the corner in time to see Lucky Jones the nucleus of a writhing, twisting clot of humanity. Malays and Chinese, it would seem, had sprung from the very cracks of the sidewalk.

Singapore threw himself into the fray with smashing fists. The door of Un Gung's opened and more units were added to the opposition. A knife slashed Singapore's coatsleeve open from shoulder to wrist and laid open the flesh at the elbow to the bone. Then he, too, went amok. The madness of battle sent a superhuman strength into sore, beaten muscles. He punched, jabbed, slugged. Faces, yellow and brown, danced about him like masks on strings. He struck at them with machine-like precision until his fists were numb, until his breath was like a hacksaw in his throat. He could not see Lucky Jones, and knew he was down; probably stabbed to death.

Then a miracle quietly happened. Un Gung's doors opened wide, but the expected savage rush did not take place. Instead, the fighters flowed, a suddenly silent stream, indoors. Those who were down were dragged in.

In a twinkling, the sidewalk was vacated of all evidences of the fray except for some scattered drops of gore, a few teeth— and Lucifer Jones who sat, looking dazed and spent, with one arm clapped to the back of his neck.

CHAPTER III

THE *BLUE GOOSE*

SINGAPORE, SEEING THAT his comrade-at-arms was not dead, at least not yet, used what felt like the last breath in his aching body to ask, "How—bad, Captain?"

Lucky Jones took the proffered hand and pulled himself to his feet. Physically, he may have been all in, but his fighting, vengeful spirit still flamed. His eyes dilated with blood madness. He muttered, "They only got my wind again. Wait till I get my breath. I'm goin' in there!" He clung, swaying, to Singapore's hand.

A Sikh policeman who looked, with his dark red turban, eight feet tall, came swinging down the sidewalk. The miraculous retreat of Un Gung's henchmen was now explained.

The Sikh glanced at them, hesitated, then, with a courteous bow, passed on. As far as he was concerned, two white gentlemen had been settling a dispute and were now clasping hands in armistice!

Singapore whistled softly in relief. He wanted no interviews with the Singapore police this night!

The big Sikh swung on and vanished. Lucky Jones growled. A double-rickshaw with a giant Mongolian between the shafts came rolling up to the curb from the direction of Raffles Plain.

Lucky Jones growled a curse and leaped; struck him savagely in midsection and jaw. It was among the minor miracles of that amazing night where this sudden burst of strength came from.

The blows landed with all the loud smacking impact of blows struck early in a fight. The Mongolian sprawled between the shafts with hands folded lovingly on paralyzed solar plexus.

The incident relieved Lucky Jones, at least momentarily, of his terrible lust for revenge; but Singapore was more than half certain that the man's hatred would blaze forth again.

"Look here," he said to the bloodthirsty schooner skipper, "at the last count, there were upwards of four hundred million people living in Asia. It is going to take you a long time, bucko, to kill them all. We have got to do some fast thinking. What are we going to do with your pal?"

"I'm going to bury him at sea."

"Where's your hooker?"

"Anchored midway between Tanjong Ru and South Mole."

"Well, let's get him aboard; otherwise, we will both be held as material witnesses in a murder case for an oriental eternity. And that's a hell of a long time. If you want more revenge, take it later."

Lucky Jones said shakily. "This is my personal party. You blow along before I start some more trouble."

Singapore's answer to that was to pick up the shafts of the rickshaw and drag the vehicle around into the lane. He stopped beside the dead man.

"I have heard about you," Lucky Jones said huskily. "You are one great guy,"

"Grab his shoulders," Singapore answered.

THEY LIFTED the dead boy into the double seat of the rickshaw, strapped him in so that he would not roll out, and, each seizing a shaft, started off. Thoroughly familiar with this old oriental seaport, Singapore laid a course through back alleys to Rochor Canal Road, across the Kalang Road bridge and so to Tanjong Ru. In this strangest of oriental cities, it was the strangest of funerals.

It was doubtful if Lucky Jones was at any time aware of the direction they were taking. He still smoldered with vengeance. He was going to put to sea and bury Kelvin Broome, then he was coming back, armed, to shoot Un Gung in his tracks!

Singapore did not argue with him. He had learned that Lucifer Jones was a man not to be lightly opposed.

Tanjong Ru is a spit of land poking like a great finger into Singapore Strait—a peninsula covered with fantastic beefwood trees.

The two men, drawing their strange hearse, emerged from the beef woods and came upon the white beach which tipped, like a fingernail, the outshore end of the point.

Beyond lay the roadstead. Riding lights of ships from all parts of the world twinkled mysteriously over the dark water. A spiced offshore breeze was bowing. It reminded Singapore of the smell of Yokohama and Calcutta and every port in between. A reaction from the night's excitement was setting in. He felt bone-weary and more than half sick. He kept thinking of the dead man's kid sister back there in Arizona, hopefully waiting for him to come home and deliver her from a "pipsqueak old lawyer." The bad luck of others always made him feel sick and mad.

But he said briskly, "Where's your schooner, skipper?"

Lucky Jones was in a daze of smoldering hatred and remorse.

"Beyond that second light," he finally answered. "That's a Jap tramp. The *Blue Goose* is around under her stern, there."

A question popped into Singapore's mind. What was this chart that had been stolen from the dead man? But he did not voice it, and walked down to the water's edge. He had seen, fairly close inshore, what appeared to be the evil red eye of a cooking brazier. That would mean that a sampan was out there. He called out in Malay, and, receiving no answer, shouted in coast pidgin.

There was a sleepy reply, after an interval. The high poop of a sampan with the tall, waving figure of a man at a sweep were silhouetted against stars and riding lights—a ghost on a ghostly sampan.

Water gurgled under a blunt bow. Teak grated harshly on white sand and sent shivers of pale green-blue out over the water. Singapore and Lucky Jones stowed the dead Viking aboard and left the rickshaw to its fate.

As they got under way, Lucky Jones took up again his refrain of hatred and revenge.

"I won't leave this lousy port for good until I find who took that chart. Whoever took that chart killed this lad. I'll find him."

"You don't suspect anybody," Singapore said impatiently, "but the Octopus, do you?"

"Hell, I know it was Lauzanno! I saw the kid showing it to him on deck. He was too trustful. He was as romantic as a schoolgirl. He thought Lauzanno was the real article. And when I get Lauzanno, I'll strangle him!"

"What was this chart?"

"It showed where sunken treasure is. The wreck of the old *Singing Spray*."

SINGAPORE RANSACKED shelves of dusty memories and answered. "She was one of the early clippers in the China trade. She got wrecked seventy years or so ago up in Micronesia, in a typhoon, and all hands were drowned."

"Not quite," stated Lucky Jones. "She was wrecked exactly ninety years ago up by the Xulla Islands, in the Moluccas, in a passage north of Bouro and south of Botjan."

"That's in the Banda Sea."

"Above the Banda Sea," he was corrected. "The *Singing Spray* was carryin' American trade stuff and a half million in bullion to Java."

"I've heard the story," Singapore said.

"You think it's phony?"

"I've heard lots of treasure stories," Singapore answered.

"This one is true."

"Yeah? Listen. I've heard stories of the wrecks along the Paracels Reef that made my mouth water. I've heard stories of sunken treasure scattered from Vladivostock to Rangoon. All you had to do was go down there and pick up the bright, shiny gold right out of the water!"

"This one ain't that kind of a story. This one is true. How would you like to team up with me and go look for that treasure?"

"Not me," Singapore said emphatically. "I am too busy looking for my old man—he's really my stepfather—to bother with other treasures. He ran off from me and my mother when I was two years old and took with him a will of my grandfather's leaving me about a million dollars. I have almost had my hands on him, and I will not quit until I do lay my hands on him and get that will. That is treasure enough for me."

"How long have you been lookin' for him?"

"Seven years. I've chased him all over China, Japan, Indo-China, the South Seas and India. I tracked him here—and lost his trail once more. I lost it in Un Gung's. A fellow said I'd find him there."

"What is a few months out of seven years?" Lucky Jones argued. "I have two complete diving outfits, and two Chinos who are the best pump hands in the business. Have you done any diving?"

"Plenty, but I'm not interested."

"Look at it this way," Lucky Jones urged him. "I am not going after this treasure for myself, but for the kid's folks. It was his chart. He was going home to see his folks and get them fixed up, then he was going to meet me in Batavia and we were going out and dive for that gold. Come along with me. Half of what we recover is yours; the other half we ship back to Kel's people."

"What makes you so sure you'll find gold?"

"I'll tell you how Kel came by that chart," Lucky answered. "There was an old guy down in Tongatabu who was a hundred and ten if he was a day. He had a face as yellow and wrinkled as a dried-up mango. He showed the kid papers to prove he was the *Singing Spray's* cabin boy. There is not question about that. He was the only man aboard of her to get away when she went down. He hung onto a spar and a current swept him down to Amboina before he beached. He went native and drifted around the islands, ending up with a black wife on Tongatabu. He outlived four black wives. We checked this up. It's all true. The kid nursed him through a spell of malaria while I was overhauling our diving gear, and the old guy gave him this chart out of thankfulness."

"He must have drawn the chart himself."

"He did. It is so old it is like eggshells. Kel pasted it down on linen and carried it next to his skin. He was so jealous of the chart he only showed it to me once."

"Could you find the wreck without the chart?"

"No. Now, answer one of my conundrums, redhead: If this story is phony, why was this Octopus so interested in that chart? People knew the *Singing Spray* went down with bullion, but not enough people to count on two fingers know where she lies. I don't. The kid did. And whoever has the chart does."

"The Octopus," Singapore agreed.

"You change your mind, Singapore, and come along!"

SINGAPORE DID not answer at once. There were disturbing pictures in his mind. An adventurer since he had been able to walk, this was adventure gilt-bound. It promised mystery, excitement, danger. He saw himself on sea bottom, in the clear, crème de menthe green of the Banda Sea—most romantic of all seas—groping around rotting wooden ribs for chests of gold while a deep sea pump throbbed in his ears. He loved deep sea diving. It was exciting work.

"How deep water is she in?"

"Thirty fathoms. Will you do it?"

Still no decision from the redhead. Another picture was storming his imagination. He was seeing a sixteen-year-old girl with tears in her eyes—tears and stark despair—as she read a cablegram saying her brother had been buried at sea. No details—*"Regret very much to say that Kelvin Broome died and was buried at sea last night."* One didn't notify parents and sisters that their best beloved had been stabbed to death in a Singapore hop joint and tossed out like a bag of rags into a wet alley.

A sliver of the old moon was riding the eastern horizon and picking out high spots here and there. It glowed dimly on Singapore Town, etched out a lady liner and a cluster of rusty tramps and played upon the raked masts of a small, graceful sailing ship that floated in the night mist like a dream ship. Her slim hull was steel-blue. Her lines were a yacht's. How a man could learn to love a ship with lines like hers!

"Is that your ship?"

"Yes, sir! Are you comin' along?"

"What does she measure?"

"Ninety foot on deck. Twenty beam. Twelve draft. She handles with one finger. She's a good girl in any weather. There isn't a mean kink in her. Wait till you take the wheel! She points like a racin' yacht. She's as quick as a cat, I don't care how much green there is aboard. You're lookin' at a schooner, mister!"

Singapore loved ships as some men love horses and dogs. Here was a small ship worthy of any man's devotion. He was drawn to Lucky Jones accordingly.

"Come on, redhead! Change your mind and come along! Say, you ain't afraid, by any chance, of the sharks and octopus in the Banda Sea? They're big and fast and tough and hungry in those waters!"

"You can meet up with a big octopus in thirty fathoms," Singapore agreed.

"I caught a twenty-foot shark, tiger, right off Serwati! Think of that before you say yes or no, Mr. Shay!"

"Wait a minute," Singapore growled. "You aren't dealin' with a kid now. Supposin' we draw up a gentleman's agreement. Supposin' we say that I'm goin' along, *if* we can find that chart. Well and good. But I go along for what fun I get out of divin' for the gold. What gold we find goes to the kid's folks, minus actual expenses. Is that a deal?"

"It's a deal," the other man said heartily. "I seem to keep learnin' new things all the time about you. You are white all the way through, Sam Shay! Maybe," he went on, "you have some ideas for findin' needles in haystacks."

"I am groping," Singapore answered. "While you sail your hook out of the mud, I will slip ashore and snoop around. You say you have Chinese boys aboard?"

"Yep!"

"Good. I want to borrow a complete Chino outfit, from hat to shoes, to wear over this suit. How long will it take you to sail out, bury your pal, and come back to this anchorage?"

"I will be back by sun-up."

"I'll try to be," Singapore said.

"If you don't show up, where do I look for you?"

"You could try the morgue, but you won't. Right now you promise me to stay on board this hooker and leave that town alone. This will be ticklish work and I've had plenty of back-to-back fightin' for one night."

The skipper of the *Blue Goose* looked wistfully across the water at the oriental city beginning to glow brighter in the light of the crescent moon. His eyes blazed, then became sane again.

"Okay," he submitted. "But just where are you goin'?"

"Octopus hunting!"

CHAPTER IV

THE BEACH AT TANJONG RU

SINGAPORE TOOK NO bait along on this perilous expedition. For equipment he carried nothing under his borrowed Chinese costume but a stout heart and a pair of battered but willing fists. If he succeeded in finding Pierre Lauzanno, the Octopus, he would have to rely on his clever thinking. The odds seemed several thousand to one against him. It was a dangerous errand and might well prove a futile and fatal one.

He went ashore at the foot of Bras Basah Road and told the sampan *fokie* to stand off and on until he returned. Before starting up the road from Raffles Reclamation, he rolled up the pantlegs of his white ducks. If a bold scheme worked out correctly, he would discard the Chino costume at one stage of the proceedings and finish the job a la American.

Fully aware that discovery would mean swift death, Singapore made straight for Un Gung's dive, slipping into the fantan room with a half-dozen young Chinese bloods looking for quick fortune. And it was fortunate that Un Gung's was so badly lighted.

With heart triphammering high in chest, he drifted from fantan room to roulette room, glanced into the scene of the recent shambles, looked around the bar and visited the opium stalls. No human octopus was in evidence.

Half sick with disappointment, Singapore spent another hour in the joint, hoping that Pierre Lauzanno might have gone away and would return. Then he slipped out onto Bridge Road again and went on down to The Halfsplice, another dump of the same odor, and investigated, in turn, Charlie Ching's and three nameless grogshops. In The Jade Grin, he mingled with French, British, and Jap sailors, looked into the large red-and-gold room where dancing girls were in evidence, and made the mistake of slapping an insolent Eurasian hanger-on in the nose for kicking him in the ankle.

A British bosun intervened, called Singapore a bloody, stinking Chinese something-or-other, and Singapore was compelled to drop him with a belly-and-jaw punch which he had learned by studiously observing the technique of one Jack Dempsey in a fight picture he had seen one night in a Siamese theater.

AN INTERNATIONAL fistfight was the result. Singapore saw an open door and made a rush for the open air, leaving behind him a howling, shouting, cursing mob who slugged, kicked and bit one another after the fighting customs of their countries.

It was a close squeak for Singapore and left him in a state of acute nervousness. Rearranging his costume in the black shadow of a tamarind tree, he limped back to Un Gung's, half-sick again over the realization that the odds against his finding the human octopus had jumped to about a million to one.

And he hardly believed his luck when he saw the powerful, black-haired giant he was looking for in the fantan room, tossing down money on the little numbers, and roaring curses.

Singapore stifled his enthusiasm and slunk into a smoky dark corner, slipped his hands into his sleeves, dropped his chin on his chest, and watched, trying to look as Chinese as a porcelain Buddha.

Eventually Pierre Lauzanno tired of fantan and sauntered into the roulette room, via the bar, pausing long enough to pour into his mouth enough Javanese *arrack* to paralyze a horse. Leaving the bar, he took the *arrack* bottle with him.

The Octopus began systematically playing black and combinations, and losing consistently. Singapore, occupying another obscure niche, watched him throw away money and watched him drink. He marveled at Lauzanno's capacity. In a space of two hours he saw the man put away enough of this potent liquor to send any two men under the table. While he played, he cursed, roared, shouted, yelled. The more he lost, the louder he roared. This was Pierre Lauzanno at play.

Singapore saw slate gray as a door opened and closed. Dawn was on the way! His nervousness increased. His heart began hammering again. If the Octopus carried his play on into broad daylight, Singapore's scheme was ruined.

And suddenly Lauzanno roared, "I've had plenty!" Decisively, he turned from the table and started for one of the rear doors. Singapore idly followed, Lauzanno went toward the room in which Singapore had first glimpsed Lucifer Jones and the Viking. A poker game was in progress now—Un Gung banking a game for four British sailors.

Lauzanno went on down the hall through which Singapore had, only a few hours before, been kicked and pushed.

Un Gung looked up. His cold, inquiring eyes lingered on Singapore's face. For a moment, Singapore thought he would suffocate. His back prickled at thought of a knife. Then Un Gung glanced away, and Singapore, with the sweat of awful suspense streaming off his forehead, limped on down the corridor after the Octopus.

The iron door opened, admitted pearl-gray dawn light. It clanged shut. Singapore ran to the door and threw it open. Pierre Lauzanno stood in the middle of the lane, preparing to light a white Burmese cheroot. He brought up a flaming match from the seat of his pants, and cupped his hands.

Singapore glanced up and down the lane. Save for himself and the Octopus, it was empty. With hands tucked into sleeves, ready to be extracted at a moment's notice, Singapore edged dose to his quarry.

Lauzanno glared over the tops of his cupped hands, and roared past the cheroot: "No *cumshaw!* Beat it, you louse!"

Singapore edged still closer. Pale, malignant eyes were fixed on him warily. They narrowed. Then they flew open wide and his mouth gaped.

"You—" he began, in a strangled voice.

SINGAPORE SLUGGED him full on the point of the jaw, and so sure he was of the effectiveness of the punch that his arms were open to catch his victim as he fell. Two hundred pounds of limp man sagged in his hands.

Hastily Singapore rid himself of his Oriental masquerade. It would never do for a Chinese to be seen dragging an unconscious white man around Singapore.

The pearly mist of dawn was shot with the pale promise of a fiery sunrise as Singapore dragged the stunned man down the lane to Beach Road.

A rickshaw and a British police officer arrived simultaneously.

The officer glanced from Singapore to his unconscious burden. He frowned and said, "Blotto?"

"Boiled like an owl," Singapore answered. "Hey, rickshaw!"

The policeman's eyes were narrow. "What ship?"

"Schooner *Blue Goose*."

Pierre Lauzanno groaned. Singapore's heart raced. The cop grinned and said, "I'll give you a 'and up with 'im." And did so.

Singapore mopped a fresh deposit of sweat from an overworked brow as they rolled away. The groans of the Octopus became louder.

"Chop-chop!" Singapore snarled at the coolie.

Lauzanno gave a faint but definite squirm as the rickshaw rolled to the foot of Brah Basah Road. He opened his eyes as Singapore and the coolie lifted him out of the seat. Cold, malignant eyes rolled backward, downward, then steadied and settled on Singapore's hard blue ones. Lauzanno wavered on his feet.

He staggered out of Singapore's hands.

"You—" he began once again in a hoarse voice.

Singapore slugged him again. The rickshaw coolie and the waiting sampan *fokie,* accustomed to the queer whims of white men, sullenly obeyed Singapore's sharp commands; carried the unconscious man into the sampan's stern.

CHAPTER VI

TREASURE CHART

STEPPING ABOARD THE sampan from the retaining wall, Singapore gazed into the dawn mists ahead. They were pierced by the promised fire. Steel ships rode on vapor. The mist was rolling in billows of pink and lavender. Lateen sails appeared.

The mist seemed to part. Then white sails above a steel-blue hull materialized. A soft breeze filled and rounded them, and Singapore heard the bellowed orders of Lucky Jones.

"Stand by to lower your jibs. Lower away! Stand by to let go your anchor. Let go!"

There was a faint splash. Pierre Lauzanno opened his eyes and moaned.

"Make one move," Singapore growled, "and I'll let you have it again!"

He systematically explored the man's pockets; found a few bills, a few coins, a few soiled letters in a girl's handwriting.

"Where is it?" he snapped.

"I don't know what you mean."

"The chart you took from that kid."

The pale, malignant eyes stared at him.

"What chart?"

Singapore grunted with relief. By professing ignorance of the chart, Lauzanno had betrayed his knowledge of it.

"Where is it?"

"You're way over my head, Singapore. And—look! I have an idea you are going to be very sorry for this."

"You might be surprised," Singapore said quietly. He stood up and shouted, "Ahoy, there!"

Lucky Jones deserted the wheel and came running along the deck.

"Ahoy! What have you got there?"

"Gent by the name of Pierre Lauzanno!"

"The chart?"

"Not yet."

"I'll kill the dog with my bare hands!"

"You'll stand by and let me handle this!" Singapore retorted angrily.

The schooner captain was pale and his lips were as hard as rope. As Singapore saw the amok look in his eyes, he lost some more of his patience.

"Give me a hand with this slob, and if you muss him up, I'm through!"

Lucky Jones growled, "Oh, all right, all right; but what the hell? If he killed your pal, what would you do?"

"What I'm goin' to do!"

He pushed the dazed scoundrel up to the schooner's deck and paused long enough to pay off the *fokie*. When he climbed aboard, Lucky was holding up their captive by the elbows, glaring into his face and Lauzanno was glaring coldly, malignantly back.

"Sit him down on that hatch cover," Singapore directed.

Lucky Jones obeyed with much more alacrity than Singapore thought necessary. He carried the man in a savage rush and threw him down hard enough to knock the wind from him.

"You slobs are gonna be sorry for this," the Octopus said

"Stow it!" Lucky snarled and picked up a belaying pin. "Now, where's that chart?"

"Look here," Lauzanno answered harshly, "you two tough

eggs can beat me and kick me until I'm nothin' but holes—but will I talk? Take a good look and answer yourself!"

Singapore knocked the belaying pin out of Lucky's hand as it came up and over. He said:

"You big pirate, I'm doin' this! Stand by, now." He had to glare Lucky down, then he swung to Lauzanno and said, "Mister, you were right. We are one pair of tough eggs. We don't say you stabbed that kid. We do say you were the only man in Singapore last night who knew what that chart was. We have got you cold. Take your clothes off!"

"Go to hell!"

"Whistle up your *serang* and those Chinos," Singapore directed Lucky. "I want him stripped."

"Save the bother," Lauzanno snapped. "I'll shuck my own clothes off."

HE DID so. A hairy body was presently entirely exposed in the golden light of the risen sun. Singapore went through each garment as it was shed, but he found no chart.

He placed the flat of his hand against a davit and looked at Lauzanno dreamily. Those who had had experience knew that this was by far the most dangerous, most sinister expression that the red-haired young man used. But Lauzanno, lacking the experience, looked up at him with his loose-lipped grin.

"Lucky," said Singapore, "I want you to take a good look at this specimen. Don't leap—just look! Do you know the habits of the deep sea octopus, Lucky? This specimen here has them all. Take them one at a time. Take a good squint at those eyes. Queer, ain't they? Oval and slanted. They ain't dark or large, but they're small, cold and full of murder."

The Octopus grinned at him. Singapore went on.

"A deep sea octopus .has a hooked beak like that, too. It uses the beak to tear its victims in shreds. It changes its color like a little tropical lizard to match its background. Our friend here can't change his color, but how he can pretend to be what he ain't! Same thing. The deep sea octopus has an ink sack that he puts to pretty clever use. In a fight, he clouds up the water with this ink, then he leaps backward by flipping his gill plumes, and comes at you from around behind—while you're still starin' at the ink cloud! Our friend here hasn't an ink ejector, so he uses smooth conversation. He fools you. He gets you lookin' at what he's been sayin', then he slips around and knifes you in the back!"

"You guessed that part right," said the Octopus.

Singapore, looking at him dreamily, went on. "An octopus has eight arms or legs. Our friend here has only two arms and two legs. But they are as good as eight. Lucky, did you ever cut off an octopus's arm? There's no blood, just a little bluish ooze. If you cut off one of our friend's arms, would we find blood, or blue ooze?"

The oval, pale, small eyes were twin points of murderous hatred now. Singapore said sharply, "Lucky, rig up a net!"

"What for?"

"I want to find out how much this guy is like his sea goin' brothers!"

Lauzanno rose halfway from the hatch cover.

"Sit down!" Singapore snapped. The Octopus sat down; snarled, "I won't forget this soon, Singapore!"

"You won't ever forget it," Singapore said quietly.

Lucky Jones had shouted to the *serang*. The Malay came trotting up the deck with a cargo net. Lucky grinned and said, "Now what, Mr. Shay?"

"Rig up a single block on the end of your main-boom. I want a line running from inboard, through the block to this net, outboard."

"Okay." These interesting details were swiftly arranged.

Lauzanno leaped up from the hatch cover and roared, "You won't get me into that net!" He lunged at the red-haired tormentor.

Singapore struck him with that useful belly-jaw punch he had learned in a motion picture theater in Bangkok. When Lauzanno opened his ugly eyes again he was enmeshed like a huge fish in the cargo net. The *serang* and the two Chinese boys, all grinning delightedly, were holding the inboard end of the rope which ran through the block on the end of the boom and supported the net.

"Now," Singapore said quietly, "swing the boom out!"

THE BOOM was swung out. Pierre Lauzanno, intricately enmeshed in the net, began to roar curses.

Singapore glanced at the three men holding the rope.

"Hold it until I give you the word," he said. Then, to Lauzanno, "Do you feel like tellin' me where that chart is?"

"I'll never tell you!"

"Okay," said the redhead. "Let him down!"

The three men let go the rope. It paid out swiftly. There was a pearly splash as Pierre Lauzanno struck the green water like a yellow ball. He fought to extricate himself. His head appeared. He spouted sea water and curses. Then, in his struggles his head disappeared below the surface. His hind quarters appeared and glistened in the sun.

Lucky Jones was leaning against the boom, gurgling with laughter.

"Haul him up!" Singapore ordered.

The three men hauled in the rope. The net came up. Lauzanno spluttered, gagged, cursed, sucked in whistling breath and declared as he gripped meshes as an ape grips the bars of its cage, "I'm going to get you, if it takes the last drop of blood in my veins, the last beat of my heart, the last thought in my brain, the last move of my last moving finger!"

It was a flowery Oriental threat which Singapore had heard often enough before, but never spilled by the lips of a white man.

"Where's—that—chart?"

"Drown me," was the wrathful answer, "and find out!"

"Lower away, boys!" the redhead sang.

With a great splash, the man in the cargo net re-entered the native element of the sea-going breed of octopus.

Again there was wild floundering, gasping, cursing, and a pitching view of all parts of Lauzanno's anatomy. His struggles were becoming feeble when Singapore ordered the net to be pulled up again.

The prisoner gagged and gasped as before. Sea water spewed from his mouth. His eyes rolled horribly.

The low voice of Singapore: "Where's—that—chart?"

"Drown me!"

"All right," Singapore said. "Drown the rat!"

Splash! Lauzanno did not struggle this time, but lay inert, perhaps waiting with an acquired Oriental fatalism for death.

The net and the man it contained went down and down until it could barely be seen.

"Let him stay there," Lucky growled. "Let him drown!"

The *serang,* close to the side, suddenly began to babble. The one word, *octopus,* stood out.

Singapore cried: "Can you beat that! Haul the guy in!"

It was true enough. They had, with Mr. Lauzanno's quite unwilling assistance, bagged an actual octopus; not a deep sea octopus, but a fair-sized adolescent that was too small to be called octopus, too large to be called squid.

The writhing, eight-armed fish clung to the round yellow ball of flesh which was Pierre Lauzanno. Its countless suckers were fastened to various exposed areas of the Lauzanno anatomy. The head hung straight down, like a counter weight. Snake-like arms waved about, found new areas on which to clamp suction discs.

The man in the net was not cursing or roaring now. He was screaming with terror.

"Lower away!" Singapore shouted. "We'll have every police boat in the harbor over here!"

Lauzanno suddenly stopped screaming. His voice, pitched

to a hoarse whisper, implored, "Get him off me! He's sucking the life out of me! For God's sake, get him off me!"

"Where—is—that—chart?"

"I'll tell you! Get him off me—and I'll tell you!"

"Nix," Singapore said mercilessly. "Tell us—and we'll get him off you!"

"Give me your word you won't kill me!"

"We won't kill you."

"It—it's in that alley back of Un Gung's!" the agonized man panted. "It's under the red sandstone slab near the base of the date palm. It's there. I put it there."

"So you admit you killed the kid?"

"No, no, no!" Lauzanno bleated. "One of the Chinks did it! All I did was take the chart!"

"Bring him aboard," Singapore grunted. "Lucky," he said, as the men hauled the big boom in, "I'll tell you how we'll work this. We will pry this strange octopus off our octopus, and we'll leave our octopus in the net while you slip ashore and see if that chart is there by the date palm. We won't kill the eight-armed octopus until you come back with the chart. If you don't come back with the chart, we will sic this octopus on our octopus again. Okay?"

"Okay," Lucky Jones agreed.

"Look at their eyes!" Singapore cried. "Compare them! Do you see what I mean, Lucky?"

"I see what you mean," Lucky growled.

It took five strong men using countless fathoms of rope more than a half hour to free the frantic man in the net from the suction discs of that greedy Singapore harbor octopus!

LUCKY JONES was absent on his shore-going mission less than an hour. In his absence, Singapore listened to the insults oozing like tangible filth from the lips of the man in the cargo net until he grew weary; then set about a personal tour of the *Blue Goose*.

She was, as his first glimpse last night had told him, a beautiful little ship, and he noted with approval that she showed evidences everywhere of loving care. Such a princess of the sea was certainly deserving of the best. Her deck was holystoned to the whiteness of parchment. Her bright work gleamed in the hot equatorial sun. Her sails, her standing and running rigging were in fine condition.

Going below, he was delighted with the condition of her cabins, galley and dining room. Whoever had built the *Blue Goose* had spent money lavishly. Her staterooms were panelled in Philippine nara-wood, shading from amber to deep purple, and this was waxed to a satiny sheen.

A hail caused him to hasten on deck. A sampan was fishtailing toward the schooner from the waterfront, and a black-haired young man was standing in the stern. When Lucky Jones saw Singapore, he waved a folded yellow paper in his hand.

That would be the stolen chart. It meant that the treasure hunting exposition would at least get under way. Fraught with peril and disappointments though it might be, it was, to Singapore, a shining road to adventure. Gold—thirty fathoms down! Jade-green water and the throb of a deep-sea pump in his ears!

He gave Lucky a hand up over the side and told the sampan boy to stand by for a shoregoing passenger. He only glanced at the ninety-year-old chart and asked, "No question about it?"

"This is it," Lucky Jones said with a wide grin.

Singapore went to the net and released the cursing prisoner.

"You can get into your clothes and go now, Octopus," he said. "I won't forget you. Clear out of here now."

The naked man fixed him with his small, malignant eyes.

"Listen, you!" he growled. "I won't forget you, either—or your pal, here. Some day not so far off, I'll be crossin' trails with you guys again. When it happens, think faster and act faster than I do. That's all!"

Lucky, with fists clenched at sides, was breathing hard through tense lips.

"Get off—quick," he said. "Scram!"

The Octopus wasted no time, and the last glimpse the two men on the schooner had of him was of his pale, oval eyes staring malignantly at them over the cabin of the receding sampan.

The owner of the *Blue Goose* said, "That's that; but we should have killed him, Singapore; we should have killed him. He won't forget. If we ever cross trails with that guy again— What the hell? How do you like my ship?"

"She's a princess."

"How's for some breakfast? I've got civilized food on board. How's for some coffee, ham and eggs and wheat cakes, while we study the chart and lay some plans? I should say we had better lay here and outfit. I want an expert to go over the diving gear, and we will have to lay in what provisions we need. In that way, we can avoid puttin' in at Java."

"How soon can you water, provision and get the divin' gear overhauled?" asked Singapore.

"By tonight."

"It's none too soon. Lucky, has it occurred to you that Lauzanno has got that chart memorized?"

"What of it?"

"If the chart was worth so much to him, why won't he try to use the information? What's to stop him from goin' down to those islands and takin' a whack at that treasure?"

"He better steer clear," Lucky growled. "If I find him there, I kill him!"

Singapore stared at him, then burst into laughter. "Lucky," he said, "you are one hard egg."

"Now let me tell one," Lucky said grimly. "I would bet this ship that that rat knifed the kid and then stole the chart. I should not have listened to your lip, redhead. I should have stuck a knife into his guts, or caved his skull in with that belayin' pin. You are dead wrong. I say that lettin' him free means trouble. Look! What will we do with this octopus here?"

"Slaughter him."

"It's all the same," Lucky said. "If that other human octopus follows us down to where the *Singing Spray* lies, I will slaughter him unless he slaughters me first!"

CHAPTER VI

TWO OF A KIND

PIERRE LAUZANNO KEPT his eyes on the slim, blue schooner as the sampan carried him through a litter of small shipping to the Tanjong Pagar dock, but it could not be truthfully said that he seethed or smoldered with vengeful thoughts. Pierre Lauzanno never seethed or smoldered. The thoughts that marched through his mind now were as cold as a parade of the northern lights. And while he thought, his eyes remained as cold, as malignant, as those of his deep sea prototype. In the very extremities of fury, Pierre Lauzanno remained cold.

Reaching Tanjong Pagar dock, he paid off the *fokie* and walked to a line of waiting gharries. His pale eyes ran down the line, selecting the strongest-looking horse of the lot.

He bargained with the *syce* for the long trip to Johore Bharu. A figure agreed on, he entered the gharry and sat with shades drawn, in darkness, letting his thoughts rove. Singapore Sammy would have found another comparison here: in such a manner, in its murky, undersea cave, the deep-sea octopus dwells, pondering its malign thoughts, planning, plotting, scheming. For no animal on earth or in the waters of the earth is so diabolical in the execution of a plan as the octopus. Not without reason has it been named the Terror of the Deep. And this human octopus, in the darkened gharry, was planning a deed which would, if it came off, warrant naming him also terror of the deep.

It was past noon when Lauzanno's gharry reached the elephant stables of the Maharaja of Johore, on the outskirts of Johore Bharu. The man he sought and presently found was one of the maharaja's elephant men; a slender, bronzed-face, white-haired man of sixty with eyes as hard, as polished, as blue glass marbles.

There is an old oriental saying: *"Rats know the ways of rats."* What Singapore Sammy had strenuously tried and failed to do, Lauzanno casually did. That is, he sought out and found Singapore's father. And something more than the whim of the moment had led Lauzanno to him. He and the old elephant man were kindred spirits. They had undertaken more than one shady enterprise together.

Bill Shay—oddly enough his own last name was the same as Singapore's—was a rogue as clever, as unscrupulous as only the Far East can produce. In his salad days an elephant man with American circuses, he had deserted young Sammy and Sammy's mother to answer the siren call of the Orient—and had been diligently answering it ever since.

HIS TWO passions were pearls and elephants, or as Singapore expressed it, "The old rat is nuts about pearls and nuts about pigs." He had served rajas and sultans as elephant trainer; he could have amassed a fortune larger than his present one if he had stayed honest and become a reputable pearl dealer. He was a liar, a thief, a murderer and, on occasion, a polished man of the world.

Pierre Lauzanno said simply to this old vagabond: "Your redheaded whelp is in Singapore."

And the blue marble eyes blazed at him. "Where?" he snapped.

The Octopus smiled his loose-lipped smile. "Easy, Bill," he said. "Easy. I have plenty to tell you."

"Where," the old man wrathfully demanded, "is that rat?"

"I'll tell you everything. Let's sit down under a tree."

So they sat down in the shade of a breadfruit tree and Lauzanno said, "I didn't know you felt that way about him, Bill. I thought he was givin' you a big laugh, the way he trailed you everywhere."

Bill Shay nodded. "That was changed a few months ago. Yes; it was fun leading him here and there. For seven years, I led him from the pearling grounds of the South Seas to the elephant grounds of Rangoon; and from the caravanserais of Pekin to the pearling grounds of the Persian Gulf. It was fun, keeping just one jump ahead. But all that was changed this spring by what happened in Siam. It's me now that wants to find him. And when I do, I am going to slit his throat. Where is he?"

Lauzanno's pale eyes were dancing.

"You can't reach him just now, but I have a plan. It will wait. What happened in Siam?"

The old elephant man glared at him suspiciously. "You didn't hear about my pink elephant?"

"No! Did you find a *phoouh?*"

"I did! It has been my biggest ambition to find a pink pig and deliver it to the king of Siam for the sacred elephant temples. You know what it means. If I had delivered the *phoonk,* the king would have given me my pick of all the pearls and diamonds in his vaults. He would have made me a noble of Siam. I would have been wined and dined. And the morning I found the *phoouk* was the morning that redheaded whelp caught up to me—him and twenty soldiers and war elephants he had borrowed from Prince Poot Alla! Out of those seven years of playing tag with him, it had to be that morning!"

Bill Shay glared at a mango bird which had flown down and was pecking at the hardbaked ground a few feet away.

"He got the pig. Then I tricked him—got it back. I started hellbent for Bangkok. And he stole it one night out from under my very nose. He started driving it over into Burma, but it died in the Karen Hills. But that wasn't all. The king's brother and Prince Poot Alla grabbed me when I reached Ang Tor. They swore I was in the plot. They strapped me to a bamboo rack and built a fire under me. They kept a slow fire going under me for a day and a night, torturing me for what that whelp had done! They smoked my eyes shut so I couldn't see for a week. Then they staked me out in the sun and left me to the ants for another day and a night. They crawled into my nose and ears and into my mouth. Then they turned me loose—so blind, so swollen from antbites that I was no good for a month. I came here to wait. I knew he would come to Singapore in time. But this time he won't have to look for me. I'll find him!"

The old elephant man's eyes were glittering and red with hate.

"Yes," the Octopus agreed, "you can find him. He is sailin' today for the Molucca Passage to look for sunken treasure. He and a rat named Lucifer Jones."

"What ship?"

"The schooner *Blue Goose*. Wait, Bill! You can't catch him now. Cool down. Give me a chance to talk."

"What's this treasure?"

"The wreck of the American clipper *Singing Spray* which went down in a typhoon in the Sapahalu Strait in 1840." Lauzanno added eagerly: "Bill! You and I can get that treasure!"

Bill Shay answered with profane insults. Then: "You ought to know," he said, "that I am too old a hand to fall for yarns of sunken treasure."

"Listen," the Octopus pleaded, and told Bill Shay about Lucky Jones and the *Blue Goose;* how Kelvin Broome had shown him the old chart.

"I got Broome and Jones into a blackjack game at Un Gung's. This redheaded whelp of yours came in in time to join in a fight. When the light went out, I went after Broome; put a knife in his back and got the chart."

"Where is this chart?" Bill Shay snapped.

LAUZANNO RELATED the very unpleasant events which led up to his loss of the chart. He stated that he knew the chart by heart. Then coldly, profanely, he told about his ducking and the attack on him by the harbor octopus.

Bill Shay interrupted by bursting into laughter. He laughed until tears spurted into his eyes. He slapped his leg and roared, "Pierre, I would have given a lot of money to see that octopus throw his arms around you!"

Lauzanno smiled his loose-lipped smile and his eyes were heavy-lidded.

"You may live to see something funnier. I will pay those two back in the same kind of coin, if it takes me fifty years!"

"Get on with your story," Bill Shay said.

So the Octopus continued. The old elephant man listened with narrowed, calculating eyes; stopped him presently with the question, "How deep is this wreck?"

"Thirty fathoms."

"What do you want me to do?"

"Charter Ling Fang's brig, the *Java Lady*."

"Don't be a fool, Pierre."

"Listen! The *Java Lady* has just come in from a pearlin' cruise and has several complete divin' outfits—"

"Thirty fathoms," the old man muttered. "A hundred and eighty feet. That is too much water for a man of my age, and too much water for a man of your habits. It takes young, healthy arteries to stand that pressure. I am too old. You are too immoral. You are fifty per cent pus, Pierre. You drink too much, smoke too much, and spend too much time with the ladies. You have no wind."

"I am as tough as iron. I'll match my endurance with any bucko you name."

"Yet that young whelp of mine handled you like a feather! No, Pierre; I can't see you or me picking up gold in thirty fathoms. Did you ever hear of the bends?"

"Yes! But there is a decompression tank in one of the *Java Lady's* cargo holds."

Bill Shay became thoughtful. Then he said irritably, "Well, what is your plan? Do we go down there and jump those two, scuttle their ship and get the gold? That would be a waste of time. Why not wait till they get the gold, then kill them off and scuttle their ship?"

"No," said the Octopus. "Do you know what happens to a diver workin' in that much water when his air hose is cut unexpectedly?"

The elephant man nodded. "They call it the squeeze," he answered. "The sudden loss of pressure inside the suit causes the weight of the water to crush him flat. His innards squeeze up through his neck into his helmet. Every man who spends much time in deep water has the squeeze on his mind. I know a dozen Australian pearl divers who have clauses in their wills stating that if they are squeezed, they are to be buried in their helmets. They do not want to be taken out of their helmets with an acetylene torch! A fall that lets a diver down too fast, a broken air hose, a leaky safety valve or a split suit can cause death by the squeeze. Half the deaths in diving are from the squeeze."

Pierre Lauzanno was looking at him with his loose-lipped smile.

"You have said it all," he answered. "I would not be satisfied to kill them with a knife, and then to scuttle their ship. They are goin' to suffer the way they made me suffer. I nearly died of another kind of squeeze when that octopus grabbed me this mornin'. I got this idea then. You say you want to get rid of that whelp of yours. I will not stop until I have got rid of him and Jones too."

BILL SHAY shook his head. "That octopus must have squeezed your head. Your scheme is crazy and dangerous. It depends on too many factors. Any one of them can go wrong and spoil everything."

"It is safe and it is sane," Lauzanno coldly argued. "Both of them are amateur divers. Both of us are old hands. The risk of gettin' the gold above water is far greater than gettin' it below.

Our best chance is to get them and the gold is at the bottom. I have worked it out in my mind to the last detail. This wreck is lyin' north of Pangar Island."

"In charted water?"

"No. Ships never go near Pangar. They keep close to Tahabu or go between Tahabu and Selawe, in Grayhound Strait, even if they are goin' to Jilolo. Now, listen. Pangar rises sheer five hundred feet from water's edge on all sides. We will anchor south of Pangar, which puts Pangar between us and the *Blue Goose*. We will post a lookout on Pangar to signal us when they have found the gold. We will know that by the baskets, which won't be sent down until they find the gold. It may take them weeks to find it. All right! Fine! They have the work of findin' it—we have the fun of takin' it! I have thought of everything! We cannot fail."

"What makes you so sure they'll both go down at once?"

"Sharks and currents. Any two men with sense would go down together to look out for each other in case of grief."

"When they both are down and send for the baskets, then what?"

"Our lookout on Pangar signals us when the baskets go down. Thirty fathoms is a long way down. They would have to come up slow, even if their pumpers warn them we are comin', or they get the bends. The minute the baskets go overboard, we up anchor and sail around and lay alongside the *Blue Goose*. Our crew holds guns on their crew. Our two friends are under water, safely out of our way. We go down with knives to cut their air lines."

"Impractical and fantastic," the old man said firmly. "Why not run alongside, as you say, shoot down their crew and cut the air lines right there on deck?"

"No. That is not what I want. I want to them suffer, as they saw me suffer. I want to see them lookin' up as we come down along their air lines. What can they do? Nothin'! Each of us hangs onto one of their air lines. We will look down at them for a minute, then let them watch us cut their air lines."

Bill Shay slowly nodded his head. "It is a madman's idea," he said. "But a madman can often get away with a mad scheme. Yes—it's a mad scheme but I like it. After what I went through in Siam, because of that *phoouk,* I would like to watch that redheaded whelp when his air line is cut in thirty fathoms!"

The pale, oval, malignant eyes of the Octopus seemed to glow with a frosty light.

"If you could have heard them laugh when that harbor octopus was slidin' and slippin' its slimy suckers all over my body!"

"I know how I felt on that bamboo rack," the elephant man answered.

"Have you made up your mind?" Lauzanno growled. "Will you charter the *Java Lady?*"

"We will go to Singapore," Bill Shay replied, "and have some palaver with Ling Fang now."

CHAPTER VII

BANDA SEA

WHILE THE *Blue Goose* slipped southward over the equator, through the Rhio Archipelago, and into the blazing blue of the Karimata Sea, a lasting friendship was ripening under the tan awning stretched over the after deck. The redhead and the buccaneer leisurely checked over the diving gear, made plans, studied charts, and supervised the Chinese boys in the manufacture of baskets for hauling the treasure to the surface. These baskets were similar to those employed for bringing pearl shell to the surface, but stronger. In off moments, the two young men drank bottled Japanese brew off ice, swapped yarns, or simply snoozed in stark naked comfort in airy Bombay wicker chairs.

They were two of a kind. Neither knew what a home was.

Both had been on the go since they were youngsters. Each had fought, begged, stolen and bummed his way all over the world. And each was hard as flint.

Having no perspective on himself, Singapore was sure that Lucky Jones was the hardest individual in the Far East. And the better he came to know him, the surer of this he became. It was not merely surface hardness: Lucky was hard clean through. But this was, to Singapore, the right kind of hardness. It was the hardness of a diamond, clear, scintillating and perfect.

It did not occur to Singapore that he and this first pal that he had ever had were in any degree soft-hearted. That they should turn over what treasure they found, if any, to Kel's people, was merely playing the game. That Lucky would fight and be willing to die for a friend was, to Singapore, the very essence of hardness. It was a code of living that he understood and heartily approved.

And while these two, whom fate had cast together in one of the toughest dives in the Far East, were growing to know and like each other, a black menace like a thundercloud was gathering over them. The *Java Lady*, with two of the most unscrupulous rascals in the Orient aboard, was ploughing along in their wake, two days' sail astern.

As the blue schooner, with fair winds, soared on down into the Java Sea, the Flores Sea, the Banda Sea, the two friends lounged in their lazy chairs, forgot that Pierre Lauzanno existed, and watched the most beautiful islands in the world swim by.

JEWELS OF the tropical seas these isles are, as luring as the call of any siren to the man with red blood and an adventurous heart. They are mystery islands—the islands that men in stuffy offices dream they will some day visit and explore—and never do! Even their names are like notes struck on an oriental temple gong: Kangean, Manggar, Sangkapura, Allor, Gunung-Api, Buru! Cannibal islands, treasure islands, islands rich in undiscovered gold, of wistful brown maidens, of romance and bizarre adventure! If there is a Call of the East, here, in these enchanted tropical islands, are its lips.

All real men who see these beautiful islands sense their lure and their mystery. Yet if Singapore and Lucky Jones harbored such thoughts, they certainly never expressed them! Such comments as they made were terse, practical, hard and humorous. For both Lucky and Singapore were terse, practical and humorous.

Lucky would say, "That's Manggar, over there. A good shot could run up a fortune on that dump, shootin' leopards. Manggar is crawlin' and lousy with leopards."

Each one had some practical or humorous comment to make on every island they passed.

"See that green wart over there? That's Panga. A guy I knew was shipwrecked there once. All he had to eat was clams. Breakfast, tiffin and dinner—clams, clams, clams! He ate so many clams that when a ship finally took him off, he smelled like a seagull. He told me that when he got back to his home town— it was Boston—the folks gave him a banquet. And what do you think was the first dish they set in front of him? Cherrystone clams! Tie that!"

"I knew a guy once," Singapore narrated, "who was shipwrecked down in the Fijis. It sure was a desert island, too. He was twenty-three years old when he was shipwrecked. The very next mornin' he took a stroll down the beach and happened to kick a rock. He looked at his toenail and it was gilded!"

"Gold?"

"Yep. That doggone beach was lousy with nuggets. Then he found oysters growin' in a bed in a cove—a landlocked, shark-proof cove it was, at that. And every time he opened an oyster, he found a pearl!"

"I'll bet he went nuts," was Lucky's comment.

"Listen, bo. That guy was a bum. But the sight of all that wealth reformed him. He began thinkin' of his dear old maw, and his hard workin' brother, and the gal he had left behind

him. Think of it! He was a multi-millionaire at twenty-three!
So he says to himself: 'I'm gonna go home and buy my maw a
limousine and a yacht and a mansion, and my brother a ticket
to Paris, so's he can see life. And I'm gonna bedeck my sweet-
heart with strings of pearls and diamonds and rubies and sapphires and emeralds. I'm gonna know the feel of little cherub
fingers a-pluckin' at my heartstrings.'"

"Yeah?" Lucky cynically broke in. "And just then somebody
give him a sweet kick in the pants, and the dream was out!"

"Nix," Singapore grunted. "It wasn't no opium dream. It was
all real. He was a multi-millionaire. All he had to do was gather
the gold into a big pile and collect the pearls in another big
pile."

"Did he go back and buy his maw luxuries and bedeck his
gal in costly ornaments?"

Singapore sadly shook his head. "Nope. He was on that island
for forty-two years before a ship came along. For forty-two
years he was a multi-millionaire—and he couldn't spend a
dime!"

"That was a tough break," Lucky commented. He stared out
across the sea. "Redhead," he said presently: "I was just thinkin'
of that guy Lauzanno—those mean, pale eyes o' his."

Singapore growled: "Supposin' he comes to Pangar. Just supposin'."

The two adventurers exchanged a long, probing look. Then
Lucky drew his right thumbnail swiftly across his throat.

THE *Blue Goose* crossed the Emperor of China Reef, passed
well to starboard of the island of Hagedis, slipped through the
Buton Passage and entered the northwestern bight of the Banda
Sea on the last leg of her journey. She reached her destination
one afternoon at dusk, and dropped anchor in the uncharted
Strait of Sapalahu, between Tahabu and Mangali Islands, which,
on some charts, are named the Sula Islands, and, on others, the
Xullas. This small archipelago lies at the southern end of

Molucca Passage, under the frowning tropical heights of Celebes and about eighty miles due south of the equator.

To starboard, as they dropped anchor, loomed the tiny, high island of Pangar. Early next morning, they went ashore and explored Pangar, in hopes of finding a fresh water spring in case the supply in their tanks went bad. The island was mostly coral rock and white sand. Coconut palm trees flourished in abundance. The milk from the coconuts was useful, but there was no fresh water on Pangar.

This was the first of a long series of discouragements and disappointments. Returning to the schooner, they secured sounding gear, grapples, and a wooden firkin, the bottom of which had been removed and replaced with a disc of glass. Through this they could see a considerable distance down in the clear, green water. It was an amazing green—the color of kingfisher jade.

With Singapore at the waterglass, Lucky taking soundings, hauling in the grapple, and making a detailed chart of bottom conformations, and Sing Lee, the pump expert, at the oars, they proceeded to make certain annoying discoveries.

First of all, and of major importance, they found that a reef of gray and white coral ran parallel to the beach its entire length at about a half mile offshore. This long backbone of coral came, at some places, within inches of the surface at low tide. To complicate matters, the reef was not shown on the ninety-year-old chart or on any other chart. The sole survivor of the wreck of the old *Singing Spray* had indicated the rock on which he thought she had foundered. Certainly, a reef of such dimensions hadn't grown in ninety years. Coral reefs take thousands of years to grow.

While the reef was fairly straight, running almost due east and west, its height was very irregular. It consisted of countless little peaks and depressions. A fairly deep draught ship could have sailed over some of these depressions. This fact seriously complicated the problem. On which side of the reef had the

Singing Spray gone down? Had she broken her back on it, and gone down on both sides? Had she piled up on the offshore side, sunk slowly and been carried far into the Sula Gulf or far into the Molucca Passage? Strong currents swept west with a making tide; strong currents swept east with an ebb tide.

They would have lost faith utterly in the chart if it had not indicated landmarks so faithfully. And, except for an occasional high or low spot, the bottom was consistently thirty fathoms.

And the bottom was mostly white sand, although Lucky brought up on his grapples sufficient coral branches to inform them that a large part of the bottom was coral forest.

All this was very discouraging. It meant, for one thing, that even if they found the wreck, it would be so thickly encrusted with coral by this time as to be unrecognizable; and they would probably have to blast to get at it. Lucky had very little dynamite aboard, and blasting was slow and laborious.

Another feature, especially annoying to Singapore, was the sharks. He hated sharks. The twenty-foot man-eater Lucky had caught one time off Amboina, a few hundred miles west of Pangar, was, he declared, a minnow compared with these devils. They were the boldest sharks Singapore had ever seen, bolder even than the man eaters in the Gulf of Siam. Garbage thrown overboard by the Chinese cook attracted them in schools. Singapore one evening counted nineteen of them, all swimming close to the schooner, rolling over and showing their white bellies as they gobbled up floating tidbits. They showed their teeth and seemed to sneer at Singapore.

THAT WAS the evening he went to the arms locker and got out Lucky's submachine gun. He sprayed hot lead into shark's bellies until the sea was pink all about the *Blue Goose*. And he derived no small satisfaction from seeing how cannibalistic sharks are. No sooner did he disable one, than its able-bodied companions rushed and savagely tore it to shreds.

It seemed to Singapore that before darkness came he had

slaughtered every shark in the East Indies. And next evening there were more than ever!

Lucky experimented by lowering into the water a fifteen-foot length of old, discarded air hose. It made Singapore feel queer inside to see the way three sharks savagely attacked the hose and reduced it, in a few seconds, to ribbons. But Lucky paid out more hose and left it dangling there. He said he wanted to teach the sharks how little nourishment there was in an air hose! But the sharks were poor pupils. They shredded all the hose he put out!

"The sharks don't worry me," Lucky said, "near as much as the octopus. This looks to me like octopus water. You will often find big caves, grottoes, in these coral formations, and an octopus always lives in a cave."

"Wouldn't these dead sharks bring an octopus up?"

"Nope. A big octopus will generally stay in his cave until something passes that he can pounce on."

They laboriously went on with their charting. One afternoon, toward dusk, while they were immersed in this slow, tedious task, the *serang*, aboard the schooner a half mile away, shouted, "Sail-ho!"

A black brig, almost hull down, was making up the bight, all sails set and drawing. The rowboat returned to the schooner and Lucky, through a glass, discovered with interest that the brig was the *Java Lady*. He could not, of course, read the name on her black bows at that distance, but he would know her anywhere by the cut of her black, patched sails.

"She's a pearler," he said. "She belongs to a Chink in Singapore by the name of Ling Fang. I know him well. I lent him a cook one time in Tahiti."

"What's she doin' down here?" Singapore grunted.

"There are pearls in the Gulf of Tomini and in Jilolo Strait. She will change course and pass to westward of Taliabu if she's goin' to the Gulf of Tomini, and she will change course and pass to eastward of Mangali if she's going to Jilolo Strait. She might be makin' for either."

"Or," Singapore growled, "she might be under charter to the human octopus!"

"Yes," Lucky slowly agreed, "she might be under charter."

For some seconds the two treasure hunters stared into each other's eyes.

"If Lauzanno is aboard that ship and comes monkeyin' around here—" Lucky began. He did not finish.

They watched the black brig. When the *Java Lady* was about four miles away, she changed her course and bore southeasterly. That decided Lucky.

"She isn't comin' here," he stated. "She's headin' for the pass between Ceram and Ombira, which means Jilolo Strait."

Assured by this logical deduction that the black brig carried no menace to them or their venture, they returned to their charting of the reef. They could not know that the black brig, once it was safely beyond eyeshot on the other side of the island, came into the wind and that less than an hour later, two men— Bill Shay and Pierre Lauzanno—were on the island and staring down at them through marine glasses, watching every move they made and perfecting the details of their murderous plan.

AS THE days passsed, Lauzanno and Singapore's father lounged comfortably in the shade of an areca-nut palm and watched the two young men in the rowboat hunt for the treasure.

That search might have consumed months—might never have produced results—if the redhead had not suddenly been visited by a very bright idea. It happened one day just when they were preparing to knock off work because of the terrific noonday heat. The rowboat was over the reef and approximately equidistant from each end.

Singapore was staring down through the waterglass at what he and Lucky had supposed was a deep depression in the ridge of coral. The jade-green water shaded off into darker greens and finally into dark, impenetrable ultramarine; The rough wall of the reef was shaded likewise as it dropped down to the ocean floor.

The tide was in the last hour of its ebb and running out rapidly.

Singapore was watching the sounding lead on the end of the knotted line as Lucky paid it out. As it dropped down into the ultramarine depths, he suddenly saw it swing like a pendulum. But it did not swing back! The tidal current, setting strongly offshore from Pangar Island, was pushing the lead decidedly toward the north, or into the Strait.

To cause such a sharp inclination of the lead, the current, Singapore reasoned, must be tremendous. How come? It wasn't nearly so strong anywhere else along the reef, at other depressions, even toward the end of ebb tide.

And it suddenly dawned on the redhead that this depression in the coral ridge was not a depression at all, but a fissure, and that, in all likelihood, this fissure, or cleft, extended in a narrow V all the way to the bottom. As they had taken no transverse soundings on the reef itself, except a few random ones, he suggested to Lucky that they now do so—and presented his arguments.

Lucky listened without much enthusiasm.

"In other words," he said, "you're sayin' that the reef is not continuous but is open at this point. I don't believe it, but we'll sound across."

This they did, under pressure of rising excitement—to find that Singapore's guess was correct! A fissure extended through the reef from top to bottom at this point, in the shape of a narrow V. It was no more than a hundred feet wide at the top and it seemed to be about fifty feet wide at the bottom. Through this natural doorway, the sea flowed in and out as the tides changed. It was, in fact, a gateway of the sea.

Yet neither of the two hard boiled young men would voice the belief, the growing certainty, that they would find what remained of the *Singing Spray* lodged down there at the bottom of that doorway. It was simply too good to be true.

"It just can't be there," Singapore said pessimistically. "But if it should be, I'll tell you somethin', bo. There won't be much coral on it."

"Why not?"

"Because it's fast water, and coral don't like fast water!"

Lucky would not agree with this. "It's still water down there every time the tide changes. A few minutes a day for ninety years can grow a lot of coral, redhead. We'll look-see."

Lucky roared through cupped hands at the *Blue Goose*—roared so loud that the two men watching him from the island heard every word he said.

The *serang* brought the schooner as close to the natural sea gateway as safety would permit, and Lucky told him to put out a stern as well as a bow anchor, so the schooner would not swing over the reef when the tide changed.

When the *Blue Goose* was placed just where he wanted it, Lucky and Singapore went aboard. Standing in the bows of the schooner, Lucky heaved out grapples as far as he could beyond the reef and dragged the bottom of the doorway. His first cast hooked an unyielding object.

"Coral," said Lucky. "Give me a hand, redhead."

They both hauled on the line, but it would not come. They were compelled to resort to a winch.

The rope almost snapped before the grapple came up, bringing with it a curved "log" of coral a yard long and about a foot thick. Lucky made the first important discovery. Examining the end of the coral "log," he suddenly exclaimed: "It's wood, redhead! This is nothin' but a thin coral formation on what looks like oak! Look at the shape of it! This is the rib of a ship!"

But Singapore, suddenly pale and too excited even to speak, was pointing with a shaking finger at one of the grapple points. It was faintly but unmistakably tipped with gold!

CHAPTER VIII

BONES OF THE DEEP

THE TWO MEN under the areca-nut palm on Pangar watched these developments with the greatest interest.

"They've struck it!" Lauzanno announced.

"We'd better get back aboard," Bill Shay said. "They won't waste any time gettin' ready to go down for the gold. We'll post a lookout here to signal us when they get ready to send the baskets down. We will just have time to get into our diving gear."

Pierre Lauzanno followed him down the steep path they had cut into the wall on the fat side of the island, smiling his loose-lipped smile.

SINGAPORE SAT on a hatch cover beside Lucky Jones. The breastplate was lowered over his head and bolted down. The Chinese pump boy laced his heavy shoes. Lucky, already dressed for that descent into thirty fathoms, had only to have his face-plate locked down.

The helmet came down over Singapore's eyes and rasped against his breastplate. Then the face-plate swung open and he sucked in deep lungfulls of the torrid air.

Lucky said, "As we are gettin' air from separate pumps, we will each have a boy, workin' under the pumpers' directions, to take our signals. We will each take a shark knife and each have a bar sent down for breakin' open boxes, if we find 'em. They are pretty sure to be crusted thick with coral. Now, you guys be sure to keep those basket ropes clear. If we find gold, we will have to work fast. We will try to get it all in one trip. Now, let's go over our signals again."

These were the signals which the two divers were to send up to the surface as the occasion dictated:

Breast Rope:
1 pull——everything okay.
2 pulls——send down basket.
3 pulls——send down a rope.
4 pulls——I am coming up.

Air Pipe:
1 pull——Ease up—less air.
2 pulls——More air.
3 pulls——Take up the slack.
4 pulls——Up!

"It's too bad," Lucky said, "that these suits are old fashioned and haven't telephones. But we probably won't need telephones. I hope we won't need anything but baskets—plenty baskets!" They had arranged to have bars sent down when they should signal for baskets, then the baskets would be sent. "Sing Lee, are those ladders lashed okay?"

"Yes, sir."

"Shot ropes ready?"

"Yes, sir."

"You got your distance line there, redhead?"

"Yep!"

"All right. Start the pumps."

Singapore stared out uneasily over the placid green water as the air whistled around his ears. It was a little too early for the sharks. They generally didn't put in an appearance until a little before dusk.

He made sure that the breast rope and air pipe, running under the right and left arms respectively, were properly secured to the front of the corselet by their lanyards. His fingers felt the rolling hitches and were assured.

As his face-plate was clamped closed, he placed one finger on the outlet valve spindle to detect leaks. There were no leaks. He adjusted the pressure valve and drew deep breaths. The first few minutes in a diving suit always made him feel queer—as a man might feel in a small, close cell.

Lucky pressed his closed helmet to Singapore's, for speaking, and Singapore heard Lucky's muffled voice, saying, "Sam—you got your shark knife there?"

It was in Singapore's hand, whetted to an edge sharp enough to shave with. "I'm all set," he said.

"Let's go!"

Singapore, with a Malay's hand under one arm to guide him, walked heavily to the iron ladder which went down the schooner's side. His feet weighed a ton. The Malay boy placed his first foot on the top rung of the diving ladder for him as Singapore turned around, and helped his hands find the sides of the ladder.

Very carefully, Singapore went down the ladder. His helmet seemed to float an instant in the water, and the green water line rippled across his face-plate. Then he went down and down.

The water at first was almost as clear as the air, and objects were seen with perfect visibility. The red copper anti-fouling paint on the bottom of the *Blue Goose* was like a big red Zeppelin when he looked up at it.

The surface of the water was a magical ceiling of the most beautiful deep green he had ever seen.

HE REACHED the end of the ladder and took firm hold of the shot rope which extended down to a fifty-pound weight lying on the bottom.

The men on deck lowered him and Lucky down slowly, giving them a chance to get used to the pressure as they went down. Singapore didn't mind the pressure. In fact, he rather liked it as it grew heavier and heavier against his body.

A pink fish with a snow-white snout and sapphires for eyes swam inquisitively to his face-plate, peered in, flapped its rainbow tail and flashed away. Then Singapore dropped down into a large school of fish, which played fearlessly about him.

Some were almost transparent, taking on the color of the water. Others were pink, blue, purple, black, gold.

Singapore had been too occupied with other matters to notice the reef. He was absorbed by the brilliant, blue, inscrutable depths below him. Blue, the blue of finest sapphires— nothing but blue. The green was all gone now—all up above. It seemed to him they had gone down miles.

He realized suddenly that they had stopped, and twisted about to see the reef. He knew that those who were lowering them were giving them a chance to get used to the pressure. His heart was acting O.K.

Singapore gazed through jewel-blue water at the reef. From above, through the waterglass, it had appeared no rougher than rough plaster on a wall. This was giving way to little cups and pockets. Farther down, he saw, these cups were larger. If that kept up, there would be caves farther down.

He remained motionless with the rainbow-hued fish darting about him, tapping against his hands, ticking against the helmet.

He wondered what they were waiting for up on the schooner. A jerk came on his breast-rope. He gave an answering jerk: everything okay.

Singapore went down more miles into the amazing brilliant deep blue. It was strange, how the light got down here through so much water. The bottom of the schooner looked small and far away now—like a toy red Zeppelin. He could just see it by leaning back and throwing his head forward and around.

Lucky's helmet clicked against his and he heard a remote watery voice: "Hey, Stupid! Look at that reef now. Watch out for an octopus!"

And from that moment, Singapore only observed the wonders of this undersea world as incidental to the main business of watching for the bottom—and an octopus! Watching the reef, he saw the pockets become larger and larger until a man could have crawled into one, and, as he sank down, they grew still larger until they were large caves in which sinister shadows lurked. Any one of those caves might house an octopus!

His heart was hammering a little, and he wondered if this was pressure or excitement. It was scary business, dropping below those caves. Supposing an octopus slipped out and dropped down! That wouldn't be so funny.

His pumper was sending down too much air. Singapore gave one yank on the air pipe and the pressure eased off.

THEN HE saw the bottom. It gleamed blue, and, because of that, he knew he was near white sand. He hoped there wouldn't be much coral. To his relief, there wasn't. He came down the shot line the rest of the way and attached to it his distance line. Lucky did the same.

Lucky grinned at him through his faceplate. Through the blue murk Singapore grinned back.

"We have got to work fast," Lucky said. "The tide will be setting in for the beach pretty soon. We want to get all we can done in still water while it stays that way. How do you feel?"

"I could take you on for ten rounds," Singapore said.

Lucky made a playful pass at him, then said, "Have you got your bearings?"

"Yes. We're facing Pangar. That deep blue ahead must be the pass through the reef."

"That's how I figure it. Let's take a look-see. Watch out for a shark or an octopus."

The base of the reef, ahead of them, rose up like the wall of a forbidden city. Looking up and down and from side to side, Singapore could faintly make out the outlines of the sea doorway at the bottom of which, if their reasoning was sound, the wreck of the *Singing Spray* should lie. He wondered if they would find skeletons of those courageous men who had gone down in that typhoon ninety years ago.

They made their way around a depression in the white bottom to the nearest part of the reef. The distance was about eighty feet. It was hard work, and going back they would have the tide to contend with. Singapore was already out of breath.

Lucky paused at Singapore's side and said, "We'd better rest here a second. I don't like these caves at all." Singapore was looking at one of the caves. It was shaped like a mouth, opened part way in a laugh. Inside was blackness. Singapore stepped back as he saw a mass of black sliminess. At first, he thought it was an octopus cave, then a giant, black claw appeared, followed by the largest crab he had ever seen. It was a repulsive black spidery monster—in fact, a giant spider crab. Others scuttled out after it—a half dozen of them.

Lucky poked his helmet into the cave and said: "Come here and look at this formation." Singapore did so. Putting his head beside Lucky's, he said, "If you get scared, big boy, you can crawl in here and hide."

"Notice the roof of it," Lucky said.

Singapore looked at the roof. In the queer blue light filtering in, he saw that the roof was domed.

"Look," said Lucky. He put his head into the laughing coral mouth, and Singapore saw the silver air bubbles of his exhaust valve rising into the dome until a little "puddle" of air had been formed up there.

"A guy I knew," Lucky said, "used to come up drunk every time they sent him down on salvage work on a wrecked steamer. They couldn't figure it out. This is how he worked it. He went into a room that had a low door and no windows—I mean, there was lots of space between top of door and ceiling. By standin' in the room long enough, he forced out water and filled the top of the room with air. When the water had been forced below his face-plate, he opened his face-plate, uncorked a bottle of rye and drank as much as he wanted. Then he closed his face-plate—and when he went to the surface, he was tight!"

Singapore removed his head from the "laughing cave" and suddenly gasped as he started toward where he hoped the wreck was lying. A shifting of clouds over the sun, or the sun striking down at a changed angle had completely altered his surroundings.

THE BLUE murk had brightened. The water was now like one great sapphire. The coral all about them had changed to a vivid, deep, startling blue. Never, above or under the sea, had he seen a view of such wild beauty. In this sapphire half-world, of which so few men ever catch a glimpse, he saw castles and cathedrals of coral as barbarically beautiful as the Taj Mahal, or the gilded temples of Siam by moonlight. It made him feel giddy. And he wondered if the pressure was too much for him—if, perhaps, his brain was painting pictures with the help of the excessive oxygen he was taking in.

Then he realized that the castle on the left was nothing but the left hand side of the pass through the reef, and that the cathedral at his right was merely the right hand side of the pass.

His imagination was tricking him again—or was it? This time he saw clearly—unless it was a mirage—the bones of a ship! Or rather of the after-half of a ship! They were lying straight ahead of hand side of the pass.

He shouted to Lucky and Lucky shouted back. There was no question about it: that queer shift of sunlight or cloud had lighted up for them part of the little that remained of the *Singing Spray!*

Nothing much here was left of that gallant old clipper but half of the backbone and the ribs. This fragment of her lay, as Lucky had predicted, in white sand. The *Singing Spray* had obviously broken her back on the reef, and finally the after half of her had sunk down on this side. In the course of the years the swift flowing tides had picked her bones and, sweeping through the pass, the tide had kept the bones of the *Singing Spray* clear and clean of all seagrowth except a little coral.

He heard Lucky's voice shouting huskily. They fought together against the wall of blue water and came up under the stern of the wreck. Lucky warned him to watch out for his own air pipe and breast rope. Singapore was so excited he hardly heard him. The weird blue light had shown him that, scattered along the *Singing Spray's* backbone, were some objects caked with coral—objects square in shape!

He heard Lucky say, "Her strong room would have been about here!"

Singapore squeezed through the space between coral-crusted ribs, taking care not to cut his suit on the knifelike edges. A skull, half-buried in sand and lightly crusted with coral, gave him a start. Its black eye sockets seemed to be staring up at him, and its teeth, gray with coral, grinned at him.

Lucky was slowly, ponderously kicking at one of the square coral objects in the mound, and Singapore's heart was playing tricks again—beating high in his chest. For a moment, the pressure of the thirty fathoms almost overcame him. He tried to breathe evenly. But in a moment he forgot all about breathing as he kicked at what he desperately hoped was a box full of gold ingots or coin.

The tough coral at length gave. He kicked again. Suddenly, the box collapsed and small bars of gray-green metal spilled out and tumbled down over his feet. His heart sank. He picked one of the bars up. Gray metal! Lead—or at the best pewter!

They had come all this way, risked sharks and octopus, spent days in the broiling sun—to find, in the end, a few boxes of pewter!

He had been looking forward to the letter that he and Lucky would send to Kelvin Broome's mother and father and kid sister, back there in Phoenix. He said disgustedly, "Hell." Then Lucky was swinging toward him. He reached out, grasped Singapore's shoulder and began slowly, heavily to pound Singapore on the back.

"It's nothin' but lead!" Singapore blurted.

"Lead, my eye! Look!" And as Singapore looked, Lucky bent down and picked up the skull of that long-forgotten sailor. He scraped one of the gray bars against the sharp coral where the skull's teeth were. Then he showed the scraped metal bar to Singapore.

Where the coral had scraped, was bright glowing yellow! Gold! Singapore had forgotten that gold, submerged in salt water for ninety years, would show considerable surface corrosion.

His heart lurched again. There is no thrill quite like that of finding at the end of a long and difficult search, pure gold, be it ingot, coin, or nugget!

For a moment his senses reeled. The brilliant blue about him threatened to go black. Singapore fought against the tide of faintness. A half million in gold bullion at his feet!

Lucky reached up and pulled his breast-rope twice. Singapore quickly followed his example. He wanted a bar to smash in the boxes with—and baskets, and more baskets, in which to load the gold!

In his giddy enthusiasm, he failed to notice an oval shadow that flitted across the magical blue of the sea bottom.

SO CERTAIN were Bill Shay and Pierre Lauzanno that the two objects of their recent long scrutiny had found the wreck of the *Singing Spray* that they did not wait for their signal man on the hill to give word that baskets were going down.

Lucky and Singapore were hardly on the bottom when the *Java Lady* was rounding the island. She would drift down nicely on the light wind to where the *Blue Goose* was anchored.

The lack of watchfulness on the part of the crew of the blue schooner was not difficult to understand. They were expecting no visitors, and all their eyes were focused on fhe growing pile of gold bars on the deck. Basket after basket came up and was dumped. And when they were not staring at the mound of gold, they were paying attention to ropes, air pipes and pump gauges.

So it was that the *Java Lady* was well within easy pistol range when the crew of the *Blue Goose* became aware of her presence. Then there was no time to act. A voice from the brig's foredeck yelled, "Keep away from those ropes and air pipes! Stand back from that rail!"

Rifles in the hands of grim looking men backed up these orders. Two men on the black brig were in diving suits, ready, except for closing the face-plates, to go down.

CHAPTER IX

OCTOPUS!

SINGAPORE AND LUCKY were loading baskets as rapidly as their tiring muscles would permit. Singapore was certain he could not stand the exertion at this pressure much longer. He thought again for a moment that he was about to pass out cold. He felt weak. His heart was floundering again. Pressure, over-exertion, and excitement had reduced his strength to the point where he must soon go to the surface or suffer serious consequences.

He was straightening up, after loading a basket with the corroded bars, when he saw what he was sure must be a new kind of mirage—a queer kind of deepsea reflection. Very dearly, he saw a man in a diving suit above him. And this man was very dose to his air hose!

Squeezing his eyes, he looked again. This time he was certain he saw a mirage, for, where there had been one man before, there were now two. He was so sure that he was seeing, in the tricky blue light, a fantastic reflection of himself and Lucky that for a moment he did nothing but stare up curiously.

Then his floundering heart turned a complete and sickening flip. In the hand of each man he saw glinting a knife. His own knife was at his belt. His hands were empty!

In bewilderment he looked at Lucky. He was still half-certain that his brain, crowded with oxygen, was making him see things which did not exist. His neck and knees began to ache painfully.

The two strange divers, it seemed to him, were coming down closer. He attempted to reason that two divers could not be there. Where could they come from? There were only two diving suits on board the *Blue Goose*. His fast-numbing brain refused to consider that another ship had come and let down these divers.

Then Lucky was beside him, and he, too, was looking up. Through the bubbling of his exhaust valve, he heard Lucky's voice. It sounded dim and far away. Lucky was violently gesticulating. He caught a glimpse of Lucky's face as his face-plate swung around for a moment.

It was distorted with terror!

Then, and not until then, did Singapore realize just what the situation meant. A strange diver had slid down each of their air pipes with a shark knife in his hand! And even as Singapore watched, that knife near his air pipe came up with the obvious intention of cutting the flow of air.

He knew then what it meant. One of those men must certainly be Pierre Lauzanno. Who was the other?

JUST WHAT would happen to his anatomy if that air pipe was cut flashed through Singapore's mind in a split second. He had seen men who had died of "the squeeze." For a moment, he was on the verge of screaming with sheer terror. There was absolutely nothing he or Lucky could do to avert hideous death. His agonized brain reflected: "Anyhow, it won't take long."

Nothing to do now but wait. The air would stop coming down into his helmet. Then the weight of thirty fathoms would strike in on him in a blow mercifully swift.

A death-like shadow floated over his eyes. Then something touched him lightly—very lightly—on the left knee. It seemed to fondle his knee, to caress it lovingly.

Then the brilliant blue scene executed a swift and amazing somersault. The startling blue castle on his left, the magnificent blue cathedral on his right flew upward and over and down.

He was being snatched through the water at a terrific speed. All about him were silver bubbles from helmets.

The thing which had clutched his left knee tightened. One word blotted out every other terror in Singapore's mind.

OCTOPUS!

Swiftly he reached for the razor-sharp knife in his sheath. He swept it down in a wild arc; severed the black tentacle which had wrapped about his knee.

He began to fall through the water. Another black snake shot down and coiled about his waist. He felt bones give; almost snap.

Then, for the first time, he caught a glimpse of the terror. It seemed to fill the entire underwater world—a bulbous mass in the center of waving, squirming arms. That central mass, the body, must have been yards in diameter. It was enormous. And high upon it he suddenly saw its eyes—pale, oval eyes—hideous eyes which coldly glowed with murder.

He slashed savagely at the tentacle enfolding his waist, and slashed it through, only to have a third tentacle take its place.

Once again he was borne at terrific speed through the water. He was jerked this way and that. His head, helpless, banged about inside the helmet. He was bleeding from a deep cut over one eye. The blood ran down into his eye and down his cheek, dribbling off his chin and down his neck.

He fought, hacked with the knife; knew that the terror was forcing him nearer and nearer the sharp, horrible beak in its maws—the beak with which it hacked its victims into hunks and devoured them.

At first, as if in a dream, then for clear moments, he saw that not alone he had been attacked, but the three other divers— Lucky, Lauzanno and the other diver.

One thrashing blow of the powerful black arm sent Singapore smashing against the reef. He felt his breastplate buckle; felt a rib give and snap. A pull on his breastrope increased. It was no use.

And he knew that he could not keep up his fight much longer. He saw one of the divers hacking at an arm; saw the arm weaken and let the diver down.

Then he was thrown so violently in contact with another of the divers that his face-plate cracked. For an instant, he stared with absolute unbelief into the face of his father. Then his father was snatched away, as if catapulted.

A cloud of blackness suddenly descended about him. That was the octopus ink. It was as if night had suddenly fallen.

Singapore gave one final hack with the knife, severed a tentacle half through—and began to fall. He realized that he was free, at least momentarily, from the terror. He reached up to give his air pipe the four quick jerks which meant "Up!" Then his hand came away. Where was Lucky?

At that moment, there occurred four pulls on the air pipe. Did he want to go up? His answer was ironical—one pull on the breast rope: *Everything okay!*

Where was Lucky?

HE CAME heavily to his knees on the white sand and looked frantically about him. One of the divers was twenty feet away, on hands and knees, with helmet hanging down, evidently too spent to move.

Singapore fought his way through the water. It was harder than before, and he realized that the tide had turned, was beginning to sweep through the pass toward Pangar.

A glimpse of that rocky island flitted across Singapore's aching brain. How he had disliked that arid little island! What a paradise it seemed now!

He dropped down as a long waving black arm struck at him from the inky cloud above.

A man dropped down just in front of him. In the murky light, Singapore could see his face. His father again. The face-plate was spattered with blood.

Before Singapore could reach him, Bill Shay reached up and

jerked his air pipe—and shot upward with the speed of a rocket! Singapore saw him shoot clear of the octopus and on up toward the surface.

He reached the diver who had fallen; hoarsely shouted, "Is that you, Lucky?"

The answer, low, vague, muffled, came, "My air line is pinched. I'm done for!"

Singapore looked wildly about. He saw that Lucky's breast-rope and airpipe, some fifty feet away, were in a hopeless snarl about an arm of coral which grew out like the branch of a tree from the side of the reef. It was just above the cave that had reminded Singapore of a laughing mouth.

His eyes ran up the airline, and as they did, he saw that another diver—it must be Lauzanno—was enfolded now in the stumps of the octopus' arms. He was, in fact, the nucleus of a tangled web of tentacles. He was struggling feebly.

And as Singapore watched, he saw those mighty, snakelike arms draw their victim toward the beak-like fang in the bulbous horrible mass of the thing's body.

Horrified, he watched the helpless man drawn into that rapacious black mouth; saw the hooked beak plunge into his body and tear out a lump of flesh. Red from the helpless victim spurted out and stained the water.

Then the terror, as swiftly as it had struck, retreated up the reef wall with its human meal—vanished into a round black cave opening where it would feast at its leisure.

Singapore, while he watched, was fighting his way against the tide to the tangle of air pipe and breast rope. He felt for his knife. It was gone. He snatched at the tangle; realized that he could not possibly free it with his hands. And he now saw that the bubbles rising from Lucky's helmet had tapered off to a thin silver thread. Air could not be forced through the pinched tube! And if he pulled on it too hard, the knifelike coral would cut the tube.

CHAPTER X

TREASURE SHIP

WHILE THE LIFE of his friend hung on the slenderest of threads, Singapore thought more swiftly than he had ever thought in his life.

If he could find a knife, he might hack through the tangle, taking care not to cut the air pipe; but there was no knife available. If he seized Lucky in his arms and signalled "Up!" the airpipe would break and Lucky would be killed by the squeeze.

Then a fantastic scheme occurred to him. He returned to Lucky and dragged him to his feet. Half-carrying, half-dragging him, he transported him to the "laughing cave"; dragged him into it.

Then he gave two sharp pulls on his pipeline: *More air!* Promptly he felt the increased pressure; bubbles spurted from his exhaust valve and began to form an air-pocket against the domed roof of the cave. He signalled again for more air. The pressure increased until his lungs felt as though they must burst. But the pocket against the domed roof was growing. It came down to the top of his faceplate when he sat erect. Little by little, the waterline lowered.

Lucky was now limp. His face, through the face-plate, looked green. Singapore propped him against the cave wall. In a moment the air bubble would be large enough so that he could open Lucky's face-plate. But he did not dare until the water was below the bottom of the rim. Lucky's face was bruised and bloody, too.

Weakly, he wondered if that octopus would forage forth again; wondered whether an octopus died when so many yards of its arms were slashed and hacked off.

THE WATERLINE danced at the bottom of the rim. He

waited another eternity, then quickly opened Lucky's faceplate and his own. He shouted: "Lucky!"

Leaden lids lifted; dazed eyes stared at him.

"Lucky! Stay where you are! Don't move! This air in here will last you a long while." But would it? Would it last long enough for him to get to the surface and back down again with the necessary gear to save Lucky's life?

The greenness of Lucky's face turned to a sickly white pallor.

"Don't move!" Singapore cautioned him. "Sit right where you are!"

Lucky's lips moved. "All right, redhead."

Singapore waited a few minutes longer, until the air pocket had come down to Lucky's shoulders. Then he closed his own face-plate and backed out of the cave. He gave four jerks on the air pipe. Up!

The redheaded adventurer gave only a passing thought to the bends as he was quickly hauled to the surface. He should have gone up slowly, with a long pause half way, to permit the compressed nitrogen in his blood to expand slowly and properly. It is the too-rapid expansion of this nitrogen into bubbles in the blood which cause the hideous cramps—"the bends"— and sometimes painful death.

But Singapore's one thought was to get back to the cave with rescue gear as rapidly as possible. When his eager hands found the iron ladder and he swarmed up above water, he opened his face-plate, and shouted to the pale and wild-eyed *serang:*

"Ax! Rope! Wrench! New airpipe!"

And when these articles were brought to him, he said, "Connect up this air hose and start pumping now! Disconnect Lucky's old airhose when I signal!"

The *serang* stared at him incredulously; he could not know of a life-saving air pocket in a cave thirty fathoms down; but he obeyed.

"Lower me fast!" was Singapore's last command before he

closed his face-plate, climbed down the iron ladder at the schooner's side, and went under again.

Singapore's return to the "stationary diving bell," which was what that cave, in effect, was, consisted largely of a fight against the tide which swept through the passage in the reef. The tide was running strong now, and would run stronger with every passing minute.

Twice, as he attempted to gain the laughing mouth, he was swept irresistibly past. Then, at risk of cutting his suit on the coral, he clung to the wall and inched his way to the opening. His first act was to thrust inside the bubbling end of the new air hose. Lucky reached down and pulled it inside.

Singapore crawled in, detached the old air hose and coupled on the new one. Then he went out, hacked off the old air hose and the rope above the obstruction on which they had snarled, and fought his way back to the entrance just as Lucky emerged under his own power.

In deciding on the speed of their ascent they deliberated briefly on the three most important factors: The octopus—or another octopus; sharks, and the bends.

Lucky, with his greater diving experience, decided on a slow ascent. Singapore had no voice in the matter. He was out—cold!

WHEN SINGAPORE returned from his journey into Darkest Wonderland, he way lying in his Bombay chair under the tan awning. He heard the hiss of tiny bursting bubbles, and knew that the *Blue Goose* was under way.

He was so weak that he felt that he could never lift a hand again. Yet he was surprised at the responsiveness of his muscles when a whisky glass full of sparkling amber liquid floated down within reach.

Lucky Jones, wearing nothing but a pair of shorts, stood over him, grinning. Singapore grinned feebly in return. There was moisture in Lucky's eyes.

"Kid," he said, "I hand it to you. That was the cleverest, smartest and bravest piece of rescue work I ever heard of. If you hadn't thought so quick—and acted quicker—I would be that octopus's next meal! As I have said before, you are one great guy."

"Boloney," Singapore replied.

"Do you want to know what all happened?"

"I sure do."

Lucky pulled up a chair and sat down. "It seems that while we were down there, the *Java Lady* hove alongside and our old pal Lauzanno and some old gink—"

"My old man—of sorts," Singapore interrupted.

"I suspected that. Anyhow, they went down with the honest, humane intention of cuttin' our airpipes. Why they picked that way to kill us, God only knows. But that seems to have been their general idea. And before they could cut the airpipes, down comes old man octopus. Accordin' to the *serang* the octopus got Lauzanno—a plain case of dog-eat-dog, you might say—but your old man got clear and, without waitin' to make sure his pal was alive or dead, had his airpipe and breastrope chopped clear with an ax—ordered anchor weighed and sails up—and off he sailed."

"We're gonna follow him," Singapore said grimly.

"That's just what we're doin', buddy."

"How about the gold?"

"We got it all aboard."

"Like hell we did. There's still a stack down there."

Lucky chuckled. "All right, redhead. Say the word and we'll put about and go back there and get it!"

"Not me," said Singapore. "I'm no hog. How much did we get?"

"I've just been weighin' it up. There's about five hundred and seventy some odd pounds of it. In terms of American dollars, that's about one hundred and eighty thousand bucks—or a fair mornin's work for a pair of bright lads!"

"The rest of it," Singapore said, "can stay down there. Do you want it?"

"Not me, redhead. We might go after it some day with a clam—but I doubt it. There's too much water there, and the current is too tough."

"How long will it take to overhaul that brig?" Singapore asked.

"With luck—by sundown. She's carryin' every stitch she owns, and so are we."

"It's gonna be fun," Singapore said, "writin' that letter to Kel's folks. I'd like to see the look on his sister's face when that bank draft falls out. A hundred and eighty thousand bucks ought to save that gal from a lot of old pipsqueak lawyers!"

THE *Blue Goose*—now a treasure ship in her own right—slipped on down into the Banda Sea and so into the sunset. She did not overhaul the *Java Lady*. When night fell the *Java Lady* was still well in the lead and it seems likely, in view of the quickness of her disappearance, that she ran all night without lights, thereby violating the most stringent of maritime rules, but enabling Bill Shay to escape.

An octopus had taught the old elephant man that he loved his life much more than he hated his red-headed offspring!

ABOUT THE AUTHOR

THE DECISION TO become a writer of fiction was made for me by fate. In 1914, in Panama, where I spent a week when I was a wireless operator on a little steamer that creaked up and down the Central American coast, I met an author who painted the joys of free-lancing so vividly that I could not resist the call. We were drunk. I was twenty. Since then, I have been trying to catch up with all of those joys he mentioned.

Starting to write stories in 1914 and, four years later selling my first one, marks up, I suppose, a very poor batting average. But in those years I was getting experience, seeing the world, and acquiring knowledge. I "punched brass" as a wireless operator all over the Pacific. I entered Columbia University in 1915, and one year later left because I didn't believe in higher learning. I still don't believe in it. I became a newspaper reporter, later a magazine editor.

Then came the war, which I won practically single-handed by writing high-pressure publicity to induce patriotic Americans to send books to Washington for camp libraries for soldiers and gobs. Books came by the carload, by the ton: McGuffy's readers, old almanacs, spellers, arithmetics, out-dated novels and just trash. The soldiers and sailors who read those books soon hated the war so bitterly, that they promptly got busy and ended it. That's how I won the war.

After the war, I wanted another look at China, and was sent to the Far East by *Collier's* to write articles on China, the Philippines, India and Malaya.

266

The first story I sold was written while I was editing a motion picture trade paper. It was bought by the *Argosy,* and it was about a wolf named Murg. Don't ask me why. In the intervening years I have written millions of words. Perhaps it is Murg who sits so patiently at my door!

I started writing fiction under the pen name of Loring Brent, because it would have annoyed the owner of the motion picture magazine to learn that I was writing fiction out of hours. He thought I fell asleep at my desk because I was working so hard for him! When my income from fiction exceeded my salary, I quit the job. Since then I have been free-lancing exclusively, except for a two-year period when I lived in a Florida swamp town and added to my writing the duties of postmaster, game warden and deputy sheriff. Out of that experience came a long series of stories about a Florida town I called Vingo.

I have enjoyed most writing stories about certain established characters. Apparently the most popular of these have been the Peter the Brazen, the Vingo and the Gillian Hazeltine stories. I stopped writing about Peter the Brazen (a swashbuckling wireless operator on ships in the China run) about ten years ago. He was, incidentally, the subject of the only novel I have had published in America. I am now starting a new series about him.

When I am not traveling I live in Westport, Connecticut. My interests are horses, sailing and flying. I took up flying about a year ago to write some articles on how it feels to learn to fly, and was badly bitten by the bug. I can make a three-point landing about five times out of ten.

I like New York, but would prefer to live in Honolulu. I smoke sixty cigarettes a day. I like murder trials. I have never mastered the noble game of poker, although I once wrote a book about it. In my spare time I study law and medicine. I have two young sons and a still younger daughter; an able crew for my sailboat—except that there is usually mutiny aboard the lugger!

TARZAN AND THE JEWELS OF OPAR
BY ARGOSY'S GREATEST AUTHOR
EDGAR RICE BURROUGHS

WAR LORD OF MANY SWORDSMEN
W. WIRT

CLOVELLY
BY WORLD-FAMOUS AUTHOR
MAX BRAND

DRINK WE DEEP
THE SCIENCE FICTION CLASSIC
ARTHUR LEO ZAGAT

THE GUN-BRAND
BY NORTHWEST FICTION LEGEND
JAMES B. HENDRYX

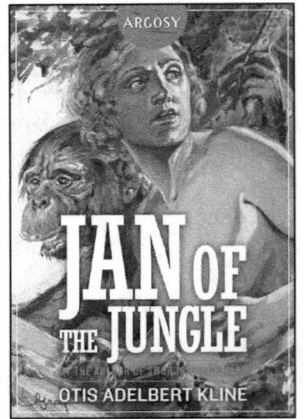

JAN OF THE JUNGLE
OTIS ADELBERT KLINE

THE BLUE FIRE PEARL
GEORGE F. WORTS

THE MOON POOL & THE CONQUEST OF THE MOON POOL
ABRAHAM MERRITT

MINIONS OF THE MOON
THE SCIENCE FICTION CLASSIC
WILLIAM GREY BEYER

ALIAS THE NIGHT WIND
VARICK VANARDY

THE ARGOSY™ LIBRARY

SERIES 3 INCLUDES:

* BURROUGHS * ZAGAT * MERRITT *
* BRAND * KLINE *
* BEYER * HENDRYX *
* WIRT * VANARDY *
* WORTS *

THE BEST FICTION
FROM THE FRANK
A. MUNSEY LINE

1. GENIUS JONES by Lester Dent
2. WHEN TIGERS ARE HUNTING: THE COMPLETE ADVENTURES OF CORDIE, SOLDIER OF FORTUNE, VOLUME 1 by W. Wirt
3. THE SWORDSMAN OF MARS by Otis Adelbert Kline
4. THE SHERLOCK OF SAGELAND: THE COMPLETE TALES OF SHERIFF HENRY, VOLUME 1 by W.C. Tuttle
5. GONE NORTH by Charles Alden Seltzer
6. THE MASKED MASTER MIND by George F. Worts
7. BALATA by Fred MacIsaac
8. BRETWALDA by Philip Ketchum
9. DRAFT OF ETERNITY by Victor Rousseau
10. FOUR CORNERS, VOLUME 1 by Theodore Roscoe
11. CHAMPION OF LOST CAUSES by Max Brand
12. THE SCARLET BLADE: THE RAKEHELLY ADVENTURES OF CLEVE AND D'ENTREVILLE, VOLUME 1 by Murray R. Montgomery
13. DOAN AND CARSTAIRS: THEIR COMPLETE CASES by Norbert Davis
14. THE KING WHO CAME BACK by Fred MacIsaac
15. BLOOD RITUAL: THE ADVENTURES OF SCARLET AND BRADSHAW, VOLUME 1 by Theodore Roscoe
16. THE CITY OF STOLEN LIVES: THE ADVENTURES OF PETER THE BRAZEN, VOLUME 1 by Loring Brent
17. THE RADIO GUN-RUNNERS by Ralph Milne Farley
18. SABOTAGE by Cleve F. Adams
19. THE COMPLETE CABALISTIC CASES OF SEMI DUAL, THE OCCULT DETECTOR, VOLUME 2: 1912–13 by J.U. Giesy and Junius B. Smith
20. SOUTH OF FIFTY-THREE by Jack Bechdolt
21. TARZAN AND THE JEWELS OF OPAR by Edgar Rice Burroughs
22. CLOVELLY by Max Brand
23. WAR LORD OF MANY SWORDSMEN: THE ADVENTURES OF NORCOSS, VOLUME 1 by W. Wirt
24. ALIAS THE NIGHT WIND by Varick Vanardy
25. THE BLUE FIRE PEARL: THE COMPLETE ADVENTURES OF SINGAPORE SAMMY, VOLUME 1 by George F. Worts
26. THE MOON POOL & THE CONQUEST OF THE MOON POOL by Abraham Merritt
27. THE GUN-BRAND by James B. Hendryx
28. JAN OF THE JUNGLE by Otis Adelbert Kline
29. MINIONS OF THE MOON by William Grey Beyer
30. DRINK WE DEEP by Arthur Leo Zagat

www.ingramcontent.com/pod-product-compliance
Lightning Source LLC
Chambersburg PA
CBHW051638050726
47502CB00011B/1091